PHOTO FINISH

PHOTO FINISH

A McKenna Mystery

TERRY AMBROSE

PHOTO FINISH

A MCKENNA MYSTERY

ISBN: 978-0-9859540-1-7

Copyright © 2012 by Terry Ambrose

Cover photograph by Kathy Ambrose and is reproduced by permission.

Book design by Kathy Ambrose.

Dedication

To Mom and Dad, who taught me three lessons to carry me through life.

Wear a smile instead of a frown.

A kind word gets a much better result than an unkind word.

Do what you say you're going to do.

While I don't always practice these lessons, I'd like to think that I work on them all the time.

1

Harris Galvin gave me what the Hawaiians call "chicken skin" the moment I met her. The goosebumps this new girl in paradise brought on were seriously scary. Harris might be drop-dead gorgeous, but she had an aura about her—something as old as the islands themselves. Put the emphasis on the drop-dead part and make that aura what the locals call *malu make,* which is pronounced mah-loo mah-kay, and roughly translates to "shadow of death," and you had Harris, an irresistible package that said, "big trouble coming—soon."

My name is McKenna. I don't usually act this way. Spooky music, getting all weird on people—that's more wacko than me. I'm just— hell—I'm just sitting on my lanai half-drunk and muttering Hawaiian death phrases about a woman I barely know because she and my best friend are missing.

Death phrases or not, nobody was going to lock me away unless I started ranting down on Waikiki in front of the big hotels. That wasn't likely since I had no overpowering urge to give up my job managing the Honolulu Sunsetter, a sweet little apartment manager's deal that gets me free rent and a great view. So no matter how crazy this whole Harris thing made me, I had to plug along. Fact is, I'm a work in progress. Maybe progress isn't exactly the right word, I'd gone from hotshot bank skip tracer to grumpy landlord faster than you could say, "The rent's due."

Anyway, while the owners of this little moneymaker did their rich-people things, my job entailed judging Harris's suitability as a tenant, which I'd done. Despite her little black-cloud aura, Harris seemed to have her life together. She'd passed all my usual sophisticated landlord checks like not bitching about the money and not being stoned. She even had twenty-five grand in the bank and called me "Honey." My other research, a couple of quick database checks, had turned up nothing. So I figured, "What the hell?" When she moved in, I got two months' rent and a deposit. And a hug that was two inches too close and lasted three seconds too long to be considered just friendly.

At five-foot six, Harris was lithe and stood just a few inches shorter than me despite my tendency to slouch. Her voice sounded proud as she handed me a letter from National Geographic and said, "I'm a photographer and have a job lined up."

Her blue eyes reminded me of the early-morning sea—mine were more like the brown of a Malibu mud slide. She struck me as more Cosmo model than nature photographer, but what did I know?

My brain must have still been working on that hug when I'd opened my big mouth. "Hmmpf. Didn't realize that there were any unphotographed parts left on Oahu."

"Honey, I'm gonna do it like it's never been done before. My article's gonna be called Spectacular Island Waterfall Day Trips. It'll cover waterfalls throughout the islands. Perspectives nobody's seen before. The tricky one's going to be Sacred Falls."

"Tricky? More like impossible."

"I know, the rock slide in '99. Killed eight hikers, yada, yada."

"Yada, yada? You can't get in there. Not legally, anyway."

"My employer has a lot of pull. I've already talked to State Parks. Got the email approval yesterday. Now that I have an address, the letter should arrive any day."

So, yeah, she'd impressed me. Hot. Organized. I might have proposed on the spot if she hadn't kept jabbering about fame and fortune, her path to the big time. Talk about yada, yada. Sheesh, give it a rest. Given her business plan—act dangerously, get paid handsomely—I probably should've gotten three months' rent. Who in their right mind went off on a damned-fool photo safari in the mountains and expected to get paid for it? Probably somebody who didn't know you couldn't make a living that way. Count me out, I'm too smart for that.

But now, it was 7:08 PM and the sun hung at half mast on the horizon and they hadn't returned from that photo safari and, damn, I was getting worried. A picture of little Harris parts scattered over the mountainside somewhere on the north end of Oahu flashed in my mind.

Goose flesh tickled my skin again. I muttered, "Dat *wahine*, she *kine* chicken skin." Kine is what the locals call a placeholder word. Hawaiians use it to mean almost anything. It can mean "a lot," "a little," "I don't know," "I forgot," or whatever else the speaker wants it to mean. In this case, it meant that despite her good traits maybe Harris just had really bad karma.

The Sunsetter apartments border the ocean on Kalakaua Ave. With Diamond Head on the east, Honolulu on the west, and the Pacific smack dab in front. They're not hard to rent despite the utilitarian white paint and island-standard musty carpets. True, a good carpenter could shoehorn one of these units into the owner's closet, but with studios and one or two bedrooms to choose from, people who had money and were so inclined could live close to the water. They're well kept, thanks to yours truly, and this little investment let my bosses go off and sip expensive drinks on about any beach in the world while I sat here and managed their little Honolulu gold mine, a task I performed admirably. I'm definitely a go-getter—after midmorning. And you can't count my afternoon nap. Or when I might worry about other people's karma.

In any case, back to Harris. Talk about energy. And how that girl had oozed confidence. Sheesh.

"I've got the drive. I've got the ambition. My photos are better than the others, that's why I got this gig."

"Got your eye on the big prize, huh?"

"You bet, honey. Just watch me."

Well, I could certainly do that. "Maybe you are better, maybe I'm wrong. But there's a lot of Ansel Adams wannabes out there."

"Don't worry, I know what I'm doing."

I remembered thinking that she had a nice chunk of change in the bank, a great apartment, and knew where she wanted to go in life. As long as she paid her rent and didn't get herself killed—ah, hell. If she did, she'd be visiting her *kupuna*, that's her ancestors for you mainlanders.

Under my breath, I whispered, "Don't let me be right."

Deep down I liked this gutsy newcomer. Even without the hugs, her friendliness just made you want to, well, like her. Still, as her landlord, I had to hope she didn't kick the bucket before I could cash her check. I snickered. Or get a few more of those hugs.

Black cloud or not, Legs, oops—yeah, that's how I thought of her, was pretty smart. She'd persuaded me to get her a guide for her little photo safari—not something most people could accomplish, then made me feel good about it by pulling me so close I almost forgot my age. At 62, I'm old enough to be her father, which is a depressing thought that just makes me want to get drunk and listen to Jimmy Buffett all afternoon. Just the same, I'd made a commitment and that meant calling my only friend in the islands, Alexander.

Alexander's lived here all his life and he's like an umbrella drink; lots of Hawaiian, two parts haole, a shot of Chinese and a dash of Japanese. The haole part is pronounced "how-lee" and just means that a couple of the pretty Hawaiian girls who were his grandmothers jumped the racial barrier and married white people, probably sailors from the mainland. A couple of his other kupuna became enamored with Asian members of the opposite sex and so Alexander's was a very common mix here in the islands. In any case, Alexander knows almost every inch of Oahu, from the mountains to the sea, or *mauka* to *makai*, as we say here. He's got more aunties, uncles, and cousins than I can count, and if you toss in the other people he knows, they could probably fill Aloha Stadium. It was now 7:21 PM and red tinges on the horizon had grown bright and fiery. The ocean was turning pink and gray.

I took another sip as the last of the sun's fire dropped below the horizon. This part of the day, the time when the struggle between daytime and night reached its climax, had become my favorite. My ten-by-twelve lanai with its four-seater patio set and chaise lounge gave me an oil-painting view of the sunset.

An electronic version of Margaritaville began to play on my cell phone, breaking the spell. I checked Caller ID. Shit. Alexander's wife. Maybe I should switch to tequila. "Hi, Kira."

"Where's Alexander? You set him up this job, yah?"

"I'm getting worried, myself."

"You get him in trouble, McKenna, I gonna come after you."

And I knew she would. "I thought they'd be back hours ago—"

"Don't make excuses, you. This not just another case of you wandering fingers."

Kira called me a letch once just because I got my hand too close to her ass. I tried to explain that I was old and deserved a little leeway, but that response earned me a bruise on my arm that hung around for weeks. "Uh, about that, I really do apologize—again." For about the tenth time. "I'll send him home as soon as he shows up."

"You keep him. That teach him a good lesson."

Kira hung up and left me listening to a dial tone. My heart pounded in my chest; my palms felt sweaty. Confrontations just weren't my thing. It was definitely time for another round.

7:42. Not good. I slumped back into my chair.

Gentle trade winds brushed across my face, whispering their island secrets. The sky grew darker, dimming to pinkish grays and purples. White lights from a yacht streamed across the ocean on the distant horizon. The crazy surfers were long gone, having done their thing from sunup to sundown. I call them crazy because, in addition to the obvious issues about fair-skinned people getting fried in the sun, the idea of flopping around in the water close to a wave the size of a bus scares the crap out of me. I'll stick to my little lanai and sunset view, thank you very much. Now, it was just the ocean— the colors, the sounds, the smells. The here, the now. Locals say that people come to the islands to run away. Maybe they're right.

My eyelids grew heavy as the trades worked their magic. I downed a mouthful of my vino du jour, a tasty, cheap-but-effective Pinot Noir I'd found on sale at the market, then crossed my arms over my chest and settled down into the chair. I hadn't always been grumpy. Chasing skips had been a rush. I'd found a lot of people who didn't want to be found. My relationship with Jenny and her son had been—who was I kidding, that's when my life imploded. As I nodded off, a familiar image flashed in my mind—me, alone in the middle of Waikiki Beach, a "Do Not Disturb" sign hung around my neck.

A knock on the front door startled me so much I damn near fell out of my chair. It took me a minute to get on my feet. I felt like a human pretzel until about halfway to the door. That's when I realized I'd taken the long route. My little end unit has a lanai that's just ten feet from the walkway to the central courtyard, which would have been a much easier route. I checked the wall clock in the dining room on my way to the door. It was after 9:00 PM. Who the hell would be coming by now? I could only think of two possibilities. It could either be Alexander and Legs, or the cops coming to confirm my fears.

"Not the cops. Please." I blinked in a weak attempt to clear my head. "Who is it?"

"It's me, Alexander. Open up, McKenna."

Oh, good. They were back and had stopped by to tell me about the day. "Hang on, I'll be right there."

"Hurry up, I had to park on the back end of the lot and my knee's killing me. I can't hold her up much longer."

Uh-oh. Hold her up? I swung the door open, then stared at what looked like a couple of massacre-movie stunt doubles. "What the hell happened to you two?"

Alexander had bruises everywhere I could see. A cut near his right eye had bled and caked the side of his face like war paint. And Harris, well, looking at Harris broke my heart. I stepped aside to let Alexander assist her into the room.

As the two hobbled past me, Harris smiled and gave me a weak half-drunk wave. "Hi, hon."

Alexander shook his head. "She been calling me that all day, brah. Don't get your hopes up. And don't say nothin' about a hospital."

The evening trades hadn't yet cooled the room, and the air felt heavy. "She'll do better outside. Why no hospital?"

"We were outside all day." He shrugged. "We both got our reasons."

"Whatever. Put her on the chaise out there where she can rest."

Alexander made his way past my glass-topped, wicker dining table and TV to the lanai, lowered Harris onto the chaise lounge and occupied the chair I'd vacated. I tried to nonchalantly move my wine glass, but he just rolled his eyes.

"Crap, I've got to pee." I hobbled off to meet my favorite friend in life these days, the toilet.

"You don't care what happened to us?" Alexander shouted after me.

I was about to make the right turn towards my bathroom when I yelled over my shoulder, "You live to be my age and your bladder will explain it all to you." I closed the door and said hi to Bosco. You probably think I'm nuts, but when you spend as much time as I do visiting this guy, you might as well give him a name. The way I looked at it, he was better than a tech-support hotline—available 24/7 and no long wait times.

Back on the lanai, Alexander gently wiped Harris's face with paper towels. I'd barely made it through the lanai door when he said, "I never saw anything like it, brah, somebody threw a body off a plane."

2

Alexander Kapono is my best, and really my only, friend in the islands. True to his heritage, Alexander likes to talk story. He has some great ones, too, like the time he lost the surfing contest in high school because a 300-pound green sea turtle decided it wanted to surf the same wave. The way he told the story, the sea turtle lost control and began to tumble. End of contest for Alexander. And maybe the turtle, too.

The idea that someone would throw a body, alive or dead, out of an airplane struck me as ridiculous. Unless some wise guy had come up with a new tourist attraction, I doubted that anyone in their right mind would do such a thing. I studied Harris for a moment, then raised my eyebrows and pointed at her. "I thought she was with you, not in a plane."

Harris glared at me. "I'm like, tied to a rope and hanging off the side of the mountain. It was, like, a thousand feet down."

Alexander stood and crossed his arms. "I had the line, and it's no thousand feet, more like eighty, yah?"

"It seemed like a thousand. Anyway, there I was, looking at death and the most spectacular photo I've ever taken in my life and all hell breaks loose."

Talk about melodramatic, jeez. "So what did you do, drop your camera?"

"No! I kept telling myself to take the shot, take the shot."

"What if Alexander lost his grip?"

Harris got a worried look on her face. "I tried not to think about that."

"You don't weigh nothing. It was no problem."

"You weren't the one that was gonna fall. Anyway, I'm setting up for my last shot and there was this noise like a plane engine or something. Alexander yelled at me to look up and I saw a man shoving something out the door."

"Maybe it was camping gear or supplies for hikers."

"Park's closed, remember?" Alexander looked miffed that I didn't believe their—whatever it was.

Harris winced. "I've seen people haul dead weight before."

The tone in her voice sent a shiver down my spine. "Even so, who throws a body out of a plane, huh? Tell me that."

"A murderer, that's who! So I started taking shots of the plane instead of the waterfall."

Alexander said, "They had guns, McKenna. They shot at us."

"How could they shoot at you? They were throwing bodies out of planes." I looked from one to the other, then back again. "I've heard some lines before, but you two will never get that story to fly here. Alexander, this is worse than that high school surfing contest story you told me."

"McKenna! Don't you start on that!"

"I never did believe that sea-turtle story, so one day I asked your brother about it." After he'd stopped laughing, Alexander's brother had told me that the great mishap had nothing to do with sea turtles. The real story went that a pretty girl by the name of Loni Whachamajiggy on the board next to Alexander lost her bathing suit top. I said, "If you need an alibi for Kira—oh, Kira. She called. You're in the dog house."

He rolled his eyes. "Again?"

I nodded. "You've got to do better than this. I'll tell her—I'll come up with something. Long as you two didn't—you know."

Alexander glared at me. "Screw you, McKenna. You think I got this gash from some little nature walk?"

"No, I guess not. So'd you go into a biker bar by mistake? How many of them were there? Five? Six? What'd they do, try to haul off Legs or something?"

"Legs?" Harris fixed her gaze on mine, then winked.

Alexander added his suggestion. "Go screw yourself, McKenna."

Though I felt stupid for letting my pet nickname for Harris slip, I realized that maybe she felt the same attraction I did. My pulse quickened at the thought, but I remained undaunted. These two were BS'ing me.

Harris's face went white with pain as she shifted position in her chair. "Don't worry, Alexander, I've got the pictures to prove it."

"You hope you do. Your camera, maybe it's broke."

"Thank God it landed on me, not the other way around."

Now I had them. "So you did drop your camera! Even an eighty-foot drop, you'd be sushi, yesterday's beef stew, Hungarian—"

Harris said, "Enough! There was a ledge, just a small outcropping of rocks about twenty feet down. If I'd have missed that—all I'd be is legs." She snickered, then winced.

She wasn't going to let me live that one down. "So your camera doesn't have a neck strap, huh?"

Alexander butted in. "For chrissakes! She was all, 'I've gotta have that shot over the cliff.' I tied the line around her waist. I wrapped my end around a big boulder. But, when a bullet shatters a couple of feet from your head, you notice. She fell cuz the guy in the plane almost blew my head off."

This ridiculous improvisation needed lots of work. Maybe, if I heard the whole thing, we could polish it up a bit. "I'm an old man and can't keep up with both of you. One tells the story; otherwise, I'm outta here. Wait a minute, this is my *hale*. You're outta here."

"You got the pics. You tell him."

Harris said, "It all happened so fast. I was hanging off the cliff, the plane skimmed the ridge and a guy in the plane threw a body out the door. I snapped a couple of photos of the plane. I guess my lens reflected the light. The plane did this big turnaround thing and came back. This time the guy had a gun, and he started shooting at us. I heard Alexander yell for me to grab onto a rock or something and take cover. That's about the time he must've gotten that gash on his face because before I could grab anything the rope went slack."

I waved my hands. "Kira would see through this in a second. Let's try—"

Apparently, Harris was just getting wound up because she only paused long enough to take a deep breath. Nobody had cut me off like that in a long time and, in a way, I kind of admired her for it. She was a take-charge kind of girl. I half-wondered if that's what my life needed as she continued.

"Next thing I know, I'm trying to run uphill, but my feet can't feel the ground. I was looking up at the sky wondering why I felt like I was in slow-motion. That's when I realized I was looking at the opposite side of the canyon—upside down. I thought I was gonna die and had this crazy thought about why didn't I become a lawyer like my mother wanted me to be. I think Alexander thought I was—"

"Hey, my tours are always round trip."

Legs smiled. "I'm glad to hear that."

Alexander rested a gentle hand on her shoulder. "Company policy."

He leaned over the chair, and they did a big wimpy, huggy thing.

A twinge of jealousy shot through me as I watched them. For crying out loud, was this entire cock-and-bull story true? It was actually a lot better than either version of the surfing contest story. "So what's your problem? You survived, you only got a few cuts."

Harris winced again. "And stuff."

"So what are you worried about? Maybe the cops'll find these guys, yah?" I realized after I said it that as time went on I sounded more and more like a local. The longer I lived here, the more I adopted the island lilt in my speech and some of the common idioms, like "yah," which subconsciously solicited agreement when speaking. It was polite and friendly and when I wasn't feeling like a grump, I used it quite a bit. Of course, being from LA, I also used the good old American "yeah," a word that reminded me of tough guys in movies with cigarettes hanging out of their mouths as they stared down the barrel of a gun.

Harris seemed to be zoning out.

Alexander said, "McKenna, I can't report this."

"Why not? If you two witnessed someone disposing of a body—"

"She didn't have permission for us to be there. We were trespassing on state land."

"What?" I glanced from Alexander to Harris, then back.

"Right after I pulled her up, she told me the email from the state was a lie."

"It's in the works! I got a verbal approval to go in, okay? I'm like, really sorry, but I don't have the written confirmation yet. I just needed to get those pictures."

"So she's got a verbal approval," I said. "How long can it take for the paperwork to get here?"

Alexander let out a deep sigh. "What bureaucrat you know gonna give an okay to go in there after what happened today?"

I groaned. "State land. Trespassing. Tour operator."

Alexander added, "No more license."

Harris said, "Prison. Divorce."

Alexander glowered at her. I thought she was cute.

She and I exchanged an abbreviated smile as she apologized. "Sorry. I got carried away."

Alexander said, "You get the idea? Besides, this guy had a gun. Okay, maybe he can't hit anything, yah, but he might have friends who can. If the cops arrest us for trespassing and those pictures hit the news, it won't take long for these guys to connect us. We gotta be really careful."

"So somebody's gonna want to kill you? Here?" I squeaked, then cleared my throat. "In my apartment building. And you can't call the cops." I glanced at Legs. "Or see a doctor."

Alexander waved his hands as if he were fending off a swarm of fruit flies hungry for a rotten apple. "We just need some time to think this through. Tomorrow morning we can figure out how to clean up this whole mess."

Harris had a faraway look in her eyes, but she nodded agreement.

I licked my lips. "Uh, about that. You can't go home tonight."

He sighed, "I figured. Use your couch?"

"Sure." I had to admit that Harris appeared as though she'd come close enough to death to realize she was too young to die. Or that she still had things to do.

She reached out and took my hand. Though roughened by the day's adventure, her touch still felt soft and warm. She stared into my eyes.

Talk about having a stupid-me moment.

Alexander said, "You could help her out with this, McKenna."

As a skip tracer, it had been my job to find people who'd bailed on their debts. In the old days, I'd even repossessed cars in relatively safe situations. I'd found a few guys who always carried weapons and one who was rumored to have bombed a church, but in those cases I just turned my results over to tow-truck drivers who were used to stealing cars in the middle of the night, and the cops, who were used to dealing with the bad guys. Again, Harris jarred me from my thoughts. The spiders crawling down my back and arms caught me totally off guard. I shivered and rubbed my arms to warm them, but the effort was futile. Nothing I could do would shake that feeling as long as I held her gaze.

It had been so long since I felt as though I'd really accomplished anything important that I had to think about it for a long time. They both stayed silent while decades worth of incidents flashed through my mind. My parents' childhood mantra, the one brought on by my own deceptive behavior, played loud and clear. "Better safe than sorry."

Come to think of it, I'd never played it safe. And I'd frequently been sorry. I'd never hurt a soul, but I had an arrest record in California and an ex-girlfriend who'd disappeared when I screwed up our relationship. It would have been easy for me to find her afterwards, but she didn't want that, so I'd never tried. All in all, I'd become an emotional wreck and fled to Hawaii, where I'd played it safe. And still wasn't happy.

I made up my mind, there was only one thing I could do—evict Harris for something. With her gone, life could return to normal.

Quiet. Dull. Tedious.
That's when she did the one thing I feared most.
She started to cry. "Please?"

3

It had been a couple of hours since Alexander and Harris had shown up on my doorstep. During that time, I'd learned a couple of things about myself; I was still a sucker for a pretty face and a tear and tired of being a lonely old grump. I was also petrified by the thought of becoming anything else.

During my four years here in Hawaii, I'd gotten close to Alexander alone—that due more to his persistence than my receptiveness. Tonight, I had him on my clean couch, taking up the only real sitting room in the apartment other than the dining-room chairs. Harris was on the chaise lounge on my lanai, leaving me a choice of a dining room or lanai chair. I took the lanai. I could have gone to bed, but that seemed rude and if there's one adjective that doesn't fit me, it's rude.

A movement to my right jarred me from my thoughts. Alexander stood at my side and put his hand on my shoulder. In a voice as soft as the surf on the shore, he said, "Why not give her some *kokua*?"

Me? Help? My eyes rolled at the thought. I grumbled, "Like that's going to happen."

"You like her; I can see it."

He was right. I liked being around Harris. She made me feel—yeah, that was it, she made me feel again.

Alexander squeezed my shoulder. "I had to get up for a minute, saw you moping out here. Think about it. I'm going back to the couch."

He left me listening to the surf, admiring the moon's reflection off the black ocean surface and wondering what to do about Harris as I got sloshed on my third glass of wine. Every time her eyelids closed and her facial muscles started to relax, she jerked like a hula-girl doll in the back window of an old Chevy on a bumpy road. Her pain-noises were starting to bug me, but she'd nearly gotten her brains splattered on a mountainside. She hadn't asked for some guy to fly over in a plane and start shooting. Watching her suffer brought back memories of my own problems.

The last time I'd been anywhere close to someone else's personal drama was in Los Angeles. I'd had a growing case of depression, which had been brought on by a digestive disorder called Celiac sprue.

Celiacs can have a rainbow assortment of symptoms and until you know you're not able to tolerate wheat, oats, rye and barley, the symptoms will worsen. To top it off, you're basically screwed because doctors don't always know to test for it. The bottom line is that on a particularly bad day, my girlfriend Jenny's son Michael was beaten up because he wore the wrong colors, a gang's colors, to school. Like an idiot, I made things worse by ranting at him about his choice of apparel instead of driving my stupid butt to the school to obtain justice. I made the ultimate mistake of threatening to shake some sense into him. Jenny called the cops.

My dumb luck included two hard-nosed uniforms who hated domestic abuse cases. The cops and I played a short game of "I Can Top That" and, needless to say, they slept in their beds that night while I got a drunken, smelly roommate who kept calling me Ralph. The next day, when I arrived home, Jenny and Michael were gone.

Just like me, Harris had unknowingly brought this on herself. The major difference was that her situation had been completely avoidable, mine, medically inevitable. I watched her face. A wince of pain. A twitch of discomfort. Why the hell had she gone to that park in the first place? For a stupid job? To make it big in her field?

Fifteen minutes, or maybe an hour later, I'd drained the glass when Harris started. She blinked, then glanced over and said, "Help me up, McKenna."

"You gotta pee?" Just asking the question made me think that it might be my turn to go again.

"No, I'm going back to my place."

Talk about conflicted. Stay? Or go? If she stayed, we could help her. If she went, she might die in her apartment. That would be exceptionally bad news. I could lose my job if I let her die in there. And even if I didn't lose my job, I'd have a helluva time renting her place because prospective tenants were so picky about that dead body thing. "Can't do that."

"I want to download those pictures. Besides, I'm getting cold."

Having watched how much pain these two were in for nearly two hours, I kind of wanted to see those shots myself. It might also help to pull me out of the exceptionally funky mood that grew inside of me. She tried to roll herself out, but her face turned crimson. She couldn't make it up on her own.

"I'll get you a blanket." Talk about sounding stupid. I was about three sips from losing all common sense, but could recognize a no-win situation when it bit me in the behind. "Wait till morning." I could stick her in my bed and sleep. But where? Here, I guess.

Her head moved slightly from side to side, but even that seemed to cause her pain. "I'm too keyed up to sleep."

It was well after eleven, and Alexander snored like a happy pup on my couch, but wouldn't stay asleep for long if Harris didn't shut up. Women. Why couldn't they be less trouble? She probably didn't want to die in her landlord's home. I didn't want her to die in hers. I hoisted myself out of the chair, teetered towards her, and kept my voice low. "I'm stiff, can't sit in one place for more time than it takes you to say *humuhumunukunukuapua'a*. You ever wonder who named that little fish?"

"I need to see those photos."

My reaction reminded me of a drunk who'd just seen the flashing red lights in his rearview mirror and desperately wanted instant sobriety. I was way off my game. Who was I kidding? I hadn't been on my game in five years. My only hope was to stall and hope Harris didn't notice. "They were from Tahiti, you know. The first Hawaiians, not the fish. I don't know where the fish is from."

Her lower lip began to quiver, and I saw another of those damn tears. "I'm a twin."

"A twin what?" Oh. Wow, I really was drunk. "Sister?"

"I need the money from this job to help her. If I get delayed, she might—are you gonna help me up, or not?" Harris's face turned scarlet. Even like this, she was gorgeous.

"We'll take them to one of those 24-hour photo places tomorrow, then we'll call the cops. You rest now." She wouldn't go for that, but it was worth a try.

"It's a digital camera. I have to transfer them to my hard disk." Her blond hair, which she'd tied back in a ponytail, combined with the cuts, scrapes and bruises she'd picked up gave the straight lines of her face a severe appearance that told me she wasn't about to take any of my crap.

I was stuck. I'd have to get Harris back to her place and keep an eye on her. If I could keep her from dying immediately, it would be a win-win for me. She'd live and my bosses wouldn't be inconvenienced by having to fire me, their faithful, indentured servant.

I stood over her and extended my hand, then leaned back a bit to keep from doing a splashdown on top of her.

She said, "Don't let go."

Her grip felt strong and warm and weak and vulnerable all at the same time. It looked as though it would be my job to keep Ms. Photographer from killing herself. We took the shortcut, our footsteps crunching on the lava rocks that separated my lanai from the main walkway.

Harris said, "I'll be okay once I'm back in my place."

The last thing in the world I wanted now was to leave her. Alexander had been right; I did have feelings for Harris. We stumbled along like a couple of amateurs in a three-legged sack race. "We'll get you settled in, then tomorrow—"

"Nuh-uh. I have a deadline. No delays allowed." She stiffened in pain.

I scrunched up my face in sympathy. "I get along pretty good with computers. And I'm interested in seeing if this whole story is for real."

"It is."

"But before the cops will send someone up there to look around, they'll want proof that the body's real."

She shook my shoulder as though I'd just heartily volunteered for something. "That's the spirit."

Shit. She'd done it again. If I volunteered one more time, I'd be up for a damn humanitarian award. My mouth stayed shut as we made our way through the courtyard, the scent of jasmine and plumeria filling my nostrils. The dull murmur of the ocean's waves lapped against the shore in the background.

We shuffled quietly past five apartments to the end of the walkway, then took a left to Harris's unit on the end. These places had no air conditioning so the tenants slept with their bedroom windows open at least a crack. The last thing I needed was crabby tenants—crabby was my province.

Once inside, Harris said, "I'll boot up the machine." She pressed the power button, then said, "Be right back."

When she returned, she extracted the media card from her camera, which sported several nasty scratches. It looked a lot like her on the outside. I hoped its insides were in better shape. Otherwise, they might both die for nothing. "Looks like you."

"Ha, ha. It landed on me. Thank God. This thing cost me almost two grand."

"Two—jeez, what's it do, serve lunch while you shoot?" I chuckled, another good one, McKenna.

She just held onto her side and stared at me. Finally, she said, "So what do you do on computers? E-mail? Surf the net?"

"A little of this, a little of that. I was a skip tracer for a bank."

"Oh. One of those."

It surprised me that she knew what a skip tracer did, most people had no clue. "I was the guy who found the tough ones. Before we had computers, anyway. Once computers came along, the job changed."

"Got too technical?"

"In the old days, it was a rush. Like solving a puzzle. The harder the puzzle, the better it felt. Computers made it a production line. I learned to query databases instead of questioning people. Management wanted more work with fewer workers. Then, I got outsourced."

"Honey, you don't look like the kind of guy who got off on his work."

I shrugged. "I am—was. In the old days. Now, I'm sort of a techie."

"Me, I'm a people person."

"And a photographer."

"That too."

"And a twin."

She grimaced.

"Did I say something wrong?"

She shook her head. "My sister needs a kidney transplant. She's stuck with a loser husband, two kids and no insurance."

"So that's why you were willing to go to a closed park to get photos? And now you've got people wanting to kill you."

"My concern is getting more money for my sister's operation. If I don't do it, she'll die."

I didn't want to break the mood, but I realized that it had been hours since I'd been to the bathroom. "Hey, I gotta go."

"Sure, go back home, get some rest."

"No, I've gotta GO."

Harris nodded, then smiled. "You know where it's at, right?"

While in the bathroom, I splashed some water on my face to help the sobering-up process. I stood, staring at my image in the mirror. "You moron, she's a Darwin Award candidate." Maybe I was half-drunk, but Harris seemed to deserve one of those little awards that are given to those who help "improve the species . . . by accidentally removing themselves from it." Personally, I prefer one of their other sayings, "chlorinating the gene pool."

I splashed more water into my eyes, then dried my face. "Get a grip," I told myself. "And a hug."

By the time I got back, file names from the media card had filled Harris's screen and she scrutinized the list. She clicked on a name towards the end. Her screen began to reveal the photo of a waterfall crashing to the canyon floor below. We waited while the photo grew, line by line. I glanced around the room. She had flash attachments, tripods, lenses, camera bags, and other assorted paraphernalia scattered everywhere.

"Shoot, wrong one." Harris drummed her fingers as she waited for the download to finish.

"Wow. That's quite a shot." Forget the Darwin Award, Harris was a damn good photographer.

On the screen, water tumbled past the camera. The rushing blur at the top of the picture gradually became more clear until it plunged into a pool surrounded by rocks at the bottom. It looked as though you were rafting the falls. Though I knew Alexander was right, that it was only eighty feet to the bottom, I stood, mesmerized by the perception of plunging ten times that distance to the canyon floor. "If you'd have used a webcam, you'd have full motion video."

"And it would look like a low-res postage stamp. These photos are ten meg each. Unless you're doing posters, the quality is as good as film and immensely more flexible. I can use photo editing software to manipulate the photo, crop, and adjust colors."

I hadn't thought about photographers adjusting the colors on their photos before. If Harris had a few more shots like this one and a couple more answers like that, she'd move from the Darwin Award candidate category into the Wonder Woman category. Unless, of course, she died. In which case, I was going online and reluctantly making a nomination. "Is that how they get those bright-red sunset shots?"

"Sometimes. They might also use a special lens or combination of lenses. This one's pretty good, but I've got a couple that are better. This was the last one before the plane showed up."

Harris closed the window with the waterfall and clicked another file name. This time, the screen began to paint an image of the sky—a pale-blue canvas with fluffy white clouds and a miniature image of a plane. Harris grabbed her head and leaned forward. She rested her forehead on the desk and groaned, "It's too small!"

Well, I'll be. The whole story was true. I moved in closer to the photo, trying to make out the details. There was the little plane with an ant in the middle of a miniature doorway and forever suspended in midair below the plane was another ant. But, this ant had two arms, two legs, and definitely no parachute. I said, "How come you didn't just zoom in?"

"Goddammit, McKenna, I had on a wide-angle lens to shoot scenery and didn't have time to get back to my camera bag and change lenses!"

Wow, she'd gone from Wonder Woman to the Wicked Witch in two heartbeats—and I'd missed the costume change. Crap. I'd try something out of my comfort zone—sympathy "I'd be crabby too if I got caught with the wrong lens on my $2,000 camera."

She glared at me, then began to laugh.

My breath caught in my throat. I wanted to hear that sound again.

Her nose wrinkled and she nodded. "You think you're so funny. All right, funny man, can you make out the number on that plane?"

I winked at her. "I can do better than that, I'll bet I can find out who owns the damn thing."

4

No sooner had the words popped out of my mouth than I realized I'd done it again. Something about this woman just brought out my inner sucker. I don't want to demean the act of volunteering for a worthy cause; there are plenty of those. But, I hadn't volunteered to help the homeless, guard a stranded monk seal, or anything else like that. I'd volunteered to find a couple of guys with guns. How was I going to explain to her that I hadn't meant to volunteer—without revealing myself a lost cause?

But Harris smiled. She laughed. She thought I was Mr. Wonderful. I was buried up to my neck in a mating ritual as old as Mauna Kea. The only way out was to live up to my stupid boasting and hope I didn't fail. My problem was that I had no idea how to find the owner of a frigging airplane. Sure, I'd been a crack skip tracer, but this was a plane, not a person. Now, I felt like a crack moron for getting Harris's hopes up.

The admiration in her eyes drove me on; her glee at my stupidity told me that backing down wasn't an option. I had to take a guess at how to pull this off without landing myself in the dictionary as the definitive cross-reference for terms like dumb, stupid, moron and, oh yeah, sucker. I pointed at the screen. "Every plane's got an ID number, right?"

"I've never thought about it, hon."

She'd called me "Honey" from our first meeting, which is probably what she called everyone. I considered asking, but had no desire for truth. "Neither have I, but they fly in and out of airports all the time. Those guys in the towers must have some way to identify them other than, 'Hey, you in the blue plane.'"

"Like a car's license plate, huh?"

To my relief, Harris turned back to the screen and enlarged the image. She leaned toward the screen; I followed suit. I peered over her shoulder.

She said, "Hold your breath."

She didn't have a girly-girl smell, but for someone who'd traipsed around the mountains all day and dodged bad-guy bullets, she smelled pretty good, especially if you contrasted that against my fresh-from-the-bottom-of-the-wine-bottle fragrance. I spotted a series of numbers on the tail and pointed. "There!"

"Okay, okay. I'm a little slow."

She zoomed in again, and there it was—a blur of little colored squares that were completely illegible. "Crap. Back it out a bit."

As she moved the mouse, she said, "Man, talk about impatient."

Actually, right now I was about as happy as a parrot on a pirate's shoulder. She was the cutest damn pirate I'd ever seen, and I could easily be trained to say, "McKenna want a cracker." I studied the lines of her face, the bruise forming on her cheek. I could do this all night—or at least until I had to go to the bathroom again. I glanced at the clock on her desk. Five of one. I was usually in bed three hours ago. "Take your time."

Harris tried again and again; zoom in, then out. Too fuzzy, too small. She finally said, "Goddammit, enough of this crap." She stood and crossed the room, then rummaged through one of her camera bags. She gripped her forehead as she stood, pain masking her features. "Shooting pains. I think I'm tired." In her other hand, she held a large magnifying glass. She took a couple of deep breaths, then came back and examined the computer screen from just inches away. She moved the magnifying glass and her head in and out. She said, "It's still blurry, but this gives me just enough control—I think it's M7Z434."

She dropped the magnifying glass onto the desktop and slumped back in her chair. I was afraid that she might fall asleep right where she was and that scared me because I didn't know what I should do. Get her a blanket? Nibble on her ear like a good parrot? "It's time for you to get some rest," I said. I placed my hand on her shoulder and felt a surge of heat when she reached up and stroked the back of my hand with her fingers. Another shooting pain interrupted our tender moment.

Once Harris was settled in bed, I went in and checked on her. She'd let her hair down and had on a big, floppy San Francisco Giants tee shirt.

I pointed at the shirt. "Traitor."

She glanced down, then back to me. "A present from my sister." The bruise below her eye had darkened and taken on an angry purple hue in the harsh light of the bedroom lamp. She continued, "You look tired, too."

I gulped. I couldn't tell whether that was an invitation or an observation, so I said, "I'm going to camp out on your couch. Just in case those pains get worse."

She nodded. "Hold me for a minute."

I sat on the side of the bed and let her put her arms around my waist, while I stroked her bare arm. I turned off the light with my free hand, then waited. When her breathing became slow and regular, I tucked her in, then crept from the room. I left the door open a crack just in case she called out.

It was almost two by the time I found a blanket and parked myself on the couch. I'd lost half a night's sleep, but I was still wired. And exhausted. Bad combination. Somewhere between sleep and consciousness I heard Harris moan, a dim reminder of a promise I'd made earlier in the evening. Tomorrow, I had a plane's owner to find.

5

The little glow-in-the-dark clock on Harris's desk read 4:14 AM when the rain woke me. It came in like a typical Hawaiian shower; fast, hard, and short-lived—just enough to jar me from a fitful sleep. I kept having the same dream, which never quite finished. In the dream, I stood on the beach at Waikiki. An old man, bent and crooked with age and wisdom, skin bronzed from years in the sun, stood before me. He'd asked a simple question. I'd given him an answer, then he'd made a ridiculous statement about me running away.

So here I lay, wondering why his criticism bothered me so much. Each time the dream had occurred I'd climbed the ladder to consciousness before I knew what to say. Each time, I struggled back to sleep as failure gnawed at me. Then, the cycle repeated. This time, though, the wind rustled through the palms. Leaves and branches on broadleaved plants banged together in a symphony that the heavy, moist air echoed. *Lono*, the Hawaiian god of rain and wind, was back in town. You could hear Lono's murmur, rain splattering pavement. That escalated into a low hum. Roofs and plants amplified the intensity as Lono's passion approached. You could almost do a countdown. Two blocks away. Then one. Even the unpracticed ear could tell that the show was about to begin as pandemonium erupted in the night.

I watched the little red numbers on the clock advance another minute while I considered the old man in the dream. He'd had shoulder-length gray hair, had only worn a pair of swim trunks and had held a surfboard under one arm. We'd been on the water's edge at Waikiki. I had the "Do Not Disturb" sign around my neck, but he ignored it. Wavelets splashed across his toes as I said, "Who the hell are you, Duke Kahanamoku?"

He seemed amused, but obviously wasn't the father of modern surfing as he asked his question again. "Why you not want help find these bad men?"

"I don't want something to happen to my—friends." Now I had friends? Plural? Me?

The old man gently ran his hand over the board's smooth surface. "You stop running, maybe what you looking for find you." Before I could give him a piece of my mind for intruding in my life and my dreams, he turned toward the ocean. "Good surf today." And he was off.

I listened to Lono churn the early morning air and tried to conjure up a retort to the old man's statement. As a professional skip tracer, I'd never shied away from finding someone before. Never worried about how my finding them might change their lives. I'd even crossed the ethics line a few times when all roads dead-ended. But, times were different now, more rigid. More defined. Creativity like mine had become a liability. With the advent of computer programs and massive databases that tracked virtually every minute detail of our lives, finding people had become routine if you knew which databases to use and had the access. I no longer had that access, but how hard could it be to track down the owner of a plane? Was I afraid to do it? Was that why the dream kept coming back?

Maybe I was afraid. Of what? That I might fail and look like a fool in front of Harris or that Alexander had called it correctly and these men would stop at nothing to keep their secret? I stared overhead at the green smoke detector light, then at the three-foot halo it cast onto the floor. I needed a plan.

Plan A: follow through on my promise to Harris, then call the cops. If we gave them the photo and the contact information for the owner, they should bag the bad guy in no time. That would let me fulfill my promise, let her get the recognition she deserved, and keep her and Alexander safe. The mention of his name reminded me that Plan A would fail because Alexander could never admit that he'd been in that park. Okay, Plan B: make the report anonymous and still get the photo to the cops somehow. The good news was that Plan B would make everyone happy; the bad news was that I was wide awake and operating on two hours sleep.

I moved to a dining table chair and listened to the rainwater gurgle down the gutters. Raindrops smacked the palm fronds like sticks on concrete. About thirty minutes later, Lono stopped the show. It wasn't long before the sprinklers kicked in, adding their constant hiss to the morning's routine.

It was 5:05 AM when the sprinklers shut off. I did another quick check on Harris; her breathing sounded slow and regular. Peaceful. I tiptoed out the door and closed it behind me, but accidentally bumped into her desk. The soft whir of her computer broke the silence; light from the screen illuminated the room. Like me, Harris didn't shut down her machine, she just put it to sleep. Time to start on Plan B.

Now past my wine-induced, stupid-me state, I realized that the idea of unraveling the whole falling-body mystery intrigued me. Finding the owner before Legs awoke would show that I hadn't lost my touch. Uh oh. I'd better stop calling her that. Maybe she found it demeaning. I probably wouldn't want someone calling me "Stud" or "Studley" or "Stud-muffin." Not that anyone had ever called me by one of those nicknames—so how would I know?

I sat on the edge of the chair in front of Harris's computer and congratulated myself on my newfound politically correct attitude and the fact that I was making progress on beginning to put my past mistakes behind me.

I double clicked Harris's browser icon and did an Internet search for "aircraft registration inquiry." That gave me a list of sites for Canada, Asia and more. I revised my search and added "US" to the beginning of the search phrase. Presto! The Federal Aviation

Administration was at the top of the list. I clicked the link for "FAA—Aircraft Certification: Registration Inquiry."

That led me to the FAA web site, where visitors could search for a registration number. This wasn't rocket science. It had taken me less than two minutes to find the FAA's site and click the link to do a search. When the page finished loading, I stared at it, groaning. Ten options to choose from. Fortunately, only the first one made sense. The instructions said that the FAA used N as the first character of the registration number. I studied the number we'd gotten from the plane for a few seconds—duh, the M was really an N.

A click on the link gave me a page with one blank text field. Could they make this any easier? I clicked in the text box and got a message that said, "The N-Number of the aircraft of which you wish to inquire. N is implicit." How nice.

Tap, tap, tap, numbers in the field, making sure I left off the N so the FAA wouldn't secretly log me as an idiot for not following directions. The message that appeared on the screen read, "Alphabetic characters cannot follow numeric characters."

It wasn't even light yet, so I had to think about that one. Oh. I whispered at the screen, "Why didn't you just say, 'Numbers Only?'" Bureaucrats. If the Z in the number wasn't a Z, it was probably a 2. I tried that and instantly got registration details for Laura P. Daggett in Cincinnati, Ohio. What would her plane be doing here on Oahu? That couldn't be right. So we'd been wrong about the number. No problem there, either. I had the database and the access. And some time.

I looked at the N-Number again. We'd thought that the third and fifth characters had been fours, but maybe they weren't. Maybe they were nines.

This time, I replaced each "4" with a "9." Nothing. After trying a couple of different combinations, the details for a Cessna 206H registered to Robert M. Shapiro, Jr. appeared on the screen. Our pilot lived in an apartment on Kaiulani Ave. in Honolulu.

I shrugged. With this information, we could implement Plan B as soon as Alexander and Harris were up. We'd figure out how to get this information turned in anonymously so everyone could be happy, except of course, the bad guys. My bet was that it wouldn't take long for the cops to arrest Mr. Robert M. Shapiro, Jr. Who knew what crimes he'd committed. Murder—drug running—littering a closed state park with a dead body.

The palms in the courtyard rustled in a sudden gust of wind. Lono making sure we knew he was still here? Would we get another shower? I stepped outside and listened to the island sounds. Plan B might save Harris's life. Maybe it would let me keep her as a tenant. And as a—don't go there. Would it keep Alexander out of trouble, too?

The sky grew lighter, brightening from the dark shadows of night to blues and pinks and pale grays of morning. Soon, Honolulu would be alive. A half million people would jam the freeways, all eager to get to their day's destination. Me, I didn't have to do that because I lived and worked in the same place. Managing this place wasn't much of a job, but had its perks, like Suzie Wong in #14.

Suzie Wong's real name was Julia Lym and, unlike the character in the 60s movie starring Nancy Kwan, Julia was no hooker. I'm not sure when I started thinking of her as Suzie Wong, but Julia was working on a law degree and had a bad-ass belt in karate so, needless to say, I always behaved around her. Still, she was a looker and would be leaving for work soon, so my goal was to be on my lanai to say good morning. That Aloha spirit stuff played well with pretty girls and Harris was still asleep. So, why not?

On the quiet stroll back to my apartment, I thought again about Mr. Robert M. Shapiro, Jr. What was he involved in? Smuggling? Drugs? The mob? I'd heard news stories indicating that it was alive and well. But, a smart criminal wouldn't throw a body down a mountain, would he? Why not just shoot the guy or stick a knife in him? Toss the body in a Dumpster in the right area and, just like any other big city in the world, no one would think twice about it. No attention, no risk. Jeez, was that guy they threw out of the plane really dead?

The smell of freshly brewed coffee filled the courtyard outside my apartment. I opened the door; Alexander sat at the table with a cup and a bowl of cereal. "Hey, brah. She doing okay?"

"I don't know. She was asleep when I left. Broke into my cereal, huh?"

"I can't believe you eat these little cardboard things."

"Corn puffs. They're corn puffs, not cardboard."

"Tastes like cardboard."

"It's gluten-free. I can't eat that sugary kids' stuff you like cause its got wheat in it. And gluten—"

"I know, I know, it's a protein in wheat. You only told me maybe, what, a thousand times? Hey, about yesterday?"

"Right, cops and hospital are a problem because you two were breaking the law."

"You call this food?" He glanced down to the bowl, then back to me. "No, that wasn't it—well, yeah, that's part of it. I shouldn't have asked you to help her, yah? There's something about her."

A surge of heat raced through my veins. What was he going to tell me? That he liked her? Something had happened between them? Kira would kill him—and me.

He went on, "She shoulda been afraid when that guy in the plane started shooting."

"So?"

"She wasn't. Not at all, man. She was cool as they get—until I dropped her, of course."

I breathed a sigh of relief. "So she doesn't panic. Big deal."

He flushed the uneaten portion of his cereal down the kitchen sink drain. "Anyway, she didn't die in her sleep and you didn't have to call 9-1-1. I'm outta here. Get me some real breakfast."

"You going home?"

He shook his head. "Nah, I don't show up for a couple of hours and Kira will start to feel bad about blowing up. She might even wanna make up for—"

"Too much information, Alexander! Way TMI."

"Sorry brah. I'll check on Harris."

"Not yet." I planted my feet firmly, crossed my arms over my chest. Just like the old days, just like Lono, the thrill of making the announcement rushed through my veins. The look on Alexander's face when he heard the news, the surprise at how little time it had taken to find the information, would make this morning's efforts all worthwhile. I said, "I know who owns the plane."

6

Alexander's slack jaw and wide eyes gave him away. I had his full attention. On the other hand, my attention was flagging thanks to so little sleep. My primary focus had become staying vertical. Talk about a perfect day to knock down about a gallon of coffee.

Alexander said, "When did you—"

"We got the N-Number off the plane from one of Harris's photos." Now that I knew the FAA terminology, I could pass off my N-Number knowledge like a professional. "Yours truly did some detective work last night and found the registered owner of the plane. I know where he lives, so we can turn this over to the cops and you two can get on with your lives."

"How you know you got the right guy? What if the owner wasn't the one flying?"

"If he wasn't, he'll know who was. It was easy, I just did a search for the FAA web site, then I—"

Alexander pointed at me with an accusing finger. "Don't matter how brilliant you think this is, McKenna, it might not be the right guy."

"Lighten up. It's no different than if your car was used to commit a crime. Unless you've got a good excuse, like maybe it was stolen, you're in a deep pile. Know what I mean?"

"So you been playing detective for how long?"

"Not long."

"I gonna go check on Harris. She's back at her place, yah?"

"Yah. And for the record, this old fart figured out how to find the bad guys before either of you two youngsters."

"McKenna, you're right about one thing, you an old fart." He gave me the shaka sign. Now, unlike the single-digit hand salute that mainlanders are so fond of, the shaka sign involves the use of the thumb and pinky and has several different meanings, all of them expressing good feelings.

Well, lah-de-dah. Shaka sign or not, I didn't need Alexander's approval. Or Harris's, for that matter. What I needed was breakfast on the lanai and a good morning smile from Suzie Wong. Maybe she'd wear that little flowered number again. I rushed into the kitchen and got a bowl of the gluten-free cereal Alexander didn't like, soy milk and juice. Yeah, yeah, soy milk. How come I just couldn't drink the stuff from a cow, anyway? Gives me gas, that's why.

It took only a minute to transport everything outside to the lanai and compose myself for the show. She'd be leaving in about 15 minutes. Suzie usually wore a suit. Which, unfortunately, usually meant pants. But, every now and again she wore the dress. Just the thought made my pulse quicken.

Suzie had lived here for about three years. A few months back, she took a job with a large law firm. When I'd asked what she did, she'd said, "A day's work." She'd given me a quick kiss on the cheek and swayed away. With my libido in limbo, I'd gone back to my place, had a glass of wine and reveled in my manhood for about an hour before I realized that I still didn't know what she did, just that she always dressed nice—and that she was a helluva kisser—even if it was just a peck on the cheek. My guess was that she was just testing the waters.

With just enough time to scarf down my cereal, then sit back and look handsome for her pass by my lanai, I shoveled the cardboard pellets from bowl to mouth. I chewed and swallowed with impeccable precision while I contemplated what Alexander and Harris had witnessed. I glanced at my watch. Yikes! Suzie would be leaving in just five minutes.

My reflection in the sliding glass door telegraphed a big problem, my hair looked like a bird's nest, all wiry and tangly and standing straight up in back—I looked haggard. That needed fixing, and quick. I grabbed my bowl and the soy milk and took them inside, then rushed into the bathroom and ran a comb through my hair. It was getting sparse, but there was still enough to cover the top of my head. A little water helped to hold down that nasty cowlick in the back. I splashed more water on my face, dried off, then admired my image. Not bad for an old guy—would Suzie give me another smack on the cheek someday? How about Harris?

Maybe I should tell Suzie about my detective work? Explain how I'd spent much of the night doing painstaking research? The process, to a novice, could sound complex and difficult. Maybe she'd be impressed enough to give an old man a last wish. Jeez. I'd gone for five years without a woman in my life, and now there were two.

What if I could get a phone number for Robert M. Shapiro, Jr.? That would make my accomplishments even more outstanding. It was worth a try, so I pulled the phone book from my desk drawer and grabbed the cordless phone. I made it back to the lanai just in time to hear footsteps to my left and see the swish of a flowered skirt disappear around the corner towards the parking lot. Crap! I stared down at the phone and book in my hands. "McKenna, you dumb-ass. You missed her." My day had gone to hell—and it wasn't even eight.

I stood on the lanai, phone book in one hand, cordless phone in the other. What the hell was I thinking? I was over sixty—fine, sixty-two. And Suzie was twenty-eight according to her rental application. I'd done the math many times, and the answer was always the same, thirty-plus years difference between us. She probably thought of me like her father. Or grandfather. Ouch. I should focus on an older woman, like Harris. Her rental application had said that she was thirty-one. She was the best damned looking thirty-one-year-old I'd ever seen in my life.

There was only one way to resolve this, do something to get my mind off women. I plopped down the phone and the book and began looking for Mr. Robert M. Shapiro, Jr. Why couldn't he have his own name? It wasn't really his fault that he'd been saddled with the moniker by his egotistical father, but using his middle initial and that Jr. suffix seemed pretentious to me. Take that, Mr. Robert M. Shapiro, Jr.

So, where are you, *Bob*? In a city of a million people, there were just a dozen Shapiros. The 2000 census report classified less than 20% of the population as "white." It doesn't take a genius to come to two important conclusions. First, there shouldn't be many Shapiros in the phone book because the potential population with that name would be fairly small. And, second, I needed a life. When anyone quotes the latest census report, they need some serious social interaction with people.

With no Robert M. Shapiro, Jr., or a derivative, in the book, I was at a roadblock. For an old hotshot like me, though, that roadblock was nothing more than a speed bump. What about other information? I went inside and woke up my computer, typed Robert M. Shapiro, Jr. into the search box and hit the enter key. It took less than a second for the results to appear. The entry at the top of the list stopped me cold. "Obituaries—The Honolulu Advertiser."

There's no telling how long I stared at that headline. He was DEAD? How? When? I moved my mouse over the link and clicked, then read the story.

Local News. Posted on Wednesday, May 11, 2011. Obituaries. Advertiser Staff. Robert M. Shapiro, Jr., 59, of Honolulu, Oahu, died May 10, 2011. Born in Kansas City, MO. Decorated Vietnam war veteran. Former airline pilot. No surviving relatives. No service. Arrangements by Borthwich Mortuary.

Because the vehicle that struck Shapiro appeared to have been traveling at a high rate of speed, police suspect the driver might have been under the influence of an intoxicant. Anyone with information about . . .

It was a standard close for the story, so I hit the Back button and went to the next one, "Local Man Critical After Hit-and-Run."

At approximately 9 PM last night, a resident of Kaiulani Avenue said he heard squealing tires, a loud roar and a scream. The resident, who asked that his name be withheld, left his apartment and went to the street where he found a neighbor, Mr. Robert M. Shapiro, Jr., lying in the gutter.

"He looked like a broken rag doll," said the resident, "so I called police."

Honolulu PD determined that Shapiro was the victim of a hit-and-run. They believe that the accident was caused by someone under the influence of an intoxicant. One investigator speculated that the driver may have been underage, a repeat offender, or did not have insurance and hence did not stop.

This article also did the standard blah, blah close and asked for people with information to call the police. Wow. Shapiro was really, really dead. Road kill. Poor bastard. And he'd been dead for a week.

A knock on my front door interrupted my ruminations. I squinted through the peephole. Alexander and Harris stood at the doorway, so I let them in and greeted them with the news. "Robert Shapiro's dead."

The two exchanged a glance that said, "Old fart's lost it."

Alexander asked, "Who's Shapiro?"

"The owner of the plane."

"Oh, him. How'd it happen? Old age? Heart attack? Massive stroke?"

"Hit and run. A car ran him down just outside of his apartment last week, smart ass."

Harris limped past me and sat on the couch. Her crimson and pearl face, along with the way she held her side, told me that she was still in pain. "McKenna, are you saying that the owner of the plane used to drop that body was murdered?"

Alexander threw his hands in the air. "Oh, not you, too! Harris, there's a ton of accidents in this town. Probably every day someone smacks into something. Don't get caught up in McKenna's drama."

"Hey! I didn't say the M word."

However, now that the word had been introduced, the room was filled by a rousing round of silence. Alexander and I turned to Harris, who stared off into space. Lost in thought about her sister, perhaps? She nodded, as if she'd resigned herself to something, then said, "You don't find it the least bit odd that somebody dropped a body from the sky using this guy's plane, then tried to kill us because we witnessed them disposing of the evidence?"

Alexander held up both hands. "Okay, okay. It's all kine—unusual. But, you hired me to be a guide. I did that. And remember, if the cops learn that we were in that park, we're both in big trouble. Some bureaucrat might decide to pull my permits. Now, I gotta get back to my life. And you two gotta leave me outta this. I got a wife. Kids. A job. Nobody can know I was there. Besides, my wife she not gonna speak to me for three days cause I didn't come home last night."

"I thought you said she'd want to—" I shot a glance at Harris, who was smiling at me, "Uh, you know—if you showed up in a couple of hours."

He shook his head. "I lied. Wanted to make you feel better. You gotta vouch for me, McKenna; otherwise, it might be a week."

"Me? Kira hates me."

"Nah. She just enjoy giving you a bad time. You so easy."

Harris snickered. So did Alexander.

My face felt hot with the irritation simmering inside. I was easy? Well, this pushover was going to push back. "I know I said I'd call her, but that's a mighty big favor you're asking. Kira's got quite a temper; I wouldn't want to jeopardize—"

"What you want, McKenna?"

I fingered my chin and glanced around the room. "What makes you think I want something?"

"What, McKenna? Don't play me coy, you no good at it."

"A boat ride."

He stared at me for a few seconds, as if he were trying to register the request. "You want a boat ride."

"Actually a snorkel trip for me and Harris."

Alexander's jaw dropped. Harris did a double take. Alexander glanced at Harris. Harris shrugged.

Alexander rolled his eyes, "I'm bringing the kids."

Harris eyed me as though I was a steak at the meat counter. "Sounds good to me, honey."

Wow, I had a date. "Perfect! A family outing. I love it. You set it up and let us know when. We'll be there. Now, you go home to your lovely wife; I'll call her in a few minutes." And say what?

Alexander said, "Speaking of making calls. How you gonna notify the cops without letting them know it was me and Harris in the park?"

"I don't have that figured out yet. Can't call 9-1-1, they'd know the address."

Alexander shook his head. "And the business number's out. They'd probably just blow you off as a quack. Oh, wait. They'd be right."

I faked a half-smile. "Ha, ha. You're a riot. Isn't there some number to call when you don't want to get involved?"

Harris said, "Do you guys have CrimeStoppers here?"

Alexander's face lit up. "Yah! That's right, they got that anonymous tip line."

Now, we were making progress. We had a way to get the ball rolling while keeping my friends out of trouble. "I think I've seen their ads. I'll look them up."

Alexander waved. "Great, I'm outta here." With that, he made a hasty exit, leaving me alone with Harris.

Suddenly, a wave of uncertainty washed over me. What was I doing? Reporting the crime would be easy, but Harris was watching me with that hunger in her eye again. I wouldn't mind having her jump my bones, but, jeez, I was out of practice. And her obvious desire made me nervous. "Well, guess I'd better get to finding out how to contact CrimeStoppers."

Harris nodded. "I guess so."

She ran her hand over the back of her neck. I felt my temperature rise a couple of degrees. If the room got any hotter, I'd have to fetch an ice pack from the fridge. "Yeah, CrimeStoppers."

Harris put her hand on my arm just as I started toward my computer. Oh, shit, she wanted it here. Now. Maybe even in the living room. Would my plumbing still work? I needed to lock the door. The neighbors. Oh, crap, what do I do?

"McKenna?" She stared at me expectantly.

I gulped, barely able to keep from peeing my pants. Some letch I was. "Yah?"

"Alexander told me what you did about finding this Bob Shapiro. That was sweet. And you went to a lot of extra trouble for me in figuring out what happened to him. I really appreciate that. What if we, um—"

Oh, God, here it was. These young chicks.

"Well, I'm not very good at this type of thing—but with all your skills—"

I didn't know whether I had skills or not, but I sure had a lump in my pants.

"What if we—"

Sure, Legs, right here, right now. On the floor if you want. Just let me close the drapes.

"What if we tried to find out more information about who was flying Shapiro's plane?"

7

Shapiro's plane? Talk about ruining the mood.

Back when I was skip tracing, I could react to any surprise instantly. I was used to stretching, bending, and reshaping the truth to my will and even flat-out lying when necessary. Right now, I didn't know what to say to Harris, which probably meant that my reaction skills got lost along with the toaster on my move to Hawaii.

All I could muster was a deflated, "Okay." I followed that up with a really snappy, "I—I thought we were going to call CrimeStoppers."

"Well, yeah. But wouldn't it be better if we were able to tell the cops where to look for the evidence?"

I didn't say it, but the words, I thought that was their job, flashed through my mind. She wanted me to investigate a dead guy's plane? The voice of the old man in the dream was back in my thoughts. Why wouldn't he leave me alone?

Harris must have caught my change in mood because she took my hand in hers. "Look, my head's killing me. I'm still having shooting pains. And you look exhausted. Right now, I think the best thing for both of us is to get some rest. Not . . ." She dropped her gaze to the floor, then held mine. "Something else."

Uh, oh. I'd been right. She did want me. Anticipation flooded my system again. Screw it. I could call Crime Busters, Crime Dudes, Crime whatever without her knowing about it. After all, it was an anonymous tip. And if finding whoever was flying that damn plane would make Harris happy, I could do that also. I rallied my best macho voice. "Sure, anything you want." The words came out sounding as though I'd overdosed on aphrodisiacs—too much squeak, too little bravado—and too late for a do over.

Harris went back to her apartment, I looked up the number and made the call.

"CrimeStoppers."

"I'd like to make an anonymous tip about a possible murder."

"Yes, sir. Where did the murder take place?"

Uh. "I don't know. I had two friends that were at Sacred Falls Park, and they saw a body thrown from a plane."

"Sacred Falls? That's closed. When did this happen?"

"They saw it yesterday."

"What time? Do they have a description of the plane?"

It was, uh, white—had wings. I was too tired to remember what I'd seen last night. Maybe this hadn't been such a good idea, there were so many things I didn't know. "I don't know what time. It was a Cessna. It belongs to a Robert M. Shapiro, Jr.—who is deceased."

The voice on the other end of the line sounded skeptical. "Is there any proof that this happened?"

"We have a picture."

"Can you e-mail that in? Or upload it through our web site? Then maybe you could get one of your friends who knows a bit more about what happened to help fill out the tip report."

It was a nice way for him to say, "Hey, idiot, have someone who has some real knowledge report this." I didn't have all the facts. I didn't have the photo. I didn't have a brain! Harris was right; the best thing I could do now would be to take a nap. Hopefully, I could accomplish that without difficulty. In short order, the call ended with me promising to get back to them with more details. The couch looked inviting, so I planted my landing gear there and would have slept a lot longer, but the phone rang. It was some moron with a three-week old paper wanting to know if there was still a unit available. Although it irritated me that someone was stupid enough to be apartment hunting with an old newspaper, the short rest had helped recharge my batteries a bit. I sat down at the computer, determined to learn more about Bob Shapiro and who might be flying his plane now that he was dead.

My first step involved seeing whether I'd missed anything about him or his death. That meant another series of searches for Robert M. Shapiro, Jr., the same thing without the suffix, then no middle initial. Then, I tried Bob. After going through all the name-combination possibilities, I could definitely say with firm conviction that I'd accomplished, well, nothing. Just like the old days.

I'd assembled a few small, insignificant details about our Shapiro and a wide variety of facts about other Shapiros of the world. The interesting thing about Internet searches is that you can find out a wealth of information about virtually any topic. Unfortunately, that wealth is much like debris in an old gold miner's pan. It consists of a large amount of worthless sand, silt and gravel, and maybe, if you're really lucky, a small nugget or two. Today wasn't my lucky day.

Or was it? We were on an island in the middle of the Pacific Ocean. It wasn't like we were in LA with eight billion airports around. That was it! In the entire state, Hawaii had just over a dozen airports. Everyone knew the big one, Honolulu International, the only big commercial airport on Oahu. There were another five commercial airports on the islands, including two on the Big Island, one on Kauai, one on Maui, and one on Molokai. There were some additional state airports on the islands, with only two of those on Oahu.

I would have smacked myself in the head, but the last time I did that it was while trying to kill one of our giant, island mosquitoes. The mosquito got away, I wound up with a welt from the bite, and a headache from hitting myself too hard.

All I had to do was start asking questions in a limited number of places. I pulled out the phone book and checked under "Airports." The listing of numbers for Honolulu International was longer than all the other airports in Hawaii combined. Besides, if someone were going to stuff a body into an airplane and toss it out into the wilderness, they wouldn't really want to do it at an airport where millions of eyes might see them. So, unless these guys were exceptionally stupid, they must have used one of the smaller airports. And closer to the falls. That meant Dillingham Field.

The Army constructed Dillingham Field sometime around 1942 while World War II was underway. It's near Mokuleia, a small town on the northwest side of Oahu that's popular with locals and surfers. I wasn't sure who ran the airport because there was no listed telephone number for the airfield. All I knew from my Internet search was that the airfield had something called a Unicom tower. Maybe I could find someone at one of the businesses out there, an overzealous busybody who knew something. It was McKenna's Third Skip Tracing Secret: people love to talk about their neighbors.

Dillingham was big on skydiving; I knew that much, so I went back online and did a search for "Oahu skydiving." I got the typical search results, 80 million or so listings for sites that had nothing to do with what I wanted. I refined my search to "Oahu skydiving Dillingham Field." Ah, only 40 million or so. That was encouraging. Lucky for me the first page included a couple of businesses that were actually at Dillingham Field, not in Hong Kong, Buenos Aires, or some other remote destination halfway around the world. A few minutes later, I had a phone number and called.

A man with the classic lilting Hawaiian accent answered. "Sky's the Limit Charters."

Experience told me that there were two ways to approach this guy. Be honest and forthright, or lie. It was time to invoke McKenna's First Skip Tracing Secret: when in doubt, lie. I did my best to sound bored. "Hey, O'Brien down at the Honolulu Advertiser, we're doing a follow-up on that hit-and-run with Shapiro a few days back. I'm sure you read it. Can you tell me if he keeps his plane there?"

"Shapiro? Hit-and-run?"

"Yeah, you didn't read the story? He got run down in front of his apartment."

"When did this happen?"

"The 8th."

"Not possible. He took the plane out to Kauai yesterday. Can you call back later, it kine busy right now."

"Uh—tell you what, I want to get some pictures of the plane. I'll bring a photographer out there a little later today. Could I see the plane then?"

"Hey, brah, it's not my plane. You betta' talk to Bob about that."

"But he died on the 10th."

"Well, somebody flew it. I just assumed it was Bob cause he don't let no one else fly it. I gotta go." I heard his greeting to potential customers as he hung up. "Aloha, folks!"

There was only one problem with going to Dillingham Field, I'd sold my car after a close encounter with a fire hydrant and used public transportation to get around. That saved me a few thousand bucks a year, but at times like this, I needed to get creative. I hustled down to Harris's apartment and knocked on the door.

She greeted me, then invited me in. Harris yawned as we sat; even her tanned legs looked pale. "Guess I didn't sleep well."

My brain took the opportunity to delve into the "I told you so" routines it practiced so often. If it hadn't been for the adrenaline running through me, I might have just gone back to my apartment and dialed 9-1-1 for an ambulance. "I found out which airport the plane is at."

She suppressed another yawn and said, "That's good. Can we go see it?"

"You sure you're up to this. You look beat."

"I'll be okay. I just need to wake up." Her eyes were bloodshot, reminding me of a drunk's or—gee, someone who hadn't gotten enough sleep the night before.

How bloodshot were mine? "Why don't I just call this in and we can let the cops find the plane? We'll get you to a doctor, get you checked out."

"What if it's not there? You don't want to call in a tip and not have the plane where it's supposed to be. The cops would think the whole thing was a hoax and drop it. No, give me ten."

While she went off to prepare for our trip, I pondered my predicament. I was starting to care about a woman nearly half my age. I was chasing a dead man's plane around Oahu. I'd called CrimeStoppers, but hadn't had enough details to make the report credible. We'd go to Dillingham and satisfy Harris's urge. Then, we'd get her medical attention.

Harris's voice interrupted my internal planning session. "You look deep in thought."

She was positively stunning—a twelve on the ten point scale. She wore a flowered sundress that could have easily qualified her for a Cosmo modeling job. Half my age or not, I wanted to roll over on the floor and beg her to scratch my tummy. "Just thinking."

She said, "Let me grab my camera."

I whimpered, "Okay." Lucky camera.

"Can you drive?"

"Nuh-uh. Sold my car."

She stiffened as another of those shooting pains hit her.

I rushed over and held her shoulder while she staggered to a chair. "Maybe we should take you to a hospital?" I could probably get Alexander to drive me to the North side, but if I had to trouble him, Harris was definitely getting checked out.

"I just need a minute."

"You look seriously hurt to me, like maybe you need the ER."

Harris made a helpless gesture, but she appeared determined. "How far is it to this airport?"

"Not far." If you're a seabird.

Halfway to Dillingham Field, Harris emerged from her world of thoughts and asked, "Do you want to stop and get something to eat? A burger sounds good."

"I haven't had a burger in five years, ever since I was diagnosed as being unable to tolerate wheat. Bread's out for me."

"Oh." She returned to her little driving world.

I would have explained further, but she seemed uninterested. It took almost another half hour to reach the turn for Dillingham Field. To our right, where there should be oceanfront, there were houses with only the briefest flash of an ocean view between. The houses were so close together that if you wanted to borrow a cup of sugar, you could practically lean out your window and take it out of your neighbor's pantry. Still, the scenery had me in awe. Bounded by lush, green trees and fields on the left and glimpses of ocean on the right, I understood immediately why this airfield in paradise was popular with glider enthusiasts and skydivers.

I glanced at Harris. "You should check out this scenery."

Harris shook her head, then massaged her temple. "Hurts too much."

So much for paradise.

We found the turn for Dillingham Field, but a sign at the entrance indicated we should enter under pain of death. Harris said, "There must be another entrance down the road."

We drove for over a mile. We were about ready to turn around in frustration when we came across an entrance that seemed to have the welcome mat out. Two glider companies with open-air offices set up under a roof held up by stilts appeared to be open for business. We parked and were greeted by a friendly man dressed in an aloha shirt and khaki shorts who spoke over the drone of engines from a huge gray plane on the runway.

"Welcome to Dillingham Field, folks. Are you two interested in a glider flight?"

I shook my head, perhaps a bit too vehemently, because he suppressed a chuckle.

I said, "We're actually looking for Bob Shapiro's plane." I stared past the man as the revving of the engines increased.

He smiled. "Paratrooper training. Different National Guard units sometimes come here. Happens maybe a couple of times a year. We've got a nine thousand foot runway, so they can take off and land easily. That's a C-130. Impressive, huh?"

I nodded, amazed at the plane's size and power. It lumbered away from us, slowly gaining speed until it hoisted its huge belly from the ground. Slowly, it gained altitude.

The man said, "Shapiro's on the other side, almost directly across from here. I'm not sure which hangar, though." Our lack of interest in flying in something without an engine didn't seem to faze him. He probably wound up doing a lot of traffic control, given that this was the first apparently legal entrance. He added, "You could have gone in the first entrance. Those signs—they're misleading."

Duh. "So we wouldn't have been shot on sight if we'd have gone in that way?"

He smiled. "Old signs. We try not to shoot our customers—or their friends." He pointed further down the road. "Just follow the road, take the first left. You'll be at the end of the runway so watch out for low-flying aircraft."

Great. Just what we needed. A plane without power coming in to land while we crossed the road.

We started towards the car, but the glider guy stopped us. "You might want to check with Tommy at Sky's the Limit. I think he and Bob are friends."

8

Dillingham Field is a perfect location for skydiving and glider flights due to its consistent North Shore trade winds. The popularity of those activities, along with sightseeing flights, would lead you to believe that Dillingham is a large facility, which it definitely is not. The primary business is just from adventure seekers—Harris's kind of place. The only buildings here were for flight tours, glider flights, and skydiving—with a parachute.

Dillingham still has remnants of its historic beginnings, complete with bunkers and revetments—kind of a sloped wall—that the Army had installed during World War II to protect against nasty things like incoming enemy fire or explosives. I could just see the proud pilots and ground crew who worked here in the 40s charging around whenever they ran up the engines on a B-24 Liberator or scrambled the P-40 Warhawks for takeoff.

We made the turn into Dillingham Field and kept following the road until we came across Sky's the Limit, then parked out front. As Harris and I walked through the front door, I half-expected to see a guy in a jumpsuit with a parachute on his back. Instead, a small man stood behind a waist-high, green Formica-topped counter. Photos of skydivers, several that had been autographed by the person in the photo, adorned the walls. A poster on one wall gave the rules and regulations for skydiving. I'm sure it must have included something about "open your parachute," "don't die," and "don't sue if you do."

The guy that I thought had been standing must have been sitting on a stool, because he jumped up to greet us. He wore spectacles and was clean-shaven with hair cut short and combed to the left. His eyes swam behind thick lenses. He welcomed us as if he'd had an overdose of happy pills. "Good morning, folks. What brings you to Dillingham Field?"

His cheery greeting reminded me that I'd forgotten the name I'd given him earlier. I knew better. It was McKenna's Second Secret: if you lied, make a note to avoid screwing up your "facts" later on. What was the name? Think, McKenna. Smith? Jones? Oh, poop. No, not O'Poop. O'Brien.

He smiled as if he were expecting a positive response and pointed to the patch on the left sleeve of his jacket. "Gliding? Skydiving?"

I drew on the old skills and continued the charade I'd started on the phone. "O'Brien. We talked earlier; I'm trying to get the scoop on Shapiro. You are Mr.?"

Harris hadn't heard about this, but after giving me a quick glance, she seemed to take the lie in stride. Our greeter's eyes widened at the apparent recollection of our previous conversation.

"Ah, yes, we spoke earlier. Leung. Tommy Leung. You were asking about Bob Shapiro's plane."

I nodded and pulled out a little notepad that I'd grabbed just for the occasion.

"You'd need to talk to Roger Lau about that."

"Who's he?"

"Bob's maintenance man. He's always been a very good maintenance man, does a lot of work around here for various pilots and businesses."

"So this Roger Lau runs a private maintenance outfit?"

"Yes. He's extremely reliable—and a family man. He has two sons that will be going to college soon, a lovely wife. He's second-generation."

I smiled. "Meaning that, in another thousand or so years his family might be accepted."

Leung's face went from cordial to righteous indignation to scared shitless in seconds. He rushed over and took Harris by the arm, then guided her to a chair. "Here, sit. You were about to pass out."

Harris nodded and said, "Can I take your photo? And maybe one of the plane?"

And now, Mr. Leung was Mr. Cordial. He primped by combing his hair with his fingers. "Sure, sure. Glad to help. You can take it from the chair, yah?"

"That'll work, stand over there." She motioned for Mr. C to stand a few feet away, then snapped off a few shots.

Leung raised his eyebrows and focused on Harris, which confused the hell out of me. I was proud to be with a woman he obviously found attractive, and jealous for the same reason. Man, was I screwed up.

I said, "I heard that you and Bob were friends."

Leung shook his head slowly. "Nooo—not really—friends. We knew each other, talked shop. So what do you want to know about the plane?"

Based on his earlier comment about Roger Lau, Leung's denial that he and Shapiro were friends didn't surprise me. "Shapiro's dead, so who flew to Kauai yesterday? And how'd you know it went there? Did the maintenance guy tell you?"

"Don't know. Unicom. And, um, no."

"What?"

"Roger might take the plane out for flight-testing, but he would never take it on an inter-island hop unless he had Bob's permission. That would be like the serviceman taking your car home after he's done some repairs."

"So how'd you know it went to Kauai?"

"I told you. Unicom. I heard it when he took off. I remember because you don't have to file flight plans here unless you're going into restricted airspace. Bob knows he doesn't need to announce his destination to Unicom. That's just for traffic control."

"Where are they?"

"They? They who?"

This guy was beginning to irritate me to no end. One minute he was Mr. Cordial, now he was Mr. Smart Ass. Was that because

I'd interrupted his visual undressing of Harris? My reply was curt, "Unicom."

"Oh! Unicom's not a they, it's a what. A tower, really. Pilots radio in to announce they're landing or taking off. It's like an honor system. Everyone uses it religiously because nobody wants to collide with another plane."

"So Lau could have taken the plane out and nobody would be the wiser?"

"Roger would never do anything to jeopardize his job."

I fingered my notepad. Maybe I should smack this guy on the side of his skull to see if his eyes could hula a bit more.

It was Harris who saved the day when she said, "Mr. Leung, I think what my partner is getting at is that since Mr. Shapiro is dead, it's obvious that someone else took the plane out yesterday. If we could look at the plane, maybe it would help all of us figure out who 'borrowed' Mr. Shapiro's plane." She made quotation marks in the air with her fingers.

Hmpff. Brains *and a ponytail.* Nice job, Legs. It also got Leung on the right track.

He straightened his flight jacket. "Bob's plane is down the road in the hangars, second from the end."

I said, "Is this Roger Lau around?"

"Come to think of it, I didn't see him yesterday or today."

"Is that unusual?"

"Yah. Roger never misses a day of work. Like I said, he's got two kids he's ready to ship off to college. He needs every penny he can get. There's no way he'd take time off when he's got work to do."

"How do you know he's got work to do?"

"Why, he was scheduled to do some maintenance for us today. He didn't call, and he didn't show up."

9

Leung walked us to the front door and pointed. "Go almost to the end of the runway. Turn right into the hangar parking lot. He's in the second slot."

Harris said, "How'd his clients ever find him? We've been almost all the way around this field and haven't seen a sign."

Leung nodded. "He used to joke that he should just rent space from us because a lot of his clients showed up on our door." Leung's phone rang, so he excused himself and hurried back inside.

Harris drove us to the hangars, where we checked out the second stall and came up with a big fat nothing. So, it was back to see Tommy Leung. On the way, Harris said, "It's time to report this to CrimeStoppers. You didn't call them already, did you?"

Oh, no. Busted. I felt my cheeks growing hot.

She grimaced. "You should've told me. Let's finish up with Leung and go file that report."

I breathed a sigh of relief. I'd been afraid she might go ballistic if she learned that I'd done it already. Instead, she just seemed to want to get on with the inevitable. We nodded at each other and went back into the office. Leung was just hanging up the phone and said, "Is there a problem?"

It was Harris who popped off the good one. "It, um, looks like Mother Hubbard's cupboard is bare."

Leung scrunched up his face as though we were the village idiots and couldn't follow simple directions. He sidestepped a couple of parachutes as he came around to our side of the counter, then strode out the front door and off in the direction he'd pointed. "You found the hangar, right?"

I said, "There was no plane. No maintenance guy. No anything."

It took him a minute, but he finally came back into the office muttering to himself in Chinese. He started speaking to us in the same language. His cheeks flushed as he switched to English. "Sorry. But this makes no sense. That plane was just there—just yesterday. I'm sure of it. I'm calling Roger."

He grabbed the phone from our side of the counter to avoid having to do another rendition of the parachute polka, dialed, then tilted the handset up a bit and said, "I'm calling Roger's cell. He'll be able to tell me where he's got the plane." After a few seconds, he hung up the phone. "That's odd, it went straight to voice mail. Maybe he's on another call. I'll try him in a few minutes."

I said, "If Shapiro's been dead since the 10th, why would the maintenance guy be doing anything with the plane?"

"Yes, that's kine—unusual."

Perfect word, I thought. That could be very unusual, a little unusual, it happens all the time unusual or whatever else "unusual" he wanted it to mean. That's when it happened.

The thud.

I glanced sideways at Harris, but she was gone. Then I looked down.

Bad deal. Before I could move, Leung was at Harris's side. He checked her breathing, then scampered away.

I felt a twinge of anger at seeing Leung run from a woman in need. On the other hand, I didn't know what to do either. Call 9-1-1? We were on the far side of the island. Do mouth-to-mouth? She'd probably slap me. I felt relief when Leung dashed back into the room carrying a washcloth, a pillow, and a small vial.

He kneeled at Harris's side. "Give me a hand."

I wasn't feeling much like a smart ass at the moment, so I didn't clap. Instead, I behaved as instructed and helped him straighten

Harris's body. Then, he propped up her head with the small pillow. He put a cool washcloth on her forehead and popped the top on the vial. He said, "Smelling salts."

Harris stirred, then opened her eyes. "Ugh! What happened?"

"You passed out." Talk about reality knocking on your door. If something happened to Harris, I'd be back in my apartment doing my same old job tomorrow while I suffered major guilt pangs. Or worse, I could be fired and evicted because I hadn't forced her to go to the hospital. Once again, McKenna makes the perfect decision— for an idiot. Harris had to be okay. She had to.

A couple of minutes later, Harris was in a chair, sipping water. She nodded her thanks to Leung, who smiled back. He turned to me, "She should be okay now, just watch her for a minute."

I said, "You're pretty good at this."

He shrugged, "It happens. It's worse when it happens in a plane."

Uh, yeah. I would think.

Harris was still looking woozy when she said, "Let's go."

I countered, "You're not ready. A few more minutes, okay?"

She said, "I'm fine. It's a woman thing. You know, faint to get a man's attention, let him get all worked up and worried."

I have to admit I'm not the world's best authority on "women things," but it all sounded pretty hokey to me. It was as though Harris couldn't let me see her weaker side. I shrugged, "There's no rush. Why don't we stop by the ER?"

Harris took a last sip of water as she stood. "Thank you, Mr. Leung, for taking care of me in my moment of need."

Leung shook off the compliment, "You're not the first and I'm sure you won't be the last. In fact, the last time I saw Bob, he was joking about that. He had a family of four, and it was the husband that fainted."

Leung and I laughed about that; Harris merely remained cordial. "Thanks again." She whispered in my ear, "Let's get out of here."

I damn near became the next fainting victim, but the thought of smelling salts kept me going. I glanced at Leung. "One more question. Bob did a good business, right?"

"Yeah, he had at least one flight every day. Usually more. It's been much more quiet around here without his clients bugging us."

"Right. So, my question is, if Bob's been dead since the 10th, where are all his clients? Why haven't they been coming in here, asking why he's not around?"

10

In the world of business, everyone knows you can't just shut your doors without someone noticing. Even if the business has only a few clients, those that hadn't gotten what they'd expected would be angry that their vacations had been ruined. In this case, Shapiro's abandoned clients would likely wind up standing in front of Tommy Leung. When he couldn't explain why those people weren't showing up on his doorstep, we figured our work at Dillingham Field was done and left.

We were approaching her car when Harris said, "Nobody drives my car, so don't even think about asking."

I nodded and tried to pretend she hadn't just passed out a few minutes earlier. Harris seemed focused and alert; her driving was better than mine. To pass the time, I sat back and watched the scenery. Every now and again, I surreptitiously took her in as part of the scenery. That's one of the perks, and an obligation, of being a passenger in a car with a driver wearing a short dress. You have to make sure she's, uh, paying attention to her driving.

We were about a block from home when Harris, never taking her eyes from the road, said, "You are such a dirty old man." She smiled, then faced me and winked.

Oh, shit, I was so busted—again.

She continued, "But it's okay, hon, I like you. You're cute."

Scratch my tummy? "Sorry if I was staring. You're just so sensational."

She turned into the driveway and found a spot to park. As she locked the driver's door, she said, "Your place or mine?"

I stared at her, wondering if I should pee my pants, run, or kiss her.

She laughed. "For the report, silly."

Oh that. We went back to her place. She led, I followed, all the time wondering if I should go on blood pressure medication or something so I wouldn't die if my big moment ever came.

Inside her apartment, Harris booted up the computer. While we waited, she said, "I don't understand what happened to Shapiro's clients. You think the maintenance man's been running the business in his boss's absence? Maybe he decided it was time to become the pilot?"

I shook my head. "This is a helluva lot bigger than a few little tours. No, if Lau got rid of Shapiro, it's for a lot more than a few hours work." We easily found the Honolulu CrimeStoppers web site. Harris searched the page for a link to file a report and I found the reward information. "Hey, they offer a thousand bucks for good tips."

Harris nodded. "They usually do. My sister needs that money."

She continued searching the page until she found what we needed further down. She clicked the link and we both started reading the form. The questions in the first part suggested that it was targeted at drug and gang members. We didn't know the suspect's name or age. It wasn't like we'd done introductions or anything, so we skipped down to the Crime Description field.

Harris said, "At last, something I know." She began typing in the form field.

On May 16, 2011, I was hiking at Sacred Falls State Park. I observed a single-engine Cessna airplane, owned by Robert M. Shapiro, Jr., drop a body from the plane. The body fell and landed on the mountainside. I took a picture of the plane, but then someone in the plane began shooting at me. I was not hit by a bullet, but it was a near miss.

Today, a friend and I went to Dillingham Field to check on the plane and were told that the plane had flown to Kauai yesterday. The maintenance man is missing also.

She sat back and said, "How's that?"

I read her entry, then we added a couple of more facts to the form. She found a browse button and began uploading the photo of the plane.

The upload had just finished when she said, "Hey, would you get me some water, I'm parched."

Well-trained fetcher that I am, I obediently headed off to the kitchen. Over my shoulder, I said, "Where do you keep the glasses?"

She kept her eyes on the screen. "On your left."

I opened that cabinet. "Nope, plates, saucers, and bowls."

She glanced up. "Oh, sorry, on your right. I'm still not oriented to this place."

I found the glasses, filled one with water and returned.

Harris stood, took a sip and said, "Well, it's gone. It looked good so I sent it off."

"Great. Wonderful. Do they send you an e-mail confirmation? Oh, no, they can't do that, it was anonymous."

A nervous tension filled the room. What should I do next? Harris said, "If you don't mind, I'm whipped. I need to rest for a while. Is that okay?"

"I'm fine with that. I have landlord stuff to do." Not really, but it probably sounded good to Harris.

I had my hand on the doorknob when she stopped me. "Um, McKenna—have you ever wondered where that plane might actually be—right now?"

"What?"

"Well, how long do you think it's going to take the cops to do something with this report? The web site said it's not like calling 9-1-1. By the time they get around to this, if they even take it seriously, whoever murdered that poor guy could be long gone. He may be gone already."

"True, but I don't see what that's got to do with us."

"We could work together some more. You know, hang out. It might be fun." She gave me a flirtatious smile. "Track down the bad guys—do some detective work."

"These guys had guns, they wanted to kill you. I don't think—"

She interrupted, "It would just be a little computer time. We don't actually have to, like, chase them or anything. I saved the tip with a password, so we could file reports with CrimeStoppers. It would add credibility and probably get this resolved a lot faster. Besides, when we're finished, we can have a nice, quiet celebration dinner. Just the two of us."

I didn't realize that I was wearing talking pants, but the next thing I knew, my pants had said, "Sure, count me in." Right after that, it was time for a hug. Then, it was a kiss on the cheek. After that, it was a boot in the ass as I got sent back to my apartment to work so Harris could rest.

My pants started talking again. Screw the landlord stuff. Go find that plane. The nice thing about a clearly defined task is that it gets your mind off of what it shouldn't be on—like my most recent hug-experience with Harris. It wasn't hard to surmise that Shapiro's plane had to be at one of about a dozen airports. And since it wasn't at Dillingham Field, that wasn't one of them. One down, eleven to go. I sat down and hit the power button for my laptop, logged in, and did a quick search for "Hawaii airports." I could have gone back to the trusted phone book, but I needed something that was going to make me work a bit more, keep me more involved. Besides, the phone just seemed so—mundane. I clicked a link that said it included a listing of airports, but it was only the commercial locations. My second choice got me what I wanted, a list of all public airports in the state.

Of course, there could always be others that were private and not listed. If they went to one of those, I was out of luck. I'd cross that bridge only if it became necessary. I figured that I might as well start with other airports on Oahu. That meant there were only two possibilities, Honolulu International and Kalaeloa. I'd start with the smaller one just because, I assumed, it would be easier to talk to a real person. The web page gave me phone numbers, so it was time to start calling.

"Kalaeloa Airport. O'Shaunessy." If the voice on the other end could sound anymore let-me-out-of-the-squirrel-cage bored, I'd be surprised.

I donned my reporter persona again. "Hey, O'Brien down at the Advertiser. We're doing a follow-up story on a hit-and-run victim. Turns out the guy was a pilot and his plane may have been jacked after he got flattened. You got a list of planes that have come in there in the past day or so?" I sounded like a real newspaper guy and considered giving myself a pat on the back for the performance.

"Look buddy, I'm all alone here and don't have the time to go checking records."

Crap, a prima donna. "I know you're busy out there, all that itty-bitty airport stuff you have to handle, but this is an official newspaper investigation."

"Official newspaper investigation? Oh, excuse me, I didn't realize we were talking about national security."

Ouch. Another smart ass.

"If this becomes an official police investigation, I'll do some checking. Until then, you'll just have to come out here and look over the logs all on your own. They're public record, so help yourself."

So much for somewhere. I cleared my throat. How did I explain that I was a newspaper reporter without a car? "Um, well, I'm sorry if I came on too strong. Can you just tell me if you've had any new planes come in since yesterday?" I hated begging, but I wanted that intimate dinner with Harris. If I needed to play a part, so be it.

"Persistent, aren't you? Since this morning, we only had one. Two guys flew in a Cessna from Kauai."

Two guys? I remembered what Leung had said. The pilot of the plane had announced his destination as Kauai. "You're sure it was Kauai?"

"That's it. Lau was the name. I remember that one cause I got a cousin, Larry, same last name. I gotta go, another line ringing."

Well, I'll be. Lau had flown to Kauai, then back to Oahu in his dead boss's plane? Why in the world? Oh, I'd been right. Lau was doing something illegal. I couldn't go back to Harris already, she was probably still asleep. And unfortunately, I didn't know the password she'd used for the tip report. And speaking of asleep, I was still feeling like a whipped puppy myself. It was almost four, so I settled in on the couch, turned on the TV, and took a vote.

"All in favor of giving me the rest of the day off? Aye. All opposed? Hearing none, this day is officially adjourned."

I drifted in and out a couple of times and then woke up to see a Breaking News banner splashed across the screen. The reporter on scene spoke in a solemn tone. ". . . and so it appears that, despite the efforts of administrators over the past few years, violence, or at least the threat of violence, in Hawaii schools is still real. While we don't know yet if what the other students are saying is true, that the student who has barricaded himself into one of the classrooms is on drugs and has a gun and is dangerous, we do know that police are taking every precaution to ensure that no one is injured. Back to you, Jack."

"Ruben, so authorities aren't sure if drugs are involved?"

"That's right, Jack. What they are saying is that they have to assume that the student is impaired and that he may be part of a gang. They're quick to point out that students in general are more aware of the dangers of doing drugs, but that many ignore the dangers and become involved anyway. Back to you."

A sharp chill gripped my spine. It was another painful memory of Jenny and Michael. I'd failed him, his mother, and most of all, myself. I'd been sorry ever since. My left hand twitched over the off button on the remote, but for some reason I couldn't press it.

Ruben tipped his microphone towards the camera and Jack jumped right back in. Another question, probably one the reporter had already covered. "And they're also not sure if the student has a gun? What about a bomb?"

Despite the warmth of the apartment, I shivered again. This report was just way too dèjá vu. How could something like this happen here? In paradise?

"No, Jack, they're being very tight-lipped about what weapons they suspect the student may, or may not, have with him. Most likely, we won't know until, well, they bring him out."

Jack didn't waste any time, the screen blipped, Ruben was gone and Jack was into his wrap-up. I realized that my eyes were moist. Drugs. Gangs. Danger for innocent kids. I'm sorry, Michael. What more could I say? Or do?

I swiped at my eyes and nose, then sniffled and sat up. I couldn't erase the overwhelming feeling that even this island paradise was going straight to hell. It was LA all over again. I thought about Harris's example—how she cared enough to follow this through—and compared that to my own moral code. Better safe than sorry was what my parents had taught me. But, what was safe? Besides, I couldn't get any sorrier than I'd been for the past five years.

Maybe Harris was right. We didn't have to put ourselves in danger, we could just help the process a bit. I'd helped file one report with CrimeStoppers. Why not another? If I was honest with myself, it felt good. I wasn't as grumpy. I'd enjoyed the day and the company. And then, there was that thousand-dollar reward. I got up off the couch and grabbed my phone. Time to get busy if I wanted that date with Harris.

11

My plan for wrapping up the investigation and getting my date with Harris was simple: pick Alexander's brain. He was a walking encyclopedia about this island. It didn't hurt that he was related to half the people on this rock, either. If there was something, or someone, he didn't know, he could find out in less time than it took to spend fifty bucks at the gas pump. He'd married Kira right out of high school. Where Alexander was laid back, Kira was like a big-game hunter in the information forest; she never gave up on her prey until she ran out of ammo or bagged her quarry.

"Aloha." The greeting was sweet and lilting. Yippie, the Huntress was in a good mood.

"It's McKenna, is Alexander there?"

"What no good you up to now?"

"You're still mad at me?"

She snickered, "Just wary. Every time you call you want something, so what you want this time?"

Round one off, time for her to reload. In the background, I could hear the TV and one of the kids crying. It was probably Maile because she was the youngest and prone to crying jags when she didn't get to watch her cartoons. I thought I heard something about Nanakuli High School, so I asked, "Is that a news report I hear in the background?"

"Cartoons keep getting interrupted. Maile's not happy."

"I'm sorry to hear that."

Kira didn't speak for a moment, "This is McKenna, yah?"

"I saw that report earlier and it just upset me. Brings back some old memories. Anything new in the past ten minutes?" It was McKenna's Fifth Skip Tracing Secret: the best defense was a good offense.

She filled me in with a few concise sentences, something I thought the news folks should learn to do, then went back into question mode. "So why you want Alexander?"

"I just wanted to talk to him for a few minutes."

"What? About that wahine he smuggled into the park?"

"Alexander told you about her?"

"He had to after that BS you fed me when he didn't come home all night. After your story, his make perfect sense. If there anything left of the body by the time the storm blows in, it gonna get washed away. Kalanui Stream floods big time when we get lotta rain."

"I just wanted to tell him about my trip to Dillingham." And ask some questions of my own.

"So what you doing on the North side? You don't drive."

So far, I hadn't been injured in our question and answer shoot out. How long could I dodge questions? I should have just called Alexander's cell. Ah, cell phone. I grabbed mine from my hip. I tried to sound interested in a long conversation as I worked the cell with my free hand. "We went to the North side because there was a man we needed to talk to—"

I fumbled with the phone for a few seconds, then pushed the volume button. The phone rang so loud I almost dropped it, but the ring had the desired effect.

"You got another call?"

Hey, pretty good. "Yah, looks like a possible tenant." I jabbed the button again. Even louder this time. "I can tell you about this later. Have Alexander call me, okay?"

"Yah." Kira chuckled. "And McKenna, next time you gonna try the fake cell phone ring trick, remember to push the button a bit more regular, yah? And don't hold it so close to the phone, you almost broke my eardrum that time."

Ouch. The Huntress had bagged another trophy, me.

So today I'd pushed Harris into a drive that had nearly landed her in the hospital, gotten caught trying to peep at her underwear, and blown the old "fake cell phone ring trick." What else could I accomplish? Get arrested? Nah, been there, done that. Better just to stick to the basics.

Instead of calling Alexander's cell and appearing like an ingrate after I'd already left a message with Kira, I picked up the remote and turned the TV back on. The local news hadn't given up on the high school incident. As sunset approached, the cameraman was fortunate enough to catch the cops bringing out the boy who had caused the near-disaster.

The bottom line was that there was no bomb, no gun, and no drugs. The only danger was psychological and I couldn't help but wonder how many innocent kids would wear the scars of today's worry for years to come. The police did a good job of keeping the boy's face hidden from the cameras. He probably had longish hair and a bad case of acne, but all the camera picked up was his "Kill the Haoles!" tee shirt and his shorts. Even so, by tomorrow every kid in school would know who'd gone crazy today.

The scene included a choked-up mom and dad who waved off the cameras. The reporter shot questions at the distraught couple while Mom wept.

Finally, Dad spewed venom. "Haoles caused this. They took away everything we love!"

Mom grabbed Dad by the shirt-sleeve and tugged on his shoulder. She cried out, "Our boy would never do something like this."

They held each other while a policeman guided them to their vehicle. The station played it all again and did the snappy exchanges between on-scene reporter and anchor. I realized that it was now nearly dark outside, and I'd missed dinner.

I wasn't very hungry, but did want a little snack and some wine. In Hawaii, we call appetizers pupus. My current "order" consisted of little bits of steak and chicken that I'd cooked up, some sushi from a restaurant down the street and a couple of pieces of cheese. I turned off the TV and went out to the lanai with my wine and pupus. The ocean reflected the dark reds, grays, and blues of the day's end. The tide was high, so the water was considerably closer than this morning.

Streetlights glowed, hotel towers sparkled, and tourists would now be roaming the streets in search of a place for dinner or entertainment. I settled down into my chair, happy with my little ocean-front view. For the first time in years, I felt like I had something important to do. I hadn't intended to get into this mess, and caring for Harris had never been on my radar. I'd intended to keep the status quo, and keep my life in order and not get consumed by someone else's drama. But now, order seemed irrelevant. There was a flame starting to burn, and it warmed my cold insides.

I munched, drank wine, and eventually decided that I was bored. Tomorrow, I could ask Alexander what he knew about Kalaeloa Airport, and how we might get some cooperation in finding the Cessna. If I could just see the plane, just once—even from a distance, I'd feel like—what? A moron? A do-gooder? Face it, I was a rubber-necking driver who just couldn't help but stare at the accident scene. Well, in any case, if I did see the plane, I could get the password from Harris, file an update on the tip report, and be one step closer to dinner.

I was still on the lanai debating my moron/do-gooder status when Suzie Wong came in from the parking lot. She looked extremely tired but, as usual, sensational. "Evening," I said.

"Hi. Rough day?"

Her concern embarrassed me. Why hadn't I asked her about her day first? I grumbled, "Too much going on."

She looked like she might make a snide remark, but after a short silence, said, "I hear you on that one."

"You had a bad day, too?"

"You heard about that kid at Nanakuli?"

"Yah. I feel bad for the kid and his parents."

She nodded, "A negotiator talked him out. Now, my boss wants to represent him."

"Maybe it's a full moon—no, that's next week. Crap, I've had two glasses of wine, and I'm beat."

"I've been meaning to ask you something. You know that new tenant?"

The tone in her voice told me there was a catty remark coming. "Harris? What about her?"

"Something's not right with her."

Ooh, nasty. I tried to keep an edge out of my voice. "Why do you say that?"

"Isn't she supposed to be, like, from LA?"

"Yeah, El Monte."

"Then why's she a Giants fan?"

I remembered the tee shirt Harris had worn to bed. Jeez, talk about petty. "You saw her tee shirt?"

"In the laundry room. She started in about how the Giants were so gonna go all the way this year."

"Julia, come on, she's fine. She's got a twin sister that needs a kidney transplant. Hell, even I rooted for the Cowboys one season."

"That's football."

"It was the uniforms. The cheerleader uniforms to be exact."

She laughed. "You are so bad. Okay, I'll put away the claws. But, she should wear more clothes."

I guess you could say I painted the stripes on the zebra because she caught me smiling. I made a feeble attempt to cover my embarrassment, "I'm just the landlord—I can't control what people wear."

Julia jumped all over that one with a high falsetto and a fake Pidgin accent. "Poor McKenna, he got no control over nuttin', not even where his eyes go when de pretty wahine walk by."

First Harris, now Julia. Talk about being called out. Jeez. I drained the last of my glass.

Julia started to walk away, tee-heeing to herself. She stopped after a few steps and turned, suddenly serious. "Hey, did you ever get those new security cameras installed?"

"I got them in, but forgot to see whether anything recorded."

"Do it tomorrow, you look pretty tired."

Julia continued on to her apartment. She was a nice girl and, for the first time since I'd met her, I thought of her as Julia, not Suzie

Wong. Christ, what was happening to me? Next thing you know, I'd be getting a cat.

12

I woke up at six-thirty with energy that I hadn't had in years. I felt like a much younger me this morning with only a bit of grumpiness and just a pinch of self-confidence. With all this newfound joy and happiness stuff going on in my head, I might even need a larger hat size. Unfortunately, I still hadn't heard from Alexander and it was way too early to be calling his house. In our last exchange, Kira the Huntress had taken me down with her quick insight about my lame attempt at escaping the Q&A. So, my best bet was to watch the local news for a few minutes. Maybe I could pick up the weather report. I did a little channel surfing and found out that, sure enough, Kira was right. The crack meteorologist predicted a "major storm" that would bring 60% chance of "significant" amounts of rainfall later today. Who was that guy kidding? He didn't know squat. He should just say, "Your guess is as good as mine." But, then he wouldn't get paid. So, the guy used his 60% fudge factor.

It's too bad that people, for instance, people like Robert M. Shapiro, Jr., didn't have a fudge factor. He had only a 100% chance of being dead. And what about Harris's sister? What were her chances of getting a transplant? And what about Harris? I should check on her. My guess was that she was still asleep, so I'd do that after breakfast.

I poked my head out the sliding glass door and glanced up. Clear blue. Oh, goodie, we had a 100% chance of no rain for the next five minutes. I had my cereal and juice on the lanai and waved my spoon as a way of saying goodbye to a couple of the tenants as they left to fight the traffic.

After I finished breakfast, I still felt like I needed to kill a few minutes before calling Alexander or disturbing Harris, so I logged into my computer and checked the security cameras as Julia had suggested. All four sides of the building as well as the roof checked out, so this was turning into a boring morning. It was now 7:45 and I was about to go visit Bosco. He could probably use a good cleaning because I'd been a bit lax on that task lately. I'd hire a maid, but I was too cheap. I'd clean myself, but I was too busy—or so I said. I pursed my lips and thought for a moment. Could I put that to music? Maybe it would make a good Country/Western song.

I started a little verse in my head, then said, screw it. I don't like Country/Western music anyway. Too much "twang" and "y'all." I shifted in my chair. This was starting to give me gas. Ah, the old McKenna was back. Grumpy-pants and all. The phone rang in time to save me from creating more verses for my song. Alexander didn't even say hello, but launched right in.

"What happened yesterday? Why'd you go to Dillingham Field?"

"We're trying to locate the plane to help the cops."

"Help the— We? Who's we?"

"Harris and me. We. As in working together."

Alexander let out a groan. "You leaving me out of this, right?"

I remembered his concerns from yesterday. "We didn't mention you in our tip report, if that's what you mean. All we want to do is find the plane, file another tip report, and get this Lau guy brought to justice."

"Lau? Who's he? I got a lotta cousins named Lau."

"Roger Lau. He was Shapiro's maintenance man. He's flying the plane around now. He probably killed Shapiro so he could do a few drug deals, some smuggling—you know, something criminal. If we can find where that plane is, we can put a bow on this and give the cops an early Christmas present."

"I'll be there, half an hour, forty-five minutes tops."

"Why? Harris and I can handle this. I just wanted to know if you knew someone at the airport who could help us."

"I do. And I'm going with you. Roger's a cousin. From what I know he ain't done nothin' illegal. If you gonna try to pin something on him, I gonna make sure he really did it."

I felt the heat rise in my cheeks. "You don't trust me?"

"You ain't the one I'm worried about." And he hung up.

Whew, talk about hitting someone's buttons. I'd never seen Alexander get worked up so quickly. Thirty-nine minutes later, he was at my door. During that time, instead of writing another song verse I cleaned up Bosco. I even made it out to the lanai before Alexander's truck rumbled into the parking lot. Today, he had the Tundra, a shiny beauty with a tricked-out exhaust system that sounds like a Ferrari on steroids. You've practically got to have a stepladder to get into the thing.

"Kira let you have the tank today, huh?" The one time I'd seen her tackle driving the truck, she'd had to climb up and in. From outside, you could barely see a little head, much like a hand puppet, behind the wheel. She'd driven off as though she could actually see where she was going.

"I've got Roger's address. I had to drop off the keiki."

"How are the kids?"

"Roger didn't do nothing, McKenna. He's a good man." He paused and let out a frustrated sigh. "Kids are fine. Maile, she got straight A's last semester. Bubba, he gonna try out for Little League. He hit a home run the other day, drove in three to win the game."

Alexander's jaw tightened as he pushed his anger deep beneath the surface. Volunteering to play McKenna taxi was, I gathered, just a ploy to ensure that he protected his relatives, and maybe a friend or two. I suspected that I no longer counted as one of his friends, but that Alexander had categorized me as an adversary, someone to keep close so he could track my actions. In any case, talking about the kids would keep us on neutral ground. "Why'd you name the poor kid Bubba, anyway?"

"Just kinda happened by accident. One day at a family picnic I called him that when he asked me a question, next thing I know everybody was doing the same."

A moment of awkward silence cast an invisible wall between us. It wasn't like Alexander to be distant; he either liked you or he didn't. I said, "Maybe I should get Harris?"

"If you want."

Unfortunately, his attitude was beginning to piss me off. And that could only lead to trouble. I hoped being direct would resolve this problem. "I understand you think we're trying to hurt one of your relatives, but we're just trying to assemble some evidence for the cops."

"HPD don't need no volunteer detectives running around getting in trouble and wasting their time. They tight enough on resources as it is."

"I don't want to waste anybody's resources. I'm trying to help. I just want to—" I stopped.

Alexander eyed me. "See, you don't know what you want. Maybe you just want a thousand bucks. Maybe you think you gonna get laid."

"And maybe you think I'm going to blow the whistle so that you get into trouble for taking Harris to Sacred Falls. Believe me, that's not gonna happen. I won't let it. I may not know what I do want, but I do know what I don't want, and that's getting you in trouble. You're my friend and no one, including Harris, will jeopardize your business or how you provide for your family if I can help it."

Alexander stared at me for a moment, then pulled me into a bear hug.

The hug forced the air from my lungs, but I was still able to croak, "Thanks." Then, in a hoarse whisper, squeezed out, "You could let me go now." Thank goodness, he did.

"You gonna be okay, brah. Let's go get that blonde troublemaker before you get anymore mixed up."

"You are driving, right? I don't think Harris is in any shape to do that. And I don't have a car." Alexander knew the story, rather than pay a fortune to repair my car after an accident, I'd pocketed the insurance money. I'd narrowly missed hitting a kid who'd chased his dog into the street. The driver of the oncoming car must have seen the dog because he screeched to a halt. The stupid dog ran straight into the car and bounced off, four legs sticking straight up towards the sky. I was fascinated by the spectacle and didn't see the kid standing horrified in the middle of my lane. I don't know what got my attention back on my side of the road, but I saw the kid in time to swerve. The swerve maneuver was a good-news, bad-news thing because I missed the kid, but hit a fire hydrant, which pounded the underside of my car like a water cannon. It sounded like the grand finale at a Fourth of July fireworks show. The street flooded, the kid wet his pants, the dog started to float away and, lo and behold, the cops showed up to give me a ticket. Yup, I hated driving.

"You think I want to take a chance with you behind the wheel? Or her? Forget it."

We made the short walk to Harris's apartment in silence, the tension between us now addressed and released. It's odd, but sometimes it takes a little adversity to make two friends appreciate each other more. Jeez. Talk about being philosophical. Enough of that mushy, gushy crap.

And, if there was any doubt, mushy, gushy went down the tubes when Harris opened her door. What was this effect I was having on people? Until today, every time I'd seen Harris, it had been a treat—a hot fudge sundae with double whipped cream and a cherry on top. Today was more like beef stew. She'd dressed in jeans, a long-sleeved tee shirt, and her hair hung loose and straight. Her attitude seemed to match her changed attire; simple, direct, and harsh. "What?"

Whoa. Talk about meeting the inner demon. Alexander took a step backwards, leaving me in the position of unwitting volunteer sacrifice. "We, uh, thought you might want to go to meet the maintenance guy's wife."

Her brow furrowed as she seemed to process the information. "The maintenance guy? Oh, yeah, the one we think stole the plane. Sorry, my head is killing me. I've been popping pain killers like they're going extinct tomorrow. It just keeps, like, getting worse."

"Maybe you should see someone?"

"The only one who needs to see a doctor is my sister. Besides, I don't have insurance and I'm not going to pay a bundle to have them tell me what I already know."

Alexander stood behind me and his silence told me he wouldn't be offering up any of his island feel-good philosophies. No doubt he was covering my unexposed back. Thanks, buddy. "They might be able to give you something for the pain."

"What, something I don't have already? I've got plenty. And I'm not that bad—not yet anyway. So where's this maintenance guy live?"

I stood, silent. Hell if I knew.

Alexander said, "North Shore."

"North Shore." She glared at me. "Didn't we just freaking go to the North Shore yesterday? Why the hell didn't we visit this guy then?"

Maybe it was that time of the month. Time to go. "We, uh, shouldn't have bothered you. Sorry about that."

I turned to walk away, but felt her hand on my shoulder. "Please. I'm sorry. It's the pain meds and this headache. Just give me a couple of minutes and I'll be ready." She closed the door, leaving us standing outside.

Alexander said, "I told you, brah. Something not right with that chick."

If there was anything in this world that I hated, it was an "I told you so." Especially when it came from someone else. And when they were right.

13

It had only taken Harris a few minutes to get ready, during which time Alexander and I loitered around her door. Thankfully, no other tenants came by, otherwise, I'd have felt obligated to invent some excuse for us hanging around outside her door—something less ridiculous than being involved in a murder investigation, that is. A short time later, we were caught in gridlock.

Although H-1, our interstate highway, is isolated from the mainland and doesn't actually take you between states, it suffers regular bouts of traffic congestion that rival its mainland cousins. The congestion often cripples travel on the main highway through this little section of paradise. As we went from slow to go, I watched the clouds racing towards us, each a distant soldier in nature's perennial battle for life. An army of dark-gray sky-soldiers gathered strength, each prepared to blot out the sun, drench the land, and create havoc on the roads. With the storm moving in, our chances of finding out who had been thrown from the plane seemed to be dwindling as fast as blue sky. By the time we'd connected with, and then turned off of, H-2 and onto State Highway 99, my back hurt from being confined and one thought plagued me: getting involved in this whole missing-body thing had been one huge mistake.

I recalled my initial feelings about Harris, who slept in the back seat. Her greeting this morning, combined with Alexander's accusations, had unnerved me. If I hadn't been inside a moving vehicle at the time, I think I might have kicked myself.

Alexander remained intent on his driving, trying to maintain as much aloha spirit as possible while about ten thousand people wanted to pass him, cut him off, or run him off the road. We were passing Kamanunu Rd. when I closed my eyes to try to forget my back pain. My breathing slowed a bit as I relaxed. The drive had become a marathon, dealing with Harris looked like it might be another. Why couldn't things just be simpler? I shifted position and imagined the pain fading, slipping away, as if it were never there—just like before the baseball game in which I'd been injured.

When I was eight, a bunch of my friends cornered me and said they needed another player for their baseball game. I'd played softball before, and was, without a doubt, the best player on my team. But, I'd never played real baseball. A hardball. Ninety-foot baselines.

Sammy Wharton said, "Johnny Bakerton is pitching for the other team."

Johnny was twelve and big and a bully to boot. I'd seen him pitch a couple of times; he had two pitches, a fastball and a curve ball. His fastball was the finisher, the one he used to not only strike out, but humiliate the batter. "I don't know; my Mom might worry."

Steve, Sammy's older brother said, "What do moms know? Besides, if you can hit what he's throwing, you'll be a hero."

A hero. Mom had never let me play because she said it was too dangerous. I'd always poo-pooed that concern because I was eight and, well—what did she know about baseball? That's how I wound up sneaking into my room, grabbing the real baseball mitt my grandfather had given me, not the one for little kids and softball, and telling my mom that a bunch of us were going over to Sammy Wharton's to play in his tree house.

"The Whartons are such nice boys. Have fun," she said without even a glance in my direction.

I secretly wondered how they did it. Sammy was ten and his brother Steve was twelve. Every parent in the neighborhood thought they were perfect kids because they'd learned to play "Impress the Parent" very, very well. I guess part of it had something to do with the fact that no one had ever actually fallen from the tree house—and told about it.

At the baseball field, I stared wide-eyed at the diamond. I was about to become a real baseball player, not just a little kid who played softball. They even had an umpire. People watching. Some even had cameras.

I said, "Wow, people are taking pictures!"

Steve said, "My dad declared himself the official team photographer. How stupid. You're batting eighth and playing right field."

"Eighth? Right field?" I was a shortstop. I usually batted second or third. Maybe leadoff.

Sammy said, "It's your first game. That's where Steve always starts the beginners."

I was a beginner? I guess I felt suckered as I mumbled, "Sure." I trotted off for my position in Outer Mongolia. I wasn't sure where this "Outer Mongolia" was, but had heard my dad talk about it a lot.

I was starting to understand why my dad always sounded pissed off when he talked about Outer Mongolia. By the third inning, I was so bored that I started noticing weird things, like when someone spoke, their mouth moved but I didn't hear their voice until a couple of seconds later. It was pretty cool, I could make up the words, then see if I was right. But even that got boring after a couple of innings.

This was definitely a pitcher's game. Steve mowed the batters down one-by-one, only allowing strikeouts or little hits to the infield. Unfortunately, so did Johnny Bakerton. We were going into the sixth inning, and the score was tied at zero-zero.

As I was waiting for my turn at bat, I overheard Steve and a couple of the other older teammates arguing. The argument sounded heated and, at one point, Steve burst out in frustration, "I ain't got nobody else. He was a last minute choice so we wouldn't have to forfeit."

I warmed up, thinking about what he'd said. So that's what I was, a way to avoid a forfeit. There were already two outs this inning; I didn't want to be number three. The first pitch came in on the outside corner. My swing was hard, smooth. It was a perfect swing. Swish.

The catcher, another one of the older kids, said, "Nice swing—for a baby."

I felt heat in my face and chest. He had a couple of years on me and stood a half foot taller, but I wanted to smash him with the bat. The second pitch was inside and made me jump away from the plate. Johnny Bakerton smiled and sneered.

The ump yelled, "Ball One!"

I took a moment to step away from the batter's box and swung the bat a few times. I had to show Johnny Bakerton he wasn't so tough after all. I stepped back into the box, telling myself over and over to drill one into the outfield for a single. The pitch was a curve ball. To an eight-year old, it looked like the biggest curve ball in the world, like it could do a circle on its way to the plate. I stared, wide-eyed, as the ball looped past me and landed squarely in the catcher's mitt.

"Strike two!"

The catcher sneered, "Go back to softball."

Tears welled in my eyes. My insides shook. I was a failure at eight years old. I was ruined for life and would probably never get another chance to play in a real baseball game. I'd be demoted back to softball unless I did something really big.

Johnny Bakerton caught the ball thrown out by the catcher and just laughed. I read his lips, "Stupid little kid." His shoulders shook with laughter.

He was the biggest, baddest kid on the team. He outweighed me by a good thirty or forty pounds, and yet I wanted to beat him to a pulp. But, I knew what that result would be. I'd be the pulp. He'd probably kick my—what had Dad said, oh yeah, kick my ass all the way to Outer Mongolia. There was only one way to settle this.

The pitch came in low and fast. It was Johnny's fastball. The closer.

I'd seen his pattern enough to know what he'd do. I knew he'd put it right where he always did. I swung as hard as I could. My ears rang with the loudest crack of the bat I'd ever heard. Instinctively, I ran to first base. Sammy waved me on. As I rounded first, he yelled, "Go! Go!"

My heart pounded and my lungs screamed, but I ran. On my way to second, I couldn't resist a triumphant glance in Johnny's direction. I half-expected to see him standing there, furious that an eight-year-old might cost him his game. Instead, he was on the ground, doubled up, arms and hands wrapped around his knees. The catcher knelt next to him, struggling with Johnny. He wrenched the ball from Johnny's grasp and, still on one knee, threw towards second base. I was just a few feet away from the base when the ball sailed over the reach of the second baseman and into center field.

My teammates yelled from the sidelines, "Go! McKenna, Go!"

I rounded second and headed for third base. The thrill of having the only hit of the game powered my stride. My legs ached, my lungs felt like they would burst. But my heart was soaring! I'd gotten a hit off of Johnny Bakerton! The only hit of the game!

Steve was behind third base signaling me to stop. He patted me on the back and even hugged me like I was one of the guys. "Wow! What a hit. I knew you could do it!"

Right, I thought, that's why I was batting eighth. I stood at third base, my chest heaving as I watched Johnny Bakerton struggle to his feet.

Steve leaned in my direction and pointed to the bent-over pitcher. "That's gotta hurt, right in the family jewels." He laughed as he went back to his position on the sidelines.

I didn't know why he'd done it, but there was no way I'd ever make Johnny's mistake. I'd never put any of my mom's jewelry in my pants before a game.

Finally, Johnny was ready to go. I led off. Johnny wound up. I took another step. Johnny's head turned slightly in my direction, but he was committed. He threw.

Johnny had wasted batter after batter today, but a hit to the family jewels had killed his game. The weak fastball just sort of hung over the plate long enough for our catcher to pound it up the middle. I jumped towards home. Johnny ducked and threw up his glove as the ball screamed past him. I was a third of the way to home when I glanced over my shoulder and saw the second baseman knock down the ball. I was halfway home when he got control. I looked ahead, the catcher jumped up and down at home plate screaming for the second baseman to throw.

I increased my speed and glanced back at the second baseman. I caught sight of a horror-stricken Johnny jumping up and down and screaming at the top of his lungs. I pumped my arms. I breathed hard. I flew like the wind. I gloated over Johnny Bakerton's fall from grace.

I was almost home and ready to dive for the plate.

Someone yelled, "McKenna, look out!"

But, I couldn't look out. I was busy watching the ball sail in from the second baseman's throw. I poured on my last ounce of speed, took a deep breath, and looked ahead to see the other team's catcher standing like a wall between me and the plate an instant before I slammed into him at full speed.

The collision sent the catcher sprawling and me tumbling past him in the dirt. Dust choked my lungs and blinded me as I strained to get my bearings. In the background, I could hear both teams yelling.

"Get the ball!"

"Tag him out!"

"Touch the plate!"

"Get him, get—"

"In front of you—"

"Hurry—"

Scuffling in the dirt. Pain in my back and neck. Force back the tears. Johnny running toward me from the backstop. Both teams screaming for action. Ignore the pain. Johnny just two steps away. The plate was just inches away. I could barely move my arm, but managed to get my right hand on it just a fraction of a second before Johnny slammed into me and the world went dark.

"McKenna. Wake up, we're there."

I blinked and then squinted at the light.

"You fell asleep."

My back hurt in the same place it had while I lay sprawled in the dirt. "I need to move." I opened the door and stood, shaky as a newborn deer, then tested my balance. "Crap, that hurts."

Harris stood next to me and held my arm. I leaned into her a bit, relishing the attention, and her apparent change of attitude. She laughed. "We make a fine pair, huh?"

She hadn't called me honey, but her choice of words gave me an interpretation of my dream that I hadn't considered. She'd become affectionate again. Did that mean I was destined to get to first base with her? Second? Third? Might I even score? Just considering the possibility of sex made my palms sweat. Would I remember what to do? Was it really like riding a bicycle—you never forgot?

Alexander said, "You ever gonna tell me how you got hurt?"

"Huh?" I realized that I should thank Alexander for interrupting my moronic musings. I was about to embarrass myself like a teenage-boy seeing his first porno flick. I said, "I suppose, someday." Like never. Because one simple question led to more complicated ones. Questions like, why hadn't I fixed my life? I didn't know the answer. Maybe I never would.

Harris seemed to sense my discomfort. "Is this Lau's house?"

Alexander nodded. "Cousin Roger's."

It was a classic older Hawaiian hale. The home sat up on blocks, which kept the wood from touching the ground and eliminated issues like wood-rot, termites, or possible flooding when Lono decided it was time to rain for ten or twenty days straight. Panels on the sides had been painted a pale green and reddish tiles that are popular here in the islands covered the roof. Plumeria, ginger, palms and giant hibiscus filled the well-kept yard, which seemed no more than the size of a postage stamp. It reminded me of a middle-class family; two parents, kids, a dog, and a mortgage.

I said, "This is the maintenance man's home?"

"No look so much like drug dealer, yah?"

Low spots in the graveled driveway created perfect conditions for the water to pond during the slightest downpour. But there, sitting in the driveway, was a brand-new Toyota pickup, much like Alexander's. Funny, this one didn't have permanent plates.

I said, "Looks to me like Roger Lau just recently came into some serious money." We had our bad guy, time to call the cops.

14

My comment about Roger coming into money drew a glare from Alexander. I didn't want to lose his friendship, but he seemed to have blinders on.

He snapped, "Maybe I was wrong about you, you just like the others."

Harris gave my arm a gentle tug. "Come on, you two, you're friends. McKenna, looks can be deceiving. I think Alexander's right. We shouldn't just convict this guy because he's got a new truck." She pointed at a few of the other homes. "Look over there. And there. There's several new cars around here. Let's check it out. Hon, you need to work from the facts, not your emotions."

Legs, too? Why couldn't these two see how obvious this was? Maybe because I'd dealt with scumbags before and they hadn't? No matter. I could close the deal on this mess without the rookies. Alexander was already at the front door. He knocked. The screen door rattled and shook with each tap. We joined him and waited.

The inside door opened, and a heavyset woman in a faded, flowered muumuu greeted us. "Yes?"

The rookies in our little band of investigators seemed to be waiting for me to take the lead. "Aloha. Mrs. Lau? My name is McKenna. This is Harris Galvin and Alexander Kapono. We were friends of Bob

Shapiro. Your husband maintained Mr. Shapiro's plane and we'd just like to ask him, uh, your husband, a few questions."

Tears welled in her eyes, and she dabbed at her cheek with a tissue. "Roger not here."

"When will he be back?"

"I don't know. Kapono? You related to Sunny Kapono?"

"Yah, yah, he's a cousin. I haven't talked to him in long time. You okay?"

I said, "Can we come in?" Maybe we could get a look around and see whether there were other signs of sudden wealth besides the truck—art work, hand-cut crystal, new furniture. Things I couldn't afford.

She glanced at Alexander. "You Sunny's cousin, you must be okay. I'm Emma." She opened the screen door, and we stepped in.

The living room was small and square, not more than fifteen feet on a side. With the exception of a Koa-wood rocker in one corner, most of the furniture looked like it had come from a discount furniture store. "That's a beautiful piece." I gestured towards the rocker. The dark wood appeared to be as smooth as glass. The joints were perfectly matched and the back had a gentle contour that, I was sure, conformed closely to the natural shape of the spine.

"Mahalo. Roger just bought it for our anniversary."

"How long have you two been married?" It sounded like a good icebreaker to me.

"Almost twenty years. We married right out of high school, and I had Eric couple years later. Mr. Shapiro, he a good man. Roger work for him since he start his business. He really liked that new plane Mr. Shapiro got."

I made a mental note; Shapiro's plane was new. "Yah, it's quite a plane. And it's missing."

"Missing?" She got a stunned look on her face. "Since when?"

"Yesterday, we think."

"Mr. Shapiro so proud of that plane. He took us up in it right after he got it. He even let Roger fly it once. Roger is good pilot. It missing?"

I glanced at Alexander and he grimaced. Harris had blended into the background, but was scanning the room. It seemed inevitable to me that even my trainees would all soon arrive at the inevitable conclusion about Roger and the missing plane. Alexander said, "How old are your boys? They must be ready for college, yah?"

I noticed that she wasn't looking at us, but at a corner table next to the couch where a framed photo of her, a man and two boys held prominence. The men all wore brightly colored Hawaiian shirts; she wore a muumuu with a decorated neckline. The photo had obviously been taken at some sort of family event.

Alexander said, "Nice looking boys."

She sniffled and dabbed at her cheek again. She did a quick visual check on Harris, then turned her attention back to Alexander. "I hope they get to go."

"How come maybe no college?"

She choked back a sob. "Because I think my husband left me."

Alexander wrapped his arms around her and gave her a huge hug. I gave her a huge stare. This woman was either the best actress on the island or the most naive. I scanned the room while they seemed to relish their relative-bonding experience. I'd never realized how emotional Alexander was until the past couple of days. He was a regular Mother Teresa, compassion for all.

He said, "It gonna be okay. He wouldn't leave you, Sunny would kill him."

She chuckled and wiped away the smears on her cheeks. "Yah. Sunny find him, Roger gonna be in big trouble."

From the background, we heard Harris say, "Mrs. Lau, when did your husband buy the truck out front?"

"Couple weeks ago. He waited for years." She puffed up her chest and shoulders a bit, "Paid cash."

I saw Alexander wince. I, myself, suppressed a smirk, but made another mental note, told you so. Even a rank beginner could see where this was going by now.

Alexander said, "Well, there you go. He not gonna leave his new truck behind."

Mrs. Lau seemed to ponder that for a minute and then nodded. "He waited too long for that truck."

Alexander smiled. "See? Nothing to worry about."

"He not gonna get to drive it for a month when he get back."

We all half-laughed and that seemed to perk her up. I said, "Mrs. Lau, did your husband have any business dealings that you might not have known about?"

Her thin eyebrows knitted together. "That make no sense."

Good answer. The old how-would-I-know-what-I-don't-know defense. "Let me ask it another way. How much do you know about your husband's business?"

"I do the books."

Now, we were getting somewhere; watch and learn, rookies. "Any large influxes of cash lately?"

Her reaction came about two seconds later as she realized what direction I was going. Her eyes bulged in their sockets, and she shook her head from side to side. She stammered, "Get—get out! You said you—you had—questions for Roger. He not here—and now you accusing him of stealing! How dare you!"

She backed me towards the door, a pudgy index finger stabbing me in the chest. "How dare you come into my house and accuse us of something! Roger, he an honest man."

I thought I might fall over backwards, but then the wall saved me.

Alexander put his hand on Mrs. Lau's shoulder and spoke in a soft tone. "Emma. Mr. McKenna didn't mean that how it sounded."

"And how dare you come here with these haoles. You should know betta than trust them. You welcome back anytime—without him." She jabbed her finger in my direction again. "Or her, she checking out all my things."

"I meant no disrespect." Harris's contrite tone seemed to appease Mrs. Lau, but only until I opened my mouth again.

I said, "Mrs. Lau, I'm just trying to find out—"

She opened the door and grabbed my shirt. I was sure she was about to throw me into the driveway when Alexander came between us. "I'll take care of him, Emma. I apologize for his behavior."

With that, he guided us out the door and to his truck. He put us inside, got in, and we left. Mrs. Lau stood on the porch watching until we were on the road. Alexander finally said, "Why you act like a haole in there? You know betta than that."

Alexander had never called me a haole in that tone before, it had always been more of a joke. This time, the disdain in his voice telegraphed a strong message. I'd crossed an important line and become a traitor. I'd been sure that as soon as he saw I was right, he'd drop the indignation routine. Instead, this was going the other direction.

I thought about his reaction. What shocked me most was the way I felt. I didn't know why, but being right about Roger Lau now seemed less important than my relationship with Alexander.

"I gotta live on this island. Maybe you gonna leave someday, but me, this is my home."

"It's my home too." The words sounded artificial and barely made it past the knot in my throat. Tears welled in my eyes as I remembered the empty rooms when I'd arrived home after my night in jail. I couldn't go through that again. Not with my best friend.

"Then you betta start acting like it. Stop pissing people off or maybe all my cousins put you in a canoe and set you out to sea."

I put on my best Happy McKenna mask. "They wouldn't do that, would they? You guys are all about peace and love, that aloha spirit."

"Haoles don't always get same treatment. You said wrong thing to the wrong person."

"Her? Why's she special?"

"She's a relative."

"Oh, that."

"And she part Hawaiian."

"I knew that."

"That's just it, McKenna, you know it, but you don't feel it. You betta start paying attention to people's feelings. Practice some aloha spirit yourself."

I sulked in silence as we drove along, contemplating Alexander's words. I'd irritated him two or three times now in the last day or so. I had no friends left. No place left to run. Was I bound to repeat the same mistakes yet again? I did what I should have done with Jenny and Michael. "Alexander, I'm sorry."

He shook his head and smiled, "Emma, she gonna call Auntie Loni. She'll call Cousin Sunny and about five others. Me, I'd be surprised if she don't call Cousin Eddie. If you lucky, they get you booked on a freighter bound for someplace nasty by tonight. That mo betta than a canoe to nowhere."

"Doesn't sound very 'mo betta' to me."

"You rather have Cousin Eddie find you in a dark alley?"

Harris leaned forward from the back seat. In a voice soft as silk, she said, "Boys, I think we have a bigger problem. Alexander, you're right about your cousin. That's not the house of someone with lots of money. And why would he disappear now? If he had killed Shapiro, that's the worst thing he could do. Something must have happened to him, just like Shapiro. You should talk to Emma and have her report Roger as missing. And we still don't know where the plane is located."

Oh, crap, I felt another airport visit coming on.

15

If I had to cruise a few airports with Alexander to keep his friendship, I could do that. If it meant not insulting his relatives, I could probably do that, too. As long as I didn't have to look the other way when we had the proof, things would work out. They had to.

Fortunately, the traffic on H-2, another of our interstate highways, moved quickly. Later in the day it would be packed with cars like ants in a string returning to the nest with something sweet. Harris was asleep in the back seat, her head cocked to one side, her mouth open and her expression one of tranquillity only achievable by a Buddhist monk or someone zonked out. To pass the time, I stared out the side window of Alexander's truck watching landscape drift by. I guess I appeared deep in thought because Alexander finally broke the silence.

"So what you thinking about?"

"I never meant to hurt anybody's feelings."

"Deep down, inside, where it counts, you're okay. You just got something big making you crazy. You like a choppy ocean, you need let it go, your life smooth out. You hung onto it for a long time."

I wondered how he knew that. I hadn't even realized it until he'd gotten mad at me. Alexander flipped on his wipers. The front windshield got hit with a heavy mist that drifted up from the roadway. The rain began a second later. Our forward view did a continuous blurry-clear cycle as the wipers swiped fruitlessly across the windshield. Cars slowed a bit, but not enough to keep them from hydroplaning on the wet pavement.

By the time we'd merged onto H-1, we'd been through several rain showers. Each was a small cell that left everything in its wake—streets, houses, plants and people—soaking. At full speed on the freeway, the cells lasted no more than a couple of minutes. When you emerged on the other side of the rain, the sky was blue, the sun shone and, if you were looking in the right direction, a rainbow, maybe even a double, painted stripes on the sky. Despite the sun-rain cycle and the increased potential for an inattentive driver to do something stupid, like pay more attention to his cell phone than driving, we didn't have an accident and the traffic didn't snarl. What more could we ask for? Lunch? I was hungry.

Alexander interrupted my thoughts. "This whole west end full of construction."

"I had no idea." Houses, offices and shopping cropped up everywhere.

"Course not, you never get out here. You may read about it, but can't see how big Kalaeloa getting."

Until July 1990, Kalaeloa Airport had been Barbers Point Naval Air Station, named in honor of Captain Henry Barber of the British Navy, who ran his 100-foot brigantine Arthur aground off a nearby coastal point in 1796. I loved the trivia, but had no concept about the magnitude of change surrounding, and including, what had once been the largest naval air station in the Pacific theater. Hell, I thought it was doomed to be another former-military-base ghost town once the resurrection had been left to local government.

As we drove, I couldn't help but be struck by the street names: Langley, Midway, Bunker Hill. All reflected the proud military history of the area. Many base buildings had historical significance, which meant that if a landlord needed to change a light bulb, he'd need an act of Congress. And if he wanted to repaint, well, he'd have to go higher than that. Way higher.

As we entered the base, I recognized the entrance style of a controlled facility—a split in the road funneled outgoing traffic away from the incoming, but the former guard station had been transformed into a welcoming monument. Off to one side, I saw National Guard buildings. "Wow, they're here?"

Alexander shrugged. "Along with the Coast Guard. They both have hangars here."

From the back seat, I heard Harris. "Ooh, men in uniform. You can let me off."

Alexander and I exchanged a glance, from the back seat I heard a chuckle. What I had to put up with to find a little Cessna. Jeez. At the airport itself I expected traffic and people and TSA screening; what we got instead was a control tower and administration complex. I was used to places like LAX or Honolulu where you had amenities, like food. I couldn't usually eat ninety-eight percent of what most travelers grazed on in those places, but my stomach still growled like an angry dog.

Harris said, "Sounds like thunder."

"Shut up."

Alexander almost seemed to delight in my misery. We pulled into the lot, which had about a half-dozen cars in it and parked, then made our way through the double front doors. The interior walls were white, the floor an alternating pattern of beige and gray linoleum squares. Large, framed photographs of Naval aircraft decorated the wall in front of us.

"Can I help you?" The voice came from a man behind a counter to our left. He was medium height, medium build, medium complexion. I thought maybe he'd been produced in a blender and poured into an average mold so he could suffer through a normal life constrained by the bonds of mediocrity. I supposed it was possible that Mr. Average had married Mrs. Average and they had 1.8 Little Averages. I wondered what that last kid looked like.

I was about to introduce myself as O'Brien from the Advertiser when another man burst through the front doors and slapped Alexander on the back. "Cousin! Howzit?"

"Cousin Joey? Hey, I haven't seen you since—what was it? Graduation?"

"The night you stole my date. How is she, anyway?"

"Kira's doing good. We got two little ones now. She wants a third, gonna be the death of me."

"Couldn't get a better way to go, yah?" Cousin Joey must have just noticed the cut over Alexander's eye because he said, "What happened to your face?"

Alexander fingered the cut. "Bad experience at someplace I shouldn't have been."

"Brah, you didn't hit the wrong bar, did you?"

"That might've been better."

Cousin Joey winced. He shifted his weight from one foot to the other. I caught him wink at Harris. She smiled, he responded, I bristled. Cousin Joey then ignored Harris as he and Alexander exchanged manly chuckles and pats on the shoulder. Harris dropped in a few demur glances at the floor. Everyone was having a grand old time. The camaraderie and cheer were so catchy it almost made me want to jump in and hug them all.

Alexander examined the name badge on his cousin's chest. "Hey, you work here?"

"As little as possible." They both laughed again in unison. "What do you need?"

I could just see the two of them in grade school. Scary thought. A couple came through the door and slipped around us to the counter. They were both dressed in white shirts with little epaulets on the shoulders and navy pants. They both carried black notebooks with a funny logo emblazoned across the front.

Alexander rubbed the cut on his cheek. "This present came from some guys who threw a body out of a plane." He gestured at Harris. "I was guiding her in the mountains when we saw the whole thing."

Cousin Joey started, then looked at Harris, then me. "He serious?" He grinned and slapped Alexander on the shoulder. "Good one, Cousin. You almost had me. Pretty good, brah. Almost as good as the surfing contest in high school."

Alexander waved away the jibe. "We got the whole thing on film. And we think a plane that came in earlier today was involved. We want help checking it out."

"The plane stolen?"

"Maybe. We're not sure."

"Why not talk to the Sheriff? You should let them investigate."

I said, "Why not HPD?"

Cousin Joey said, "Not their jurisdiction. Stolen planes belong to the Sheriff, which is part of the Department of Public Safety."

I guess he would know, he was the airport man. "I went to the cops about the murder." Then I fibbed a bit, "They needed more proof before they could start."

Cousin Joey's gaze went back and forth between the three of us. I could see that he wondered if we were on the level or not.

Finally, he said, "This for real?"

We all nodded. The woman with the black notepad finished speaking with the man at the counter and turned away. She called over her shoulder, "See you later, Mike."

I watched her and her companion leave through the back door. Harris jabbed me in the arm. I grabbed at the spot where her fist had connected. "Hey, that hurt!"

Cousin Joey said, "Pretty nice, yah?"

Harris glared at him. I half-expected her to deck poor Cousin Joey on the spot.

He held up his hands. "Sorry. They're flight crew for some bigwig from the mainland."

It was probably my slack jaw that gave him the clue that I was dumbstruck by someone having a flight crew.

"We're promoting Kalaeloa as an alternative to HNL for private parties. We've got a long runway and no TSA to deal with. Once we get fuel on-site, it will be really attractive to private parties. And, as you can see, things are growing so much out here, this is going to become the new Honolulu someday."

Judging by the construction going on, it wouldn't be that long. I wondered how many planes they had out here. I asked, "If we give you an N-Number, can you tell us where that plane is parked?"

"Is it a transient or one of ours? Ours are in an old NAS hangar. We don't have a lot of the strict rules like over at Kaneohe."

I said, "Transient. It's based out at Dillingham Field."

He pointed to a sign-in sheet on the counter. "You gotta register here first."

I signed in the three of us, then turned expectantly to Cousin Joey. "Now what?"

Cousin Joey inspected my registrations. "Hmmm. Okay. You know what kind of plane it is?"

"A Cessna."

"Cessna makes a lot of planes. Single engine?"

"I don't know."

"Is this a new plane or something older?"

I shook my head, then remembered what Mrs. Lau had said, "I think it's new."

"Look, guys, there's a lot of Cessnas out there."

I pointed towards the door. "Out there?"

"No, man, I meant Cessna makes a lot of planes."

The man behind the counter looked up and said, "You the guy called earlier about the Cessna from Kauai?"

I recognized his name tag immediately. O'Shaunessey—the guy I'd spoken to earlier on the phone. Crap. Did he remember the name I'd given him? Cousin Joey was looking at me suspiciously. Alexander watched me with laughing eyes, probably waiting to see how I'd get out of this one. Harris pretended to whistle as she watched the ceiling. O'Shaunessey was just staring at me, kind of like he was expecting an answer.

I leaned in Harris's direction and whispered in her ear. "McKenna's Fourth Skip Tracing Secret: be flexible and go with the flow." To O'Shaunessey, I said, "Uh, yeah."

"Took off about an hour ago." He shrugged, his duty done, and picked up the papers he'd been shuffling on the counter.

Cousin Joey said, "What about a flight plan?"

O'Shaunessey shrugged, "Nah. Said he wasn't going no place controlled." He turned away and went back to his desk.

Exasperated, I threw up my hands. "How could that be? Don't you inspect these planes? Require them to go through security? Something?"

Cousin Joey said, "We use our judgment. If you don't look suspicious and have a good reason to use this airport, we probably won't inspect it. Mikey, he give a reason why he was here?"

"He said he was opening a new business out here. Just flew in for a day to check it out."

I asked, "A business? What business? Lau's an airplane maintenance man."

Cousin Joey said, "Roger Lau?"

O'Shaunessy said, "That's him!"

Cousin Joey said, "No way, Mikey. He's out at Dillingham. Roger's not opening any new businesses. He's doing good where he's at."

O'Shaunessy raised his palms in a gesture of futility, Cousin Joey buried his face in his hands while he muttered something unintelligible, Alexander shrugged, Harris ignored us, and me, I realized that I hadn't seen a restroom since Dillingham Field.

I asked Cousin Joey, "Where's, uh, your restroom?" Damn, I'd almost called it Bosco.

He pointed behind me. I nodded my thanks and hustled off to check out the john, Harris on my heels looking for the women's. The restroom reminded me of a 1940s purely functional building—brownish tile, white toilet bowl, black seat, no doors on the stall. Oh yeah, leave your modesty behind if you're doing number two here.

By the time I returned, Cousin Joey was working behind the counter and Alexander appeared impatient. I said, "Don't you ever have to go?"

Harris approached from behind me, her face pale. "That was an experience."

Alexander said, "If you two are done checking out the facilities, let's get outta here."

We were halfway to the car when Harris began to sway. Alexander and I each grabbed an arm just as her knees went weak. "I'm not feeling so good."

Harris slept in the back as we returned to the apartment. At one point, Alexander glanced at me and said, "I think she got a concussion. She needs a doctor."

"Where's the nearest hospital?"

Harris barked, "No hospitals! No doctor! Take me home."

By the time we'd picked up H-1, traffic had slowed considerably. The afternoon commute was turning grim, as was my attitude about what might have happened to Roger Lau. If he hadn't been flying the plane, who had? I said, "Roger seems like he was a good husband and father. He wouldn't just disappear without a good reason."

Alexander nodded. "Let's just hope he got himself into trouble, not dead."

16

When I'd hurt my back in the baseball game, the doctor had also warned my mother about a possible concussion. She'd gone into the granddaddy of all overreactions and kept me in bed, fed me pain meds by the handful and put cold compresses on my forehead for weeks instead of the doctor's recommended couple of days. She'd even used bags of frozen vegetables wrapped in a washcloth for a while until my father complained about the grocery bill and the lack of vegetables at dinner.

Every time she put on a cold compress, I'd tried to explain that it was my back that hurt, not my head. But, the doctor had told her that I could experience headaches, drowsiness, depression, or personality changes. She was convinced that my back couldn't hurt because the doctor hadn't found anything wrong there. And how could I be drowsy? I was in bed all day. I didn't know what depression was, but it sounded like something I didn't want. She did, however, become concerned that I might be going through personality changes because I'd been stuck in my bed for so long and was starting to argue with her about my condition.

The Wharton boys told me I would get bedpan hands if I didn't get out soon. That sounded worse than anything the doctor had told Mom about, so I launched a full-on "I'm better" assault and got my sentence commuted. What had me worried now was that Harris was exhibiting some of those symptoms my mother had watched for so diligently.

At home, we got Harris settled in on her couch with the TV remote and some water. Alexander excused himself and went to get some food for Harris. I figured he'd hit a drive-through somewhere on the way. Poor me, well, I'd have to settle for a bowl of gluten-free cereal in my kitchen—oh, yum.

About the time I got back to Harris's apartment, Alexander had shown up with an assortment of frozen dinners and lunches, some juice, soft drinks and ice cream. I watched him unpack and said, "Really healthy choices there, big fella."

"Unless you want to cook for her, this is gonna be it."

Harris called in to the kitchen, "Did you get the pizza?"

"Yah, I got the last one in the case. You one lucky wahine."

I looked at the box that Alexander held in his hand. Pepperoni, sausage, and mushrooms. Those were the big three on the front label. I checked the ingredients on the box and finally spotted the "big three" about halfway down a long list of chemicals I'd never heard of.

I handed it over. "That'd kill me."

Alexander chuckled as he put the box in the freezer, then turned serious. "McKenna, what about Shapiro?"

"What about him?"

"I was thinking on the way back from the store, if he's got a nosey landlord like you, maybe we should go visit him?"

I thought about it for a second. "I ain't nosey; I'm just naturally curious."

"Whatever you say. You want to go check it out? The rain's let up for a while."

Alexander was giving me another chance. No way I'd turn that down. I went to the window and craned my neck to see the sky. Sure enough, the one cell had moved through and there was nothing in sight. Give that about ten minutes and it would change. Hawaiian weather—if you don't like it, wait ten minutes. We'd get drenched, no doubt about it.

"Let's go," I said.

We left Harris with her frozen pizza and headed toward Kaiulani Avenue. The clouds were gathering, looking like they were at a cloud convention and just waiting for a motion to rain. I was certain that they'd all vote in favor before we got to Shapiro's apartment. We parked on the street about a block from the apartment complex and walked back. We made it before the rain-vote had been cast.

The manager's apartment wasn't hard to find and was marked by a big sign on the wall next to the door. Alexander knocked, waited, then knocked again. Just to the right of the door, I read another sign that gave the manager's hours: "Office open from 9:00 AM - 12:00 PM and 1:00 PM - 5:00 PM No exceptions."

From behind us, we heard, "He ain't in there."

We turned. A smallish man wearing a gold Green Bay Packers cap, a white shirt with blue and red horizontal stripes and khaki shorts peered at us from behind a hoe that he held in both hands as if it were a martial arts staff. Two thin white spindles that he probably called legs stuck out from the baggy shorts.

I wondered if he would pop me with the hoe. I said, "We wanted to ask him some questions about Mr. Shapiro."

"What?" He raised his left hand and cupped it behind his left ear.

Oh, great, hard-of-hearing. "We had questions about a tenant! Robert Shapiro." I spoke slowly and yelled at him.

In a loud voice, he said, "You don't have to yell." His shoulders slumped a bit as he glanced away. He looked me in the eye and said, "Shapiro's dead."

I tried a slightly lower volume this time. "I know. He got hit by a car a couple of weeks ago."

He leaned on the hoe and stared off into space. The sadness in his eyes said he'd known Shapiro well. "He didn't deserve to die like that."

Alexander asked, "Are you the gardener?"

"Gardener? No, we don't have a gardener."

That struck me as an odd answer. I wasn't sure if he hadn't heard the question or just didn't want to answer. "Who are you? What do you do?"

"What needs to be done."

I felt like grabbing the hoe from his hands and smacking this guy on the side of his head. "So where's the manager?"

"Gone."

"Gone where?"

"Don't know, moved out last month."

Alexander looked confused, "The manager just left? They didn't replace him?"

"Didn't say he didn't get replaced. Just said he moved."

"Oh, for crying out loud!" I yelled, "Who the hell is running this place?"

He chuckled. "Me."

Raindrops pelted the palms. Orchids and gardenias bounced delicately as drops large and small splattered their targets. Miniature rings began to radiate in every direction on the surface of a small pool off to our left.

He eyed me with suspicion. "You two police? I'd like to see some identification."

"No, I'm doing a piece for the Advertiser."

"Hmmm. Mr. Shapiro was a nice feller."

"We're trying to figure out who ran him down."

"Uh-huh." He glanced from Alexander to me, then back again. "Where's your camera?"

Ouch, no camera. Where was Harris with her official looking gear when I needed her? Oh, that's right, resting with her pizza and ice cream. "We're trying to expose a drug ring, can't be too obvious."

He snorted. "You ain't no paperman."

Oh great, a wise guy. "Look, um—"

Alexander said, "A friend and I saw a body dropped from Mr. Shapiro's plane two days ago."

The manager rubbed his chin and nodded. He seemed to be having some sort of internal debate. "There's something I think you boys'll wanna see in my apartment."

I hoped it wasn't a gun. He pulled a jailer's key ring off his belt. I said, "Nice key ring."

"Yup. Makes it easier to do things."

"Good idea," I said.

He held up a key. "Mine's blue. Easier to find that way."

"Another good idea." Maybe I should get myself one? It would make me look more official.

Alexander moved to one side, holding his head as if he were trying to subdue pain. At about the same time, the manager and I turned to Alexander and asked him if something was wrong.

He glanced from me to Shapiro's landlord, then back again. "You two practice this?" He rolled his eyes. "No offense, but I can't take two of you."

The manager and I chuckled together and left Alexander standing outside. Maybe the rain would make that headache of his go away.

As we entered the apartment, he said, "Name's Meyer Herschel."

"Meyer? That like the lemon?"

"You're kind of a smart ass, huh?"

I shrugged, "Guess it comes naturally. I'm McKenna."

"You ashamed of your first name?"

"I've only used one name since I was a kid."

He mumbled to himself, "Chrissakes. Can't even use a whole name. So what's your story?"

The apartment was dark and small compared to mine. The walls were all painted the industry-standard off-white and the only window, the one that looked out to where Alexander stood watching the rain, was made smaller by the brightly flowered curtains that hung on either side. Meyer pulled the curtains open. The room furniture included a rattan couch and side chair with fluffy cushions covered in a matching fabric. Fortunately, the dining room set, also rattan, didn't have the same patterned fabric. The solid, forest-green covering complimented the other furniture, but didn't make the pattern so overpowering that you wanted to run around and pollinate everything.

"I guess you could say I'm investigating Shapiro's death."

Meyer crossed the room and flipped on a light switch. The hanging lamp over the dining room table lit up a stack of boxes, all labeled with Shapiro's name. I had the sudden sensation of drowning as a wave of anticipation overcame me. My breathing quickened. It was just like the old days—before computers—before the production line and before I'd been outsourced.

Meyer smirked and leaned against the kitchen counter, just next to the boxes. At that moment, I probably reminded him of a pirate drooling over a cache of gold or a half-naked maiden waiting to be ravaged. On the other hand, given my panicked reaction to Harris the other day, I'd better stick to the boxes.

"That's what you said before. You and I both know you're no investigator, so what's really going on?"

Had my lying skills gone into the crapper? I mumbled, "You're a sharp old coot, aren't you?"

"Hoot? What's a hoot? Nothing funny here."

"No, I said that you were a sharp old coot!"

He smiled. "I ain't the brightest bulb in the pack, but I do know when something's going on. Spill the beans or, like the song says, don't let the door hit'cha on the way out."

"I'm too old to let doors bang me in the ass."

"So what's it gonna be?"

I pointed out the window and spoke loudly. "That guy? He almost got killed by someone shooting from Shapiro's plane."

"That's horse pucky. I guess you forgot, Shapiro's dead. That's D-E-A-D. He don't fly no more. Besides, he was a good guy and wouldn't ever shoot anyone, unless they deserved it."

"We know he's dead. We—no, I—thought it was the guy who does the maintenance on Shapiro's plane. He ran down Shapiro, then used the plane for some illicit activity. But now he's missing, too. Maybe dead."

Meyer pushed the baseball cap up on his forehead, then pursed his lips. "Don't make no sense. Who would want to kill both Bob Shapiro and his maintenance man?"

That was true. Who would want, or need, to kill both men? And why? If Shapiro's and Lau's deaths were related somehow, I had to get to the bottom of it. It was the only way I'd get Harris her money; it was the only way I'd redeem myself in Alexander's eyes. And the only way to get to the bottom of it all was through Meyer Herschel. I needed those boxes.

17

Meyer stood next to the stack of boxes and drummed his fingers. "Yup, I started going through these records, but my eyesight ain't so good and I just ain't got enough time, what with my duties around this place."

I stroked my chin, not because I had to wipe off the drool that might be dribbling out of the corner of my mouth, but because the answers to all my problems—the Shapiro problems, anyway—might be right here. All I'd have to do is go through those boxes, assemble some information, then file the final report with CrimeStoppers. It was my old job all over again, and it would put me solidly back in Alexander's good graces. It might even get me that home run with Harris. Now that made my palms sweat.

Having decided I needed what Meyer had, I figured the best thing would be to give him the full story so that he'd understand my rationale—except for the Harris part, of course. That would be too much information. I ran through the entire story of Harris's photo safari, being sure to leave out the hugs and her friendly manner. Meyer seemed particularly interested by the Darwin Awards, saying that he could think of several people he'd like to nominate. I reminded him that the nominee had to be dead, to which he just nodded and shrugged. Best not to get on this guy's bad side, I thought.

Finally, with the entire detailed story on the table, he set his cap on top of one of the boxes. His thin hair revealed a sunspot that reminded me of the state of Florida tattooed on his scalp. He said, "You're a helluva story teller, but I still think you're full of horse pucky."

I'd been told that I was full of many things before, but horse pucky had never been one of them. At least, not that I could remember. BS, yeah. Plain old S, sure. "What, you can't say shit?"

"Where I come from, we don't say that unless we really don't like someone. Me? I kind of like you. You seem down-to-earth. So, I think you're full of horse pucky."

"Shit. You think I'm full of horse shit?"

"Call it what you want. I ain't the one asking for favors. You want to see what's in those boxes?"

I nodded.

"Then get smart."

"So now I'm stupid? Jesus."

"That's it, you're out of here. Don't let the screen door hit your skinny ASS on the way out!"

Good job, McKenna, you've destroyed another bridge. I was better at tearing down than building up. "I, uh, apologize." The last thing I needed was to have Meyer Herschel kick me out of his apartment.

"Good, glad we got the power structure figured out. Now, just because you were so obstinate, you gotta say it."

"Say what?"

Meyer's eyes twinkled. "I'm full of—"

"Bullshit! You'd better watch out, or I'll have my friend come in here and knock you on your scrawny ass!" He took a step sideways and, for the first time, I noticed a small wooden case with a glass front sitting on his desk. I pointed at the case, "What's that?"

"Something I got in the war."

The door handle behind us jiggled. Alexander yelled, "Hey, open up!"

I peered closer at the case. "That's a Medal of Honor. Is that yours?"

Alexander yelled, "What's going on in there?"

I caught and held Meyer's gaze. "What'd you have to do to get it?"

He closed his eyes and took a shallow breath. "Stay alive." When he opened his eyes, they were moist. Crinkled lines radiated across his forehead and temples, each a reminder of an event he preferred to leave in his past. I cleared my throat. "Pretty slick, locking the door on the way in. I didn't catch that."

"I figured I could always handle you. Besides, I've got a secret weapon."

"What, that hoe you were carrying?"

He gave me a crooked-toothed smile as he extracted a small canister from his left pocket. He gripped the container tightly in his hand and pointed it in my direction. "Pepper spray. It'll stop you or your friend dead in your tracks."

I'd come to the realization that, like the "simple country lawyer," Meyer was far more cagey than he appeared. The door rattled again, and we both turned at the sound of a loud thud. Alexander was trying to break it down.

I said, "Look, I think we both want to know what happened to Shapiro. Why don't we declare a truce?"

"McKenna! You okay?" Another thud, this one louder. Then, Alexander was at the window. He appeared to be searching for something to use to break the glass.

"Is he going to break in?"

I shrugged. "He might."

"You'll have to pay for damages."

"He thinks my well-being is in jeopardy."

"Negotiation skills under fire. I like that."

I yelled, "I'm okay, Alexander." I turned to Meyer. "Can I let him in before he breaks something, like maybe his shoulder?"

Meyer chuckled, then motioned towards the door with his head. He turned suddenly serious, "Your story seems pretty farfetched to me, but I think you're on the level about wanting to learn what happened to Bob. So what do you want to know?" He stuck the container back in his pocket.

I opened the door to find Alexander standing there with both hands on his hips in the Superman pose. He was probably trying to summon up his superpowers to bust down the door. I was glad that Meyer and I had come to an understanding before Alexander damaged the building's construction—or himself. "Come on in," I said.

Alexander rubbed his sore arm as he glared at us. "What happening in here, McKenna?"

"Meyer and I have agreed that he's going to help us figure out what happened to Shapiro." I walked back into the room and announced to Meyer, "I want to see what's in his records."

Meyer stationed himself next to the boxes in a defiant pose. "What? Records? Oh, these, not yet."

"What do you mean? I thought you said it was okay."

"I asked you what you wanted to know."

McKenna, I thought, this guy is as stubborn as you, take it slow and you'll get where you want to be. "Okay, we think Shapiro was murdered. But, we don't know why, or who did it."

Meyer said, "Bob only did sightseeing trips and, what'd he call that? Oh yeah, private charters. He never took cargo. He bought that fancy new airplane so he could drop his cargo business. He kept saying that there was a market for people who wanted tours and transportation. He told me he'd already lined up a couple of small-business clients who didn't have enough money for their own plane, but didn't like wasting time flying commercial."

I asked, "Would he ever let the client take luggage or cargo?"

Meyer shrugged, "How would I know?"

I wondered if Meyer was just being cagey again, or if he really wasn't sure. I suspected it wasn't the latter. "You know quite a bit, for a landlord."

Alexander said, "He probably would take cargo, brah. My Cousin Eddie runs a charter service. He lets his regular clients rent him and the plane for a flat fee."

"So a small business could save money," I said. "They could avoid the hassles of flying commercial and be with their shipment from point A to point B. That could be of importance to someone who had something valuable to move inter-island."

"Like drugs," said Alexander.

Meyer grimaced. "Bob would never do that."

"That could be why someone had to kill him. When did he buy that new plane?"

"Maybe two months. He teamed up with Roger to buy it. Cost over half a million bucks, you know."

Alexander and I stared at Meyer. I said, "Are you sure about that?"

"That's what he told me."

Alexander muttered, "I better be nicer to Cousin Eddie."

"I'm not talking about the money," I said. "I meant, why was Roger proud of it? He was just the maintenance guy."

"Nah, he was one of Bob's backers. Bob could only borrow about half of what he needed by himself. Roger's the one who got the financing for the rest."

I glanced at Alexander and said, "Well, goddamn."

He nodded. "What else do you know about Shapiro's business?"

"Not much. He always paid his rent on time. Didn't seem to have much trouble making ends meet; maybe cause he drove that old clunker. Didn't cost him nothing to own it."

"Where's the car?" I asked.

"Most of the time it's in his carport."

"Yah, yah," I said, "I'm sure it wasn't in the carport when he drove it."

"Yup."

I said, "So Shapiro drove an old car and had silent business financial backers that helped him buy an expensive airplane. Anything else?"

"Nope."

"We need to find out who the backers are," I said. Was it something he discovered about one of his partners that got him killed? Or was it one of his clients? And was it Roger Lau who had been thrown from that plane? Or was I completely off base on that presumption, too? We needed more information.

Alexander said, "You know, McKenna, I think we gonna have to go back and talk to Roger's wife again, yah?"

"I think there's a few things Mrs. Lau didn't tell us. But first, we need to know what questions to ask. And that's where these boxes are going to help."

"I'm not sure I can let you fellows do that."

Alexander asked, "Why not? We all want the same thing."

"They're not my records. They belong to Mr. Shapiro."

"Now he's Mr. Shapiro?" I said. "And, he's dead. So, who cares?"

"He's still got a right to his privacy. And his dignity."

Meyer Herschel was being cagey, yet again. I couldn't help but wonder what was going on. Why he'd suddenly not want us to look through the boxes he'd been teasing us with already. I asked, "So what are you worried about? Cops? The court?"

He rolled his eyes. "If you two are right, it means there's someone out there going to want to destroy these records. Now who do you suppose they might be?"

I said, "That's what we don't know. We're looking for a trail."

"Exactly. And how long do you suppose it's going to take those fine fellows to figure out they might have left one?"

Alexander said, "That doesn't make any sense. They don't know there's a trail."

Meyer waved his arms in the air as if he were trying to flag down a passing cab. "Stop being good Samaritans for a few minutes and smell the manure. Think like someone who's got something to hide. You saw that news report on that wacko kid at nooky nooky high school yesterday, didn't you'?"

Alexander rolled his eyes. "Nanakuli High School."

"I saw it," I said. "So, what's that got to do with Shapiro?"

"Nothing, except this. That kid didn't go to such extraordinary measures because he was happy and well adjusted. He did that because he wanted to be noticed."

I nodded, "And these guys are the opposite. They'll do whatever they need to do to erase the trail back to Shapiro."

Alexander said, "But why come looking for you? They don't know you have the records."

Meyer's caginess suddenly made perfect sense. He was doing exactly what I might do in his shoes. He'd have emptied the apartment and gotten it ready for a new tenant. He'd store the records until the estate asked for them or until probate was settled and he'd been instructed to destroy them. I said, "They've already been here, that's why."

Meyer nodded. "Last night, about ten, I noticed a light on in Bob's old apartment. It wasn't big, just something small, like a flashlight bouncing around. I called the cops. They were here in two minutes. Since I was the one who reported the problem, they came to me first, then went up to the apartment. The cops had me stay down here while they checked it out, but they didn't find anything because they had to do half their search in the dark. That apartment's only got a light in the kitchen and the bathroom, no others."

I said, "But today, you went back in the daylight—when you could see better."

"Yup, the lock was fine, probably means they had a key. Nothing was disturbed because I took everything out a couple of days ago. But, it was the carpets that gave them away."

I laughed, "You cleaned the carpets and now there were footprints."

"I might not have caught it, otherwise. I warned the cops not to mess anything up. They were real careful, but some son-of-a-bitch left mud on my clean carpet. Now, I've got to clean it again."

I chuckled. "You swore."

Meyer shrugged. "Time and place for everything. I called the cops back, and they said there was nothing more they could do about a simple break-in."

Alexander said, "Since the records weren't in the apartment, these guys will think you've got them."

I added, "And they couldn't check it out last night because HPD was here."

Meyer seemed pleased with himself. "I knew you two were smarter than you looked. Now how do I get rid of these damn boxes without getting myself in trouble—or killed?"

18

Now that Meyer's dilemma had been laid out, the three of us stood around staring at the boxes and contemplating the Big Question. I considered how, were I in Meyer's shoes, I might unload the boxes. Quite frankly, I wasn't sure.

Meyer broke the mood when he pulled the small canister of pepper spray from his pocket. He pointed the canister at his mouth and pressed the button on top. My jaw dropped, and I started to move in his direction.

I yelled, "No!"

Alexander took hold of my shoulder and held me in place. "McKenna, you gone nuts?"

Meyer swallowed and said, "That's better." He shoved the canister in my direction. "Throat spray. Helps clear the passages. Want some?"

My mouth moved, but nothing came out. This cagey old war veteran deserved respect. And maybe he'd just answered the Big Question.

Meyer said, "You look like you could use a little cleaning out. Here." He laughed so hard that he started coughing. After a few hacks, he regained control and said, "Gotcha. I don't even know where you'd buy pepper spray. As far as Shapiro's stuff goes, I donated some of it, threw away a bunch of old junk, and stored the rest. I'm hoping I get approval to get rid of it before the storage costs get to be more than his deposit."

"Why didn't you store the records with the rest?"

"Because it seemed to me that storing important records in a damn storage unit that has no humidity control wasn't a good idea. Besides, I had one of those leak once. What a mess." He handed me the throat spray. "Try it, really, it helps."

I said, "What if you told people you just threw Shapiro's stuff away?"

"That'd be a lie."

Alexander was holding his head again. "Why me?"

"I ain't gonna tell people a lie."

I said, "You've never fibbed just a bit?"

"McKenna, I kine know where this going. Don't do this."

"It's okay, Alexander. I know what I'm doing."

"Yah, corrupting an honest man. Just cause you think lying is a sport, don't mean he does."

"Pish posh."

Meyer looked puzzled. "What's that about goulash? You late for lunch or something?"

Alexander massaged his temples, "You two are giving me a headache—again."

"You lied to me about the pepper spray!"

Meyer took a step back. "Okay, okay, you don't have to yell." He slowly stroked the tops of the boxes. "Bob was a good man. So was his maintenance guy. We all had something in common."

I caught his brief glance at the Medal of Honor, then sadness washed over him. I said, "War?"

He blushed, then rubbed the back of his neck with a wizened hand. "Not the same one, but we'd all been there. Bob and Roger were in Vietnam. Bob had a Medal of Honor, too. Roger had a Silver Star." He glanced out the window, then took a deep breath. "I think they'd both appreciate someone taking an interest. I wish I could—"

He looked at the boxes and stepped aside. "I got me some grounds work to do. I hope none of those boxes disappear while I'm off. I don't know what I'd do if they disappeared while I wasn't paying attention. It could get me in some serious trouble with the courts if I threw them away, but if they got lost—" He grabbed his baseball cap and put it back on his head, then opened the door, and walked out.

Alexander stood in the corner rubbing his temples. "I don't believe this. Two of you. Why me?"

"We don't have time for that, grab a couple of boxes."

It took us two trips, but we were able to stuff all the boxes into the back seat of Alexander's truck. Before we left, I jotted a quick thank-you note to Meyer along with my telephone number. Mostly, I wanted to make sure he knew how to reach me, just in case he thought of something new. As we drove away, I saw his reflection in the side mirror waving goodbye. I waved back, hoping that I'd get to see him again.

We schlepped the boxes into my apartment and put them on the floor next to the kitchen table. Alexander's brow furrowed. I said, "You look like something's bugging you."

"McKenna, you gone pupule. You really think that old coot gonna be able fool these guys they come back?"

"I didn't know you cared."

"Bullshit. I didn't know you cared!"

"There's a possible thousand-dollar reward for this tip. Harris needs money for her sister's operation."

"So you telling me you doing this so you can get laid, yah?"

"This is the kind of thing I used to do—find people."

He held my gaze, his eyes saying what words couldn't.

"It's the challenge. The rush of solving the puzzle."

Silence. Just silence. And that damned introspective stare of his. This was beginning to piss me off. "I owe people."

"You didn't even know Shapiro."

I almost said, "Not Shapiro, you dummy. I owe you." Alexander had supported me and my grumpiness for five years. It was payback time. Besides, I knew that Shapiro's death had been glossed over by the cops just as my symptoms had been glossed over by a doctor. It had taken a new doctor, someone who was a good listener, to finally uncover my Celiac sprue. Maybe it was my turn to listen. "Fine! I'm feeling something. For the first time in—screw it."

"Your *mana* picked a helluva time to come back."

He was right. I had picked a helluva time to start feeling strong again. I forced a laugh—it was a pitiful display of bravado. "My mana will protect me. Isn't that what you guys say?"

"No amount of spirit gonna save you from a bullet."

Well, that sure put a damper on the conversation. I cleared my throat. "I need to go check on Harris. We were gone longer than I thought we'd be."

"I'll go too. If she don't need nothing, I'm heading home."

Harris had parked herself on the couch. She was flipping through channels on the TV, a mound of potato chips on a napkin in her lap, a glass in her hand. She glared up at us when we walked in and barked, "Where the hell have you been?" Her outburst sprayed potato chip crumbs in every direction. She hid her mouth with her hand and took a quick drink.

I said, "Nice to see you too. You must be feeling better." And cranky.

"Sorry. I don't know where that came from. I've got a helluva headache, and every now and again I start yelling at the TV. I keep getting these weird mood swings. It's like PMS, but it's the wrong time of the month."

I held up my hands. "Whoa."

She blushed. "Sorry—again."

Alexander said, "You need anything?"

She waved off the question. "I'm good. I just want to rest."

We left Harris to her TV, potato chips, and soft drink. Alexander bid me goodbye, and I went into my apartment and surveyed my collection of boxes. Wow. A puzzle. A challenge. And a dangerous one. I shoved that thought to the back of my mind. The master skip tracer was back. My job was just to find these guys; the cops could do the dangerous work.

I checked the box labels. The first one read "Business #1." There were also boxes for #2 and #3. There were boxes for "Photos," "Personal - Bank," and even "Business - Bank." Sadness filled me as I thought about how many boxes my life might come down to. I probably would only have three or four, and that made me even sadder. Shapiro had been a six-box man, I was no more than four, tops.

Shapiro had business records that someone might want to review, but no one had taken the time to look them over. And the people who were included in these records wanted to destroy them. I slumped down into the chair closest to the photo box, hoping that I might at least get to know the man a bit before I started poring through the business details of his life.

I lifted the lid and peered inside. Meyer had dumped photographs bundled with rubber bands on top of a single photo album that filled the bottom of the box. Ironically, he'd neatly arranged a dozen little Kodak cartons that probably contained slides against one side.

I decided to start with the slide cartons for a simple reason. The rubber-banded photos were already in a heap, so I might as well remove the neatness before the slides toppled over and made me feel bad about messing up Meyer's attempt at organization. Sure, it was weak. And, yes, it was a rationalization. But, I was the one doing the work so I figured I could do whatever I damned well felt like.

I pulled out the neat little stack of boxes and the hand-held slide viewer and set them on the table. Uh-oh—the seventies all over again. They were all marked with a date and a title. The first was labeled "Mar 1978 - Lake Tahoe." The others all had similar dates, but different locations. Apparently, this had been Shapiro's "slide period." I opened the first box and held the slide up to the light, then the next, and the next, until I'd gone through a dozen of the slides in the box. Shapiro had been into taking scenery in 1978. Slides were excellent for that purpose and Shapiro had obviously caught the bug, much as I had at about the same time. We'd probably stopped shooting slides for the same reason. Although the photographer had been fascinated by scenery slides, everyone else saw them as BORING. I set the slide boxes off to the side in a neat little stack. That's okay, Bob, I still have mine—somewhere.

I pulled the rubber-banded stacks of photos from the box, then lifted out the photo album, which was labeled "Our Family." I was willing to bet that these photos were older. I doubted that they would help much with solving the mystery of Shapiro's death, but they would help me learn more about the man.

The album began with the usual bare-assed baby pictures. I'd never understood what people saw in those photos. Though my parents hadn't done this to me, those photos seemed to have only one real purpose—embarrass the crap out of the subject once he or she had attained some level of self-confidence in the world.

Think of the power possibilities for a parent who held onto just the right bare-baby photo. Just imagine the President's mother at a cocktail party. Say Mom has had a couple of glasses of wine, the chef has pulled the perfectly crusted creme brulee from the broiler, the waitstaff is filing into the dining room filled with heads of state to deliver the perfect dessert. Mom stands. She fumbles through her wallet. "Would anybody like to see a picture of my baby boy?" Oh yeah. Sweet.

I worked my way through kindergarten photos and up to high school. Somewhere in the middle of the childhood photos there was one of a serviceman, his wife, and baby. I assumed they were Shapiro's parents because there were several others in which the same people appeared. By high school, the photos were in color. There were still pictures of the woman, along with a young man, but the serviceman was no longer around. The last photo in the album was one of the young man graduating from college.

In all the early shots, the ones where the serviceman was included, the background looked familiar. There were lots of family outings at the beach and then one that was a dead giveaway. The coastline of Oahu, unmistakable with Diamond Head in the background. Shapiro's father had been in the service and stationed at Pearl Harbor. I wondered if Bob had become a pilot to follow in his father's footsteps. And why had his father disappeared?

I sorted through three bundles of photos held together by rubber bands. The first contained shots depicting a much older version of the young man in the family photos. The resemblance to the serviceman was unmistakable. What struck me as odd was that the familiar island background had changed. I'd flipped through several photos before I realized that there was writing on the back of each. The first description was written in a big loopy script that read, "Ginny & Bob, SD Zoo, 1992." I began checking the backs of the others, almost every one had a description and date. The bundle that I was looking at was from the early nineties. Almost every image included the woman named Ginny, Shapiro, or both. The photos spanned three years, from 1991 to 1994. The one on the bottom was actually a newspaper clipping titled, "Stephens-Docks Wed."

Shapiro's girlfriend left him for another man? I held the clipping in my hand, but stared off into space. Shapiro's life had been as screwed up as mine, maybe more. After all, he was dead and I was still here. I glanced back at the wedding couple. "Bob, you've gotten some bad breaks."

Ginny wore a low-cut, white wedding dress. She stood next to a man I didn't recognize. The man was dressed in a tuxedo and both he and Ginny smiled in the classic top-of-the-wedding-cake pose. The caption read, "Jacqueline (Ginny) Stephens married Harcourt Docks III in a ceremony at Our Lady of the Valley Chapel on April 4, 1998." The article had been crumpled up, then smoothed out. There was no publication name, so I had no idea where Our Lady of the Valley Chapel was located. Or who Harcourt Docks III was. Sure, I could find him, but at this point, why?

I secured the photos with the rubber band and put them on the table with the slides and the family photo album. Had Shapiro lost his father and a fiancee? I opened another set of photos. These were from the period between 1987 and 1991. Ginny and Shapiro had been to many places and each grouping of photos came several months apart. Interesting. The first such grouping came in May 1990, the second in July 1990, October 1990, and so on. So Shapiro had kept photos all the way through to the news story about Ginny's wedding in 1998. Had she been cheating on him the entire time?

I removed the rubber band from the third set, expecting more photos of Ginny from prior to 1987, but I was wrong. Number one showed Bob Shapiro standing proudly next to an old, beat up, single-engine plane. There were photos of him standing by the propeller, in the cockpit, and shaking hands with a man who had coppery-colored skin and stood slightly shorter than Shapiro. The man was wearing blue coveralls, which reminded me of the description of Roger Lau. I wondered if this might be Roger. I checked the back of the photo. Unfortunately, Shapiro had stopped annotating his memories. Maybe he never had. I glanced at the feminine-looking script on another picture. Had Ginny written all the old descriptions? I set the one with the coppery-skinned man off to the side in hopes that we might eventually figure out who the man with Shapiro was.

This set was also odd in that there were photos stuck into plastic envelopes. Each envelope contained about twenty photos, all of smiling groups of one to four people standing next to an airplane. On the back of each, someone had printed a name and date in deliberate strokes. Maybe these were clients of Shapiro's? Was this his writing?

In the last envelope, I came across a photo of four men. I recognized Shapiro and the man with coppery-colored skin immediately. The man looked a bit heavier in this photo and wore a white, short-sleeved shirt. The third man wore a white dress shirt, sleeves rolled up, and collar open. The fourth wore a popular Aloha shirt that came from Hilo Hattie. Few tourists made it off the island without dropping money at Hilo Hattie. They have stores on every island, run shuttles to the stores from major hotels and cruise-ship dockings, greet you with a shell lei, and give you something to drink. They just make it easy for you to open your wallet and take part of the islands back with you, even if your only intent is to stuff that part away in a drawer back home and never look at it again until you returned to the islands and, of course, another Hilo Hattie store.

I hadn't seen the other man in any of the other photos, but on the back, the deliberate printing read, "Paradise Private Charters, LLC. Principals." The men stood before a brightly colored plane. The tail of the plane was painted to look like palm trees silhouetted against a sunset. I also recognized the N-Number immediately.

So Shapiro had business partners? I thought about what Meyer had said. Roger had arranged financing. Maybe the financing had really been a partnership? Had something gone wrong in the deal? I asked the men in the photo a question, "Did one of you kill Bob?" The only sound in the apartment was the ticktock of my grandfather clock and the hum of the refrigerator in my little galley-type kitchen.

Actually, I was thankful for that because if there had been another sound, like maybe the photo answering my question, I'd probably have called the loony bin and begged them to come pick me up for two very good reasons—photos can't talk and killers never confess, unless they're about to kill you.

19

It was nearly five PM by the time I'd gone through the entire box of Bob Shapiro's memories. I was perplexed because I hadn't found the Medal of Honor or any references to a military career. I resolved to learn more about that later. The rain had been pouring down sporadically since we'd left Meyer's apartment and I couldn't help but wonder which of us had placed himself in more danger. Either way, I knew we had to figure out who the bad guys were before they discovered we had information that could tie them back to Shapiro's death. Great, now I was living up to other people's examples.

I wondered if Meyer had seen the picture of the four men and, perhaps, if he knew who they were. I dialed his number and listened while the phone rang once, twice, three times, and then went to the answering machine. "If you're calling about the apartment, leave a message after the beep." Bee-eep.

Crap, I wasn't ready for a quick message. I hung up and told myself that he wouldn't pick up the phone this close to five because it was almost after his posted hours. Or maybe he was out working on the grounds. A glance at the window told me that was a stupid idea. I decided to try him again later. Next time, I'd be prepared to leave a message.

I'd started with the photos to learn something about Shapiro as a person. With that hunger satisfied, it was time to get right to the heart of the matter. How much money did he have? I opened the box labeled "Personal - Bank." Inside, there were five years worth of envelopes marked as "Tax Return - Personal," two bundles of personal bank statements stacked together and an envelope marked "Death Certificate." The returns covered the previous four years, and there was an envelope for this year also. The envelope also contained several certified copies of Shapiro's Certificate of Death.

The current-year file held bills for the standard-type stuff: phone, electric, cable, and other ho-hum. There was also a social security statement showing his projected income. Assuming that he'd lived a few more years, he would have had the opportunity to decide whether to keep working or be a lucky stiff and kick back.

I did a quick check on the previous years' records and noted that Shapiro claimed annual net income of about $30,000. Unless he was sheltering, he was a poor bastard just like me. The difference between us was that he had a half-million-dollar airplane, and I didn't even own a car. Of course, he was dead. He could keep the plane. I ran through the personal bank statements for a year before deciding that if he was sheltering income, he was keeping his personal bank account clean. He was either very smart or just scraping by.

Financial Wizard McKenna said that the personal income box was no more than a curiosity thing and included nothing of value about why Shapiro had been killed. Nosey McKenna said there was more to learn. The fact is, I knew how much he made, so I let Financial Wizard placate Nosey by telling him to look for the source of the income. I repacked the box and put it off to the side, then tackled the "Business - Bank" box. That satisfied both FW and Nosey. I could only hope that Harris hadn't figured out how high maintenance I was.

This box also included tax returns for the same periods as the personal records. The current-year file was stuffed full of credit card and purchase receipts as well as monthly income statements for his business. I nearly fell out of my chair when I saw his monthly gross income of almost $15,000. Every month was roughly the same. Some were slightly higher, others lower. But in the end, Bob Shapiro drew $2,500, paid bills with about $8,000 and put the rest into a fund he'd labeled "Business Expansion." I did some fast math and came up with nearly $50,000 a year going into that fund.

Next, I pulled his business check register and looked over the entries. Sure enough, there was a draw to Shapiro each month for his living expenses, payments to a fuel company, Lau Maintenance, a bank, an insurance company, and various other suppliers or vendors for airplane services and parts. There was also an entry marked "BET" of between $4,000 to $5,000 each month which would be the Business Expansion Transfer I'd seen on the income statement.

His deposits were equally uninformative, just a weekly entry marked "Deposit" that totaled up to the monthly income shown on the income statement. I wondered where the business expansion fund was located. I also wondered why there were no payments to the partners I'd seen in the photo. Lau was getting paid for services. But, what about his share of the profits? And what about the other partners?

I glanced down at the box labeled "Business." If these guys had a partnership agreement, it would be here. I didn't like potentially mixing up records, but wanted to be able to compare the check register with what the partners had agreed to. I went into my office and grabbed a pile of sticky notes, came back and pasted notes with the box name on the backs of the two photos I'd removed. I stuck another one on the check register and piled the rest of the stuff back into its little cardboard home.

I opened the first Business container. On the very top was another ledger. The ledger had six columns: date, client name, deposit amount, flight completion status, total amount paid, and comments. "Goddamn," I muttered. I slapped a sticky note on the ledger and reopened the carton for photos. I removed one of the plastic envelopes and chuckled at the top photo. A family of four, all dressed in matching Hilo Hattie prints, posed for the camera. Dad and son wore matching shirts, Mom and daughter wore matching sundresses. Their name was Thomason, and the date was 7/14/09. I always got a kick out of families who bought the matching outfits. "Bet you guys wear those a lot back home."

I flipped through the client register until I found July 14, 2009. There was the entry for Thomason. They'd put down a $100 deposit, had a completed status on their flight, and paid a total of $540. The comments section showed that they'd had four in their party and had received an "extended tour."

I seriously doubted that anyone, even a psychopath, would kill Bob Shapiro because he hadn't liked a tour. That probably left out anyone in this book. I glanced outside. Dark. I'd missed sunset and dinner. What was there in the fridge? Not much other than some wilted lettuce, a half jar of peanut butter, a few gluten-free condiments and a small amount of cheese. I didn't feel like cooking and I didn't have anything to cook, even if the mood came over me in a flash, which wasn't likely. That meant some takeout from Ching's down the street. I checked outside. No rain, thank goodness.

Since I was going out, I might as well see whether Harris wanted something. Through her apartment window, I spotted her staring dejectedly at the TV. She smiled when she saw me and waved me in. A crumpled-up bag of potato chips lay on the floor next to her empty glass. "Hey, McKenna. What's up?"

"How's the head?"

"Still there."

Okay, let's try food. "I was just going out for some Chinese and wondered if you'd like me to bring you something."

"Man, I'm so chipped out. I'd love some."

"How about an order of McKay chicken, some garlic shrimp, and a box of rice?"

"McKay chicken?"

"It's a dish they named after me. After I'd become a regular, I got'em to try doing something similar to fried chicken, but with rice flour instead of wheat. Mr. Ching liked it so much he named it after me. It's a big seller."

"As long as I don't have to eat another potato chip."

I phoned in my order and began the walk to the restaurant. The stars shined through scattered clouds, streetlights glinted on the still-wet sidewalks, and traffic remained light, making the walk quiet and serene. The air smelled fresh and clean, as though it had taken only a few raindrops to remove the sins of the day.

When I entered the restaurant, Mr. Ching greeted me and guided me to a seat on the side. "Your order ready in just a few minutes, Mr. McKay. Your Mr. McKay chicken very popular."

The restaurant was, as usual, busy. His two daughters hustled between tables, wiping them clean, setting up, and then taking and delivering orders. One of their husbands was tonight's chef; another took the day shift. I noticed a new sign on the wall, which said that they reserved the right to refuse service to anyone. This struck me as odd because to my knowledge, each customer was like a welcome guest. When Ching's oldest daughter brought my order, I handed her a twenty and nodded at the sign. "Lily, how come you got the new sign?"

She rolled her eyes and replied in the perfect English of a third-generation Chinese. "My dad's lawyer got him to do that."

I grumbled, "Why's your dad need a lawyer?"

"We're incorporating. So the lawyer says we should protect ourselves in case we ever need to refuse service."

"I can't imagine your dad refusing service to anyone. You serve me."

She winked. "You're more like family, so we put up with you." She leaned forward, then lowered her voice. "It did happen once when a customer got drunk and my dad yelled at me for not being able to deal with him. I got so ticked off that I walked out. Dad went out to the table to apologize and the fat slob threw up all over him, the table, and the next table where one of our best customers was just finishing up."

"Ouch, vomit in a restaurant."

She shook her head, "My dad might not have gotten angry, but at that point, the customer yelled that there was a cockroach in his beer." She hid her mouth as she giggled, "My dad lost it and yelled back that the only cockroach he'd seen that night was drunk and had thrown up all over the Chief of Police."

Lily cocked her head to one side. I presumed that meant her dad was coming. She continued, "The drunk ran out like he'd seen a ghost. My dad apologized to the entire restaurant and said that entertainment would no longer be provided. He comped the rest of the tables with a free dessert, gave his broker a free meal, and told him he'd pay for the cleaning bill. He even apologized to me and that's never happened before."

A man and woman in their early thirties strolled in. Mr. Ching greeted them. He saw Lily and me talking and waved. I waved back and smiled. "Well, thanks for the story. I guess I'd better let you get back to work."

"I get a laugh out of that every time I think about it." She leaned over and gave me a kiss on the cheek. "Take care. I'll get your change."

I said, "You keep it. I think I forgot to tip the last time I was in."

She winked again. "I don't recall."

For some reason, my face felt hot. "I'll try to do better in the future."

As I left the restaurant, I thought about Lily's story. Free dessert. I wish I'd have been there that night. I wondered if I should find a gluten-free dessert for Ching's. Maybe they'd try that, just as they had the chicken? I was less than a block from home and considering different types of desserts when I heard the rain coming. I stepped up the pace and made it to shelter just as a wall of water swooped in. To me, each raindrop looked to be the size of a glass of water. In no time, gutters gushed, palms shed waterfalls and storm drains swallowed almost as fast as the skies dumped. Almost.

As Harris and I ate, I filled her in on what I'd learned. She seemed genuinely interested and devoid of the concussion symptoms she'd mentioned earlier.

At one point, she said, "You know, my sister loves Chinese food. She could eat it every day, morning, noon, and night."

"How's she doing?"

"We're still trying to find funding for the operation. We have maybe a month." Then, she said, "What about that Mr. Herschel?"

"What about him?"

"You don't suppose that they'll try to kill him, do you?"

"Crap. I forgot about him. I was going to call him back." I pulled out my phone and punched in Meyer's number. As before, it rang through to the answering machine. "No answer. He'll be okay, probably just has the phone turned off so he doesn't get tenant calls."

Harris nodded, but she didn't look convinced. For that matter, neither was I.

"Well, um, I guess I'd better go."

"Sorry, I'm not very good company. When you get more information—maybe tomorrow, if I'm feeling better, we could file an update on that tip report. You're making such good progress that you'll have this wrapped up in another couple of days."

Not sure how to leave gracefully, I gave her a kiss on the forehead and headed for the door. My hand was on the knob when she said, "McKenna?"

"Yah?" My heart was pounding. My throat was dry. I had all the symptoms of a moron in love.

"Maybe tomorrow. I'm sure I'll be feeling better by then."

I did my best leading-man swagger and headed out the door. Outside, I breathed in the fresh air. Was I glad to be outside or not? I didn't know. Tomorrow. Gulp. Tomorrow? Yikes? I wasn't ready. I made a hasty retreat to my apartment. Time to do something that would distract me from dwelling on Legs. The records.

Since Shapiro had acquired the new plane recently, I assumed that the partnership had been created at the same time. If that was the case, I should start at the back of the ledger and work my way forward. I opened Shapiro's little book to the last page and looked at the final entry.

"Daniels, $100 deposit, canceled, refund $100, DD has negatives in LL file, M."

What the hell did that mean? I looked for other cancellations. In the entire ledger, there were just three others. Each was marked, "canceled by customer" and had a reason like "illness" or "scheduling conflict." In the case of the illnesses, Shapiro had returned the deposit, for the scheduling conflict, he'd marked the entry "no refund." Why had Shapiro just marked this one "canceled"? Had he gotten sloppy? I doubted it. This entry had to mean something. I kept looking.

I went back three months, then six, then a year. Other than the four cancellations, every entry showed a flight completed, payment made, and occasionally, a short note like "good people," "big tipper," and even one, "jackass—never again."

It was after ten when I decided I was going in circles and put the ledger back into its box. I still hadn't come across the partnership agreement and still didn't know if Meyer Herschel was okay. Maybe I should call again? But, if nothing had happened, he'd be upset that I woke him. If something had, it was too late. It was a lose-lose situation for me. Probably for Meyer also.

I brushed my teeth and did the other usual personal business to get ready for bed, then read from the latest issue of National Geographic. I usually read for about four minutes, then nodded off. Tonight, I read for forty and still hadn't wound down.

At 11:10 PM, the phone rang. Ordinarily, at this hour, I'd let the machine pick up, but Caller ID said that it was M. Herschel. I grabbed the handset immediately and hit the connect button. "McKenna."

A weak voice on the other end responded. "I had two visitors."

20

Meyer's voice was raspy and frightened—his visitors obviously weren't friends. Without thinking, I whispered back, "Are you okay? Who was it?"

"What? Speak up, you know I'm half deaf."

Uh, yeah, and the other half obstinate. "What visitors?" I bellowed. Shit! Now I'd probably wake up the next-door tenant, an 87-year-old Japanese ex-schoolteacher who kept strict hours and guarded her quiet time by calling me whenever other tenants got the least bit noisy.

"Dunno. Two guys I ain't seen before. They said they were police. They were no more police than you're a newspaperman. Besides, the police would've had a warrant. And they wouldn't be stopping around in the middle of the night for an apartment tour."

"Are you okay? Did they hurt you?"

"I thought at one point they might try something funny, but they didn't do anything they weren't supposed to do, unless you count showing up here in the middle of the night."

"So they acted like police?"

"They weren't cops."

I sat straight up in bed. I could feel my heart pounding in my chest. Could it have been that guy whose flight Shapiro canceled? What was his name? That's right, Daniels. "What did you tell them?"

And there it was, the banging on the wall. Tomorrow, Mrs. Nakamura would give me hell for waking her up. I got out of bed and trotted off to the living room.

"Exactly what we discussed, that I destroyed the records by accident because I didn't know no better. I've got to say, I was pretty good. I begged them not to report me to the Department of Landlord Monitoring and Corrections for messing up with the records."

"There's no—" I stopped and did a quick check of all the windows. I was standing there, stark naked and hadn't thought to check the blinds, which I occasionally leave open on hot nights. Thank goodness they were all closed.

"Exactly. Cops would have known that was horse pucky."

I shook my head in amazement. In a normal tone, I said, "You've got guts." Who would think of lying to a couple of thugs when they visited you in the middle of the night?

"What? Speak up."

"I said—never mind. Did you look at the photos before you packed them up?"

"Some."

"Did you see the partnership photo?"

"Yup."

"Did you recognize anyone? Were those the guys who visited you tonight?"

"Nope. These were a couple of big, intimidating looking bozos. I never saw these two before."

Okay, what about the other guy? "There was an entry in Shapiro's flight listing about someone named Daniels. Do you know anything about that?" Laughter and voices from outside broke the night silence, the clickety-clack of a woman's high heels came, then went. It was probably the young woman from 18 with her newest boyfriend. Big hair, lots of makeup and a parade of men that made me wonder if maybe she had a sideline.

"Yup."

"Okay, what do you know?"

Meyer stopped whispering and was speaking in a low, but more normal tone. "Thought you'd never ask. I was talking to Bob one day when he mentioned that he had this flight coming up with a guy he'd known in high school. The guy kept telling Shapiro he was a licensed pilot and wanted to take the plane out on his own. Guy wouldn't let up."

"Why wouldn't the guy just rent a plane?"

"Bob thought maybe he'd gotten into drugs or something and couldn't go the normal route. I volunteered to check for public records on him. I know I shouldn't have done that, but Bob was pretty conflicted. Anyway, Daniels had been arrested and even evicted a few times because of suspicious activities. Bob told me he wanted to cancel the flight."

I recalled the entry in Shapiro's ledger. "He did. Do you suppose this Daniels could be tied to Bob's death?"

"Maybe. He beat up one of his landlords for kicking him out."

"So if somebody blew a drug deal for him, he might want revenge."

"He had a prison record too."

Daniels had been in jail? That might move him to the top of my suspect list. "Are you okay?"

"They just spooked me, that's all. I'm fine now."

Exhaustion sapped my remaining energy. With Meyer's little drama over, my brain was going into the stupid-me state. I needed rest before I did something that I'd regret later, like walking out the front door into the courtyard instead of into the bedroom. I said, "What was he in prison for?"

"Drugs. Assault."

"Revenge is a great motive."

"You got that right."

I said, "You sound beat." That was about all it took. Thirty seconds later I'd hung up the phone, climbed back into bed and turned off the light. Tomorrow looked like it would be a helluva day.

Tired or not, I was wired. For nearly two hours, I dwelled on the day's events and kept coming to the same conclusions. Somebody wanted Shapiro dead and somebody wanted to use his plane. How's that for profound? Woo-hoo. When sleep finally did come, it was fitful and filled with bad men who wanted to do bad things to anyone who got in their way.

I awoke with a start at 6:30 AM, having just been thrown from a plane flying through a massive rainstorm by a masked man with a snake tattooed on one arm and "I heart Mom" on the other. I plummeted towards the ground, the flooded streets of Honolulu ready to engulf me when I hit bottom. Ala Moana Blvd. had turned into a raging, white-water river from the downpour. I was seconds away from plunging headfirst into the torrent when I saw the old surfer again. He waved his arm as if he were inviting me to join him. I put my hands over my face just before smashing into the wave being ridden by the man in green board shorts. I stared at the bedroom ceiling, listening to my heart hammer. When it slowed to a normal rate, I got out of bed and peered through the blinds.

Outside, everything dripped and drained as the rain came down, but there was no standing water, no raging rapids. Taking a shower struck me as tempting fate; not taking one was an even worse option.

After getting cleaned up, I went into the kitchen and rounded up breakfast, which consisted of the usual oh-so-yummy cardboard cereal, then went to the rent drop box and peeked inside. So far, three checks. By the end of the day, there should be a half dozen more. By tomorrow, everyone should be paid up. I put the checks into the envelope I used for rent collections and settled in at the dining room table with high hopes of getting through the rest of Shapiro's records today.

Maybe I could find out more about my primary suspect, this ex-con Daniels. But, what about the partners? It wouldn't be the first time that a partnership went sour, but the fact of the matter is that business partners seldom go around killing each other just for kicks. That brought me back to Daniels. I still needed to find the partnership agreement, that should help clear up my dilemma.

I opened the second business box. At the top of this heap was a folder labeled "Paradise Private Charters, LLC." Inside the folder, I found the partnership agreement, dated February 15, 2011. Using the standard blah-ditty-blah-blah legal mumbo jumbo, it spelled out the terms of the partnership and included the names I was looking for: Robert M. Shapiro, Jr., Roger Lau, James Stone and Frank Willows.

The agreement called for sharing of profits. Shapiro would receive 70%, Lau, Stone and Willows, ten percent each. Interestingly, payments to Stone and Willows were not necessarily to be paid in cash. Instead, they were to receive "inter-island transportation services." Basically, the better Paradise did, the more the partners received in services. So, Stone and Willows must have their own businesses that required inter-island transportation on a regular basis. Another interesting note—there didn't appear to be any cap on services, which could be bad for Shapiro. There was no mention in this agreement as to what business Stone and Willows were in.

I went through the rest of the documents in the Business #2 box and found nothing that would help me figure out what Stone and Willows did for a living. All the documents had been prepared and filed by an Oahu attorney. Calling him would be a waste of time because even I knew the words attorney-client privilege. Yeah, a call like that would definitely qualify me as fodder for happy-hour jokes with his lawyer friends. No thanks.

Box #2 also yielded a Bill of Sale for $159,500 for Shapiro's old airplane to James Markesas. The plane had been sold on February 14th, one day before the partnership agreement was signed. The escrow company that closed the deal paid off Shapiro's old loan of $54,289.32, which left Shapiro with just over $100,000 net on the deal. The box also coughed up a sales agreement for the purchase of one new, Cessna 206H dated January 4, 2011, for $543,216. I thought my eyes might bug out at the number, convinced that adventurers would still be donning feathered wings and throwing themselves from bridges if Orville and Wilbur Wright had needed even a fraction of that amount to build the first airplane.

After I'd recovered from the sticker-shock issue, I reviewed the next piece of paper. It was a letter from Cessna indicating that they were delighted to have Shapiro want to buy one of their planes, but that there were problems with his financing options. To be blunt, they were telling him, "You don't have enough money so get lost or get help." Now I knew why he'd taken on partners. He'd been unable to close that last financial gap on his own and been so close to having a new plane that he just couldn't give it up; he'd chosen help instead of waiting.

The Business Expansion Fund register as well as the partnership checking account register were in business Box #3. According to the bank statements, Shapiro had saved almost $200,000 in his expansion fund, which he withdrew on February 16 and put into the partnership bank account. So, Shapiro had put in $300,000, Lau, $50,000, and Stone and Willows a combined $100,000. The $450,000 had been immediately withdrawn and sent to Cessna, who promptly arranged for the delivery of Shapiro's new airplane and a bank note for the remaining balance. The bottom line was that the payments on the new plane would be less than on the old and Shapiro expected a lot of new business. He had the cash flow to pay down his loan early, then focus on getting out of the partnership. It all looked good to me. I still wanted to know who Stone and Willows were, but the fact that Daniels had a prison record kept leading me back to him as the main suspect.

A knock on the door startled me. I glanced at the clock. Sheesh, half the morning was gone and now some moron wanted something. Blow them off in a hurry, I thought, then back to this. I still had more pieces of the puzzle to consider. My back sent off a few twinges as I stood, reminding me that stretching was supposed to be a part of my daily routine. I resolved to stretch right after I ridded myself of the door nuisance, whoever that might be.

To my surprise, Harris stood there waiting. In her hand she held a check, the look on her face said that she felt better. I stepped to one side. "Come in!"

She nodded and handed me her rent check as she passed. "Thought you might want this."

We both hugged and gravitated towards the controlled chaos on my dining room table.

She said, "What's all this?"

"Shapiro's records." I wasn't sure how much she wanted to know, but wanted to at least give her some details. "I've got his business records, photos, flight listing and more. I think I've got it narrowed down as to who his killer might have been."

"Great! So what's the deal, hon?"

I went through the whole story, telling what I'd learned so far. Her expression brightened when I told her about Daniels' drug conviction.

She was jotting the names on a piece of scrap paper, when the phone rang.

I picked it up and said, "McKenna."

"Sorry, I must have a wrong number."

The voice sounded familiar. It was someone that I'd spoken to in the past few days. I said, "Who are you trying to reach?"

"O'Brien. He's at the Advertiser."

"This is his message phone."

"You sound a lot like him," the voice on the other end oozed suspicion.

"Oh, yeah. People get us mixed up all the time. Don't tell him I said this, but O'Brien ain't the brightest bulb in the pack, if you know what I mean." Jeez, I'd already picked up one of Meyer's expressions.

I heard a kind of a snort. "He seemed a bit off to me."

"So what's your message for O'Brien?" Dumbass.

"Oh, that plane he was looking for, Bob Shapiro's plane, its back."

"What? When?"

"Dunno, I just came in from launching a glider and saw it. It was probably here all night. I didn't hear him announce a landing on Unicom. Gotta go, customer."

Harris said, "What was that all about?"

"The plane, it's back at Dillingham Field."

"We need to go check that out."

"Why wouldn't we let the cops do that?"

"Because it'll probably be gone by the time they get there. Besides, didn't you ever do field work as a skip tracer?"

The doorbell rang. Now what? "Hold that thought!"

I jerked open the door. Lately, I'd seen Alexander's angry side, but I'd never seen him looking grim. Behind me, the phone rang. I said, "Crap. Come on in."

I spun on my heel and ran for the phone thinking about Legs wanting to do a field trip. Didn't she get it? These guys were dangerous;

she couldn't just hug her way out of trouble if they found us. I made it to the phone just before the answering machine picked up and was sure of one thing—this couldn't possibly be good news.

21

Between Harris in the living room, Alexander at the door, and the ringing phone, I felt like a duck in a shooting gallery. And right now, this little ducky damn near broke his neck getting to the phone. I also have a cordless in the bedroom, but there's no way I could have made that before the machine took the call. As I lifted the handset, I caught another look at Alexander's face. His normally healthy complexion had turned pale and splotchy. I kept watching him as I listened. The voice on the other end of the phone was almost inaudible, and I had to press the receiver halfway into my brain to hear what the caller was saying.

"It's Meyer. There's someone in my apartment."

Oh crap, not again, I thought. But it was true; the tone in his voice said it all. He was scared. "Are you there now?" Duh. Of course he wasn't, otherwise, he'd be tied up in a corner, stabbed or shot or lying dead on the floor—

Meyer's hoarse whisper cut off my ruminations. "What? Speak up! I'm in Shapiro's unit. Those yahoos from yesterday came back this morning. I heard them fiddling with the lock and ducked out the slider. I circled around and snuck up here."

"Did you call 9-1-1?"

"No. Can't you hear? I said there was two of them."

I probably should have told him to stick his head out the window and yell, "Help, police!" But with his hearing, he'd probably think I'd told him to pack a valise. I finally yelled, "Call 9-1-1!"

He whispered, "That don't work from a cell phone, does it?"

"Fine. I'll do it." The fact is, the emergency call would go through, but was he in the right frame of mind to give clear directions? For the life of me, I don't know why I held the handset away as I spoke to Alexander. Meyer couldn't hear me anyway. "Can you take me to Meyer's? He's got more visitors."

He nodded and gave me a thumbs up.

"We'll be there in ten minutes."

Meyer whispered, "Hurry, looks like they might be coming this way."

The phone went dead. I called 9-1-1 and reported what was happening. The dispatcher assured me that she would have a vehicle there shortly. I hung up the phone and said to Alexander and Harris, "Cops are on their way to Meyer's."

Harris said, "You two go check on your friend. I'll file an update with this info for the cops. Then, I have a few errands to run. We'll catch up this afternoon."

Harris went back to her apartment; Alexander and I headed for his truck. Once on the way, I said, "What happened to you anyway? You look like you saw a ghost."

Alexander's normally a pretty relaxed kind of guy. He seldom gets flustered or stressed—he's got "island-style" down pat. Sure, he's got a little bit of a temper and had yelled a bit more than normal lately, but he blew that off quickly and didn't hold a grudge.

So there was something big bugging him. We'd driven no more than a few blocks when he said, "My great-grandfather visited me last night."

I was still focused on what might be happening to Meyer, so it took a few seconds for the words to register. I scratched my head. "Your great-grandfather?"

"Great-Grampa Kimu."

"Kimu? Isn't he the one that's been dead for, like, ten years?"

"Twelve."

"What'd you and Kira do, invite him over for dinner and he showed up late?"

Alexander snickered. "You very funny McKenna. You haoles don't understand family. Our kupuna, every now and then, they come back to counsel us, cause we get off on the wrong path."

So now Harris was acting normal, and Alexander had gone wacko. Since he was driving, and therefore in control of my well-being, I nodded my agreement. Sure, whatever you say. But the fact is; I was trying to figure this one out. Dead relatives as counselors. They show up when you take a wrong turn. Could I call on one for directions? Maybe ask where were items that had been moved in the grocery store? I said, "You know, you Hawaiians have some great customs. I like luaus. Surfing's good. Pretty girls in bikinis. Oh, that wasn't you guys, that was the Greeks, but this dead ancestor thing is a bit much. You sure you didn't spend too much time in the sun yesterday? Couldn't be that, it rained. Maybe it was the stress of seeing a body thrown from a plane? Or that bullet exploded too close to your brain the other day?"

"He told me you wouldn't believe in him. He said, 'Watch out for McKenna, he's a good guy, but he messed up. You go talk story wid him, give him lotta kokua.'"

"So that's why you came to see me this morning? Because your great-grandfather told you I needed help?" Great, help from a crazy man, just perfect.

"His father was a great chief. When he say I need do something, I betta listen."

I snickered. So the great chief was too busy playing checkers in the sky to do his own bidding. "So how come the great chief didn't come visit me?"

"Maybe I misunderstood him. I dunno. Guess you not that important."

I burst out, "What! I'm not important? Says who?"

"You need be more humble, McKenna. Besides, Great-Grampa Kimu say you need to know it was Cousin Roger got thrown out of the plane. The kupuna not happy about that. Roger was good family man. Very loyal to his wife and kids."

Now, I wasn't humble or important? These ancestors were beginning to—uh oh, I wondered if they could hear me. "I don't think I like what your ancestors think of me."

"See? It's always about you. You didn't hear nothing I said about Roger."

"Yeah, yeah. Family man. Loyal like a Golden Retriever. Anyway, we already knew that."

"Great-Grampa Kimu said he been trying to tell you, but you won't listen. You need to pass along that Roger's happy where he's at to his wife."

My jaw fell open. No great chiefs had visited me. All I had was an old duffer in green board shorts who wouldn't let me sleep. "When did I graduate to middleman for the afterlife? Talk story with a dead man's wife? Are you nuts?"

"Me? Pupule? Nope, I know just where I stand."

"From where I'm at, the view's different. I ain't having a little chit chat with Roger's wife. I can't go back there; she'd kill me."

Alexander kept his hands light on the wheel as he laughed at my reaction. He said, "You haoles, you got no respect for the past. You gonna live here, you gonna be a part of this island, you gotta learn to accept a few things. Some things you can't see unless you open your mind."

"Like dead ancestors visiting in the night."

"Great-Grampa Kimu, he giving you an invitation. You should give it some serious thought."

Serious thought? My life was turning around. I might have a relationship starting. That deserved serious thought. Talk story with dead people? I don't think so. Just because I'd renumbered the apartments to get rid of unlucky thirteen didn't make me a wacko. I decided to humor Alexander. "So what time did he—you—uh, visit?"

"Right before sunrise. Great-Grampa Kimu, he always like surfing at sunrise. I guess he didn't want to miss it."

I felt a sudden chill on the back of my neck. Surfing? Maybe it was just this talk about dead kupuna that was giving me a case of the creepy crawlies. Or the old surfer in the dreams.

Alexander said, "What's wrong with you? Now you acting like you the one saw a ghost."

This was too weird. "Me? Why would he visit me? I don't believe in all that paranormal stuff, mumbo jumbo, dead guys—"

Thank goodness we arrived at Meyer's right then; otherwise, I'd have been in a serious downward spiral headed for a crash landing. There was already a Honolulu Police Department car on the scene. We met the officer at Meyer's door, and Meyer showed up a few seconds later. He spoke in his usual loud voice, "They left just before you got here."

The officer had his little notepad at the ready. He said, "Are you the one who lives here?"

Meyer said, "Me? I'm Herschel. Meyer Herschel. I own this place, been managing it since the yahoo I'd hired upped and left without notice."

"Well, Mr. Herschel, I checked the door and windows and didn't see any sign of forced entry. If you'd like, I can check inside for you."

Meyer pointed a spindly arm at the apartment. As usual, he practically yelled at the officer. "I don't need the garage checked, they were inside the apartment!"

The officer scanned the three of us, then said, "Okay, Mr. Herschel. How about if I check the apartment?"

Meyer pulled out his giant key ring and put his key into the lock. "Good idea, but you ain't gonna find nothing."

Sure enough, the officer returned to the front door in less than two minutes. "There's nobody inside. They must have been looking for something in particular, there's very little disturbed. And your back slider was wide open."

I translated for Meyer, "The coast is clear! Open slider!"

Meyer got a stern look on his face. "Check the street for suspicious cars, Officer. They might just be waiting for you to leave."

The officer nodded and agreed to walk the street. He handed us his card. "If you find anything that's missing, call me. I'll go take a look out front." The card had a nice little HPD logo on it. Very impressive.

We thanked the officer, and he went on his way, leaving us outside Meyer's apartment. Meyer said, "I closed that slider when I went out. That means they figured out how I got away without them seeing me."

That left us with the question of what to do with Meyer. I said, "You're not safe here."

"No, I ain't got no safe here," said Meyer.

I upped the voice level. "I said, you're not safe here."

"Maybe they got what they wanted," said Alexander.

Meyer and I both shook our heads. I was sure that Meyer understood what we were saying because we were almost yelling.

I said, "No, they didn't find what they were looking for because I've got it. All of it. So they'll be back. And next time, one of them will be waiting outside the slider for you to slip out."

Meyer looked at me, "Don't suppose you got any room over at your place?"

I hadn't thought about that possibility before, but the idea of sharing my little apartment with another old geezer, well, that just didn't exactly set my heart on fire.

I swear I heard a satisfied whisper from one of Alexander's ancestors in my ear. "Gotcha."

I remembered standing in the living room last night talking to Meyer. Okay, that was one level of scary, but the thought of seeing this guy with the spindly little white legs dripping wet after a shower because he forgot to close the bathroom door was enough to make yours truly go find his own deserted island.

"You don't have somewhere else to go?" I asked.

He got a sullen look on his face and stared at the sidewalk. "I got my home in Eau Claire." He glanced up at me, then at the sidewalk. "Got a brother in Minneapolis." There was another glance up, then he continued. "Got a cousin in—nope, wait, he died. Got—"

That spirit was back in my ear. A chuckle. A whisper, "Sucker."

Alexander and Meyer stared at me when I swatted at my ear.

"You close the door when you shower, right?"

"Of course I showered today. Can't you tell?"

"Fine."

Meyer put a hand to his ear. "What?"

"FINE! My place is—fine."

His face brightened and he smiled wide enough for me to see a mouthful of sparkly gold fillings. "Let me get my things."

He went inside while Alexander and I hung out by the front door. Alexander said, "You been suckered, McKenna."

"You're the second one to tell me that."

Alexander frowned. "You're getting weird."

"Yeah? I'd rather go talk story with Roger's wife than share my apartment. But he's got nowhere else to go."

A few minutes later, Meyer was back with a brown, tweed suitcase that had leather strips on either end and a matching briefcase. The handles on both were brown leather also, but had discolored from skin oils and showed signs of wearing through. While the briefcase appeared to be in mint condition except for the handle, the suitcase leather on the ends had nicks, scrapes and one huge gouge. I hadn't seen a suitcase like that since I was in high school. I said, "What, were you packed already?"

"Yeah," he said, "I was pretty upset, too. The airlines really banged it up on the trip over."

Somewhere in the back of my mind, a chorus of little voices was singing, "McKenna is a sucker, McKenna is a sucker." I glanced at Alexander. "I think your ancestors are ganging up on me."

He chuckled as he started to walk away. In a booming voice, he said, "C'mon, roomies."

We went back to Alexander's truck, Alexander leading the way, me following him, and Meyer shuffling along after me, baggage in hand. What had I gotten myself into now?

As we piled into the truck, Meyer yelled in my ear, "We headed back to your place, McKenna?"

I grabbed at my broken eardrum. "You don't have to yell."

In almost the same voice, Meyer said, "Sorry! So we going back to your place, McKenna?"

Alexander's shoulders shook. He kept his back turned. I said, "Shut up." To Meyer, I added, "No, we're going to Dillingham Field to check on a hunch."

Meyer patted my shoulder. "It's okay, I don't need anything for lunch yet. But thanks for asking."

Alexander and I both groaned. Mine was because my new roommate couldn't hear a word I said; his was most likely because Alexander is almost always hungry and he was missing an opportunity for an early meal.

Halfway to the airfield, Meyer fell asleep in the back seat. I was tempted to have Alexander stop and drop him off at Wahiawa park or something, but Alexander's Great-Grampa Kimu would probably have disapproved, so I didn't dare ask. Meyer did wake up about ten minutes from the airfield and looked around. He seemed dazed, so in the loudest voice I could muster, I said, "We're going to Dillingham Field."

He nodded and sat quietly the rest of the trip.

22

Alexander's complete belief in his Great-Grampa Kimu had shaken me. How could someone that I'd considered completely normal believe in that sort of thing? Did he have proof—a half-eaten cookie, dirty dishes from a midnight snack? Something? Anything? Logic told me visits from ancestors weren't possible. Emotion said to not be a fool, look around, feel the mana, the power of these islands. And what about my own dreams?

The fact that I was deeply conflicted and didn't want any possible kupuna mad at me weighed heavily on my decision to trek back to the North side of the island. For all I knew, these dead guys were now friends with Madame Pele. She's the Hawaiian volcano goddess who, according to legend, lives at Kilauea, a volcano on the Big Island. Kilauea may not have much in the way of furnishings, but the Halema`uma`u crater is one helluva living room. Hale means house and ma`uma`u is a type of fern and the legend says that a jilted suitor of Madame Pele's built a house of ferns over Halema`uma`u to keep Pele from getting out of her home and causing eruptions. I say, come on, like a house of ferns is going to stop any pissed-off woman?

I stared out the front window and gave Alexander my decision. "I'll speak with Roger's wife."

"What made you change your mind?"

"I'd just never decided. Besides, I don't want Kimu ticked off at me."

"Now you making fun of my kupuna."

I shook my head as Alexander flicked on his left turn signal. "Nuh-uh. Believe me, I'm not."

Maybe I was just doing this out of fear. In addition to the legends about a young, lovely, and gracious Pele, there were stories of people in Cleveland who had mailed back volcanic rock they'd stolen from Pele's home after they'd suffered a streak of incredibly bad luck. Me, I figured I'd be smart and do my best to stay on her good side—unlike the Cleveland tourists who "accidentally" stuffed rocks in their suitcase. Maybe you don't believe in that sort of thing, but Kilauea has been spewing lava in a steady stream for years. Scientists will give you all sorts of geological techno-speak about magma, core pressure and other things that they think sound impressive. But, the fact is that they can't explain why Kilauea, which has been around for maybe a half-million years, sat dormant and then suddenly decided to start a duel with the ocean that has created almost a half million acres of new land since 1983. My money's on Madame Pele.

From the back seat, Meyer shouted, "This doesn't look like a ball field. Thought you said we were going to a ball field?"

"Dillingham Field." I called over my shoulder. "It's where Shapiro kept his plane."

"I know where he kept it." He started muttering, "Darn people don't speak up. Don't speak clearly. How's anyone supposed to understand what they said?"

I rolled my eyes. "Have you been here before?"

"Bob took me up once. He had it custom painted, you know. And this ain't exactly a big airfield."

To my surprise, what we'd come to see was in the hangar as though it had never left. The plane itself was basic white. The nose was painted a reddish brown directly behind the prop that tapered into a narrower stripe. On either side of the reddish brown, there was a strip of white, then a blue stripe that tapered until all three colors blended into a single blue line that ran the length of the plane. The tail had the sunset and palm trees painted on it, just like I'd seen in the photo. And there was the N-Number that Harris and I had spent so much time trying to figure out. That part of this journey seemed as though it had happened years, not just days, ago.

Meyer did a quick walk around the plane, then checked a panel on the side. To my surprise, the panel opened.

Meyer said, "Damn fools, they ought to lock the cargo door."

I yelled, "What do you know about planes?"

He shrugged, "Quite a bit, used to fly my own until my eyesight started to go. My wife and I used to take day trips all over the Midwest, but once she passed on, well, it just wasn't fun anymore. I sold it and my house about five years ago and bought that apartment building. Best damned investment I ever made."

I glanced at Alexander, who was standing off to the side, arms crossed over his chest. I noticed that Meyer had stuck his head inside the small cargo door and was rooting around. I put on my best "I'm cocky" attitude and said, "Best damned investment I ever made," in a low voice to Alexander. He smiled at me, then pointed back to Meyer.

Meyer's voice sounded hollow from the insides of the cargo hold. "Ain't much in here but a toolkit."

When he stepped away, I walked over to the cargo door and stuck my head inside in hopes that I might at least appear to have a clue about what we were looking for. Off to my right I noticed a small scrap of paper. I grabbed it and backed away, holding it out far enough to read without my normal reading glasses. Apparently, it was a shipping label because the only thing on it were two addresses. One here on Oahu, the other on Maui.

The Oahu address was in a largely commercial area of Kalakaua Ave. I had no idea what type of neighborhood the Maui address was in. The sender and receiver were both Stone Music, Inc.

I held the label up for Alexander to read, then said, "You know where this is?"

He nodded. "I didn't know there were any music stores there."

Alexander couldn't be expected to know every business on the island, but if Stone had more than one store in the islands, wouldn't Alexander have heard about him? "Maybe there's not."

Meyer was moving his head back and forth like a trombone slide as he tried to read the address. I told him what it was and he said, "Yeah, that Stone ships a lot of stuff. Bob never realized how much stuff Stone would want to ship inter-island. He was pretty upset about that when he figured out how much of his time he'd be spending on their businesses."

I could feel my eyebrows creeping up. If I didn't watch it, they might blend in with my hairline. "How much stuff?"

"What?"

"How much stuff!"

"I dunno, but Bob was having to do at least a flight a week. He was going to talk to them about it, but he got run down first."

I pointed my right index finger at Meyer. "Maybe he didn't get run down first. Maybe he did talk with them."

Meyer shrugged. "All I know is he was mighty unhappy about something the last time I saw him."

"And when was that?" Meyer made a funny face, so I repeated it, louder.

He closed the cargo hatch and walked toward the front of the plane. "Day before he died," he said.

From behind me, I heard Alexander. "Uh, McKenna."

"Just a minute."

A deep, loud, and ominous-sounding voice commanded attention. "What's going on here?"

I nearly peed my pants as I whirled around to see who'd caught us pawing over Shapiro's plane.

23

The man behind the voice was short and stocky, wore an airport security uniform, and had parked his official-looking car just a few feet away. He had dark hair cut short, just slightly longer than a crewcut. He wore it messy and spiky and had little chin whiskers that reminded me of mold on cheese. His hands rested on the belt buckle of his rumpled uniform in the popular Hollywood-bad-cop pose. I'd been so engrossed in my conversation with Meyer that I hadn't even heard him drive up.

Meyer looked surprised, too, but not frightened. Alexander stood with his hand over his mouth, glancing from Rent-a-Uniform Guy to me, then back again. Was I the only one smart enough to be worried about this?

Rent-a-Uniform Guy did the jerk-down-the-belt buckle routine and said, "Well?"

Meyer jumped right in. He pointed an accusing finger in my direction and said, "He brought me here. He wanted to check out the plane. Me, I'm half-deaf; I thought this was his. Well, gotta go."

Meyer started to half-trot away in the opposite direction, but Rent-a-Uniform yelled at him. "Get back here."

Ouch, flaring nostrils. Definitely not a happy face.

Meyer turned to face us, his face scrunched up like a child caught dead to rights.

"I'll remember that," I said.

Meyer lowered his gaze to the pavement, "I never liked detention." He winked. "Besides, it was worth a try."

Alexander gripped his jaw with his hand, the tightness of his grip turning his knuckles white. His shoulders shook as he glanced away.

I barked at him, "What's so damn funny?"

He started to laugh, then the guard did also. Alexander said, "Give 'em a break, Dijon."

Dijon nodded, they extended their arms and did a playful knuckle tap.

"Meet my Cousin Dijon," said Alexander.

At first, relief washed over me, then irritation. The kids had played us for suckers. I snapped, "Is that like the mustard?"

"McKenna." Alexander was getting good at that schoolteacher voice.

I gave Alexander a fake smile. Take that.

"No problem, happens a lot." Dijon held out his hand to shake, but I extended my fist instead. He nodded as we touched knuckles. Little did he know what I really wanted to do with my fist. On second thought, the only fight I ever got into was when I was in about seventh grade. I took a swing at my best friend for some long-forgotten reason. I missed. He shoved. I landed on my rear in a juniper bush. End of fight, end of story, end of any shred of dignity I ever had that year.

The conversation with Cousin Dijon didn't last long. He'd had his fun by scaring us, or at least, me, to death and just wanted to get back to his routine. As he was preparing to leave, he said, "I'll check this plane more often. Too many people showing up here."

Curious, I said, "Who else has been around?"

"I drove by earlier, there was some woman and a man. Looked like they were having a big argument, so I stopped by. They said it was no problem and left."

"What'd they look like?"

"Caucasian guy, dark mustache. Nice looking blonde, short skirt—we don't see much of that out here. I just figured they'd been out on a sightseeing flight. This plane, it's been in and out three—

maybe four times this week. I hadn't heard about the owner's death. I'll keep a closer eye out now."

I asked, "Did you see what kind of car they were driving?"

"Funny—there was only a few cars here. I did see a black sedan. Late model, very clean. It had one of those personalized plates—what was it? High Sky Fan? I think it was HISKYFN."

"That's the only one you remember?"

He nodded. "I remember it 'cause the engine was running. There was some dude in it, but I couldn't make him out. Very strange, brah."

We thanked Dijon for his help. In return, he suggested that we should report the plane as stolen if we were positive that no one had the right to fly it. However, he cautioned us that if we weren't sure, or thought that maybe someone was using it with permission of the owner, we should hold off on that. "Sheriff takes a dim view of false reports about stolen planes. They might even bill you for their time if they find out the report's bogus."

My raised eyebrows must have given away my anxiety over the idea of getting billed for anything. The old wallet was tight enough already; it didn't need more bills.

Dijon obviously noticed my reaction. "Just kidding, brah." He smiled, gave us the shaka sign, then left.

Although Shapiro was dead, we didn't know if whoever was using the plane had a little pass similar to the ones the teachers hand out in grammar school for the bathroom.

I tried to loosen up my back before we piled into Alexander's truck, but somehow, all this driving around the island had me wishing I could afford a massage. Finally, we were in the truck and driving out the entrance when I heard Meyer in the back seat. I said, "You okay?"

He was fumbling with the seat belt. "This damn thing don't want to stay locked. Every time I get the male part in the female part, it pops out. Reminds me of—"

I shouted, "Never mind! Sorry I asked."

Alexander massaged the back of his neck with one hand as we made the right onto the main highway. We were off to see Roger Lau's wife. I'd have the dubious honor of apologizing for my earlier behavior, something I probably would do poorly. I'd also get to explain how Alexander's kupuna came to visit him in the night. Just between you and me, I'm a pretty poor candidate for this whole family reunion thing. I hate reunions. Especially with dead people.

Other than the loud click of Meyer's seat belt engaging and the even louder "whoopee" from him when it happened, we passed the rest of the trip in relative silence. As we pulled up to the Lau house, my insides churned like a Kilauea lava flow.

I said, "You sure your uncle wants me to do this?"

"Grampa. He's my Great-Grampa Kimu. Don't screw this up McKenna."

"Whatever. Visit in the middle of the night. He likes surfing at sunrise. He was a happy-go-lucky kind of guy and now he wants me to tell the grieving widow that her hubby got tossed from a plane and splattered all over a mountainside. Got it. Thanks for the opportunity."

Alexander stared at me impassively. I could feel his irritation building. I glanced up and wrinkled my nose. "All right," I said. "I'll see if I can soften it up a bit."

Meyer's voice blasted into my ear from the back seat. "You believe in heaven, McKenna?"

I shrugged and made a noise like a noncommittal "dunno." I guess the older I got, the more I hoped for something meaningful beyond this screwed-up world.

"You think she does?" he said.

I unfastened my seatbelt and let out an exaggerated sigh. "Fine. I'll tell her he's gone surfing with Great-Grampa Kimu and they're talking story and having a great time." I opened the door and started to move the seat for Meyer.

He put his hand on the seat back and held it in place. "I'd better stay here. This kind of news is more personal."

I looked across the truck at Alexander. Would he go with me?

Alexander opened his door, "Someone gotta help you get started."

We had just stepped onto the front lanai when Mrs. Lau burst through the door. She wore another faded-flowered muumuu, this one also came to her ankles. An apron over the muumuu read, "Aloha Spirit." She'd tied her hair up in a bun behind her head, which did little to dispel the angry linebacker image she projected in my direction. She clenched her fists as she ground out, "What you doing back here?" She stuck her hands in the pockets of the muumuu and glared at me.

I watched the lanai floor. Hmmm, the wooden slats were worn smooth, they needed paint and, uh-oh, there were pudgy little toes pointing angrily in my direction. For once in my life, I didn't know what to say. I scratched my head and looked at Alexander, then at Mrs. Lau, then at the boards on the lanai. I scratched my head again and said, "I, uh, I came to say I'm sorry."

"I no need you here."

Fear flooded my veins. What if I blew this? A small bird with brown and gray feathers landed on the lanai and stared at me. Shit, what had I done to him? Then, the bird winked. I swear, he winked, then he nodded. That just about sent me running for the airport because legend says that the Hawaiian gods, depending on their mana, or power, can take different forms. I told myself it was just a bird. Alexander stared at me as though I'd lost my mind. Maybe I had.

"Mrs. Lau, I apologize for having said some terrible things about your husband earlier. I've since learned that he was a good man and wasn't one of the bad guys. Can we come in and talk for a few minutes? If you have some time?"

She crossed her arms over her ample chest.

"Please?"

She opened the door. We followed her in, and she motioned towards the dining room table. "So what change you mind?"

I wasn't about to reveal that I'd been freaked out by a bird and a bad dream. These two would read "spirit world" into that. Not me. Should I cross my fingers? Knock on wood?

"A couple of things." I said, "A friend of mine told me that your husband and Bob Shapiro were good friends. And that he didn't think Roger would ever do anything to hurt Shapiro."

"I told you that before."

"I know, I was just too suspicious. And I was looking for scapegoats. The other thing that happened is that Alexander's Great-Grampa Kimu told him that Roger didn't kill Shapiro."

Her eyes got wide as she stared across the table at Alexander. "Kimu Ioneki?"

He nodded.

"You know who he is?" I said.

"What you trying pull?" she asked. "Everyone knows who Kimu Ioneki is—was."

Stupid me, guess I'm not everyone. "We're not trying to pull anything. Kimu visited Alexander last night and said that I should tell you what happened to Roger."

Slowly, a sad smile spread across her face. She put both hands on the table, then said, "That Kimu. He always pick the least likely person for a job. Always he try help the underdog learn he can't win if he don't try."

"He picked me because I was—*a loser*?"

Alexander and Mrs. Lau both chuckled. She said, "One of the last things he did was introduce me and Roger. He said we were going marry and have two great *keike*. Roger had always gone out with pretty, skinny girls. I was opposite of ones he choose himself. But, we went out to make Kimu happy and Roger propose on next date. We have two fine boys. They so like their father." She took a deep breath and closed her eyes, then wiped away a tear. "So what else Kimu say?"

My eyes felt watery as a lump settled in my throat. I'd proven once before that I wasn't good at this rapport thing. Could I do better now? My thoughts were interrupted when Alexander shifted position. He nodded when I glanced in his direction. "I'm sorry," I said. "I was remembering something. Someone. What did you say?"

"You have your own loss, yah? That why Kimu ask you do this. Help you remember. What else he say?"

"Um, that he'd spoken with Roger. That Roger was with him."

She grabbed a tissue from a box on the hutch behind her, then wiped at her nose. Her shoulders began to shake as she buried her face in her hands and sobbed. Her body shook and she began to hiccup. She sat up straight and forced a weak smile. "Oh, no," she said.

I managed to get out a whisper, "I'm sorry."

"I was afraid maybe this so." She glanced at Alexander. "You sure about Kimu?"

Alexander nodded. "He very clear."

A knowing look spread across her face. She took a heavy breath. "Kimu never lie."

Alexander said, "I think Great-Grampa Kimu teaching McKenna to deal with his past. Not be so grumpy all the time."

She thought for a moment. "Kimu got more planned than that." She gazed out the window, then back at us. "I be right back."

She stood and walked into the other room. A few minutes later, she returned, seeming more composed. Her right hand clutched something in her apron pocket. "I think you should know about someone. His name Dadrian Daniels. He know Roger and Mr. Shapiro for many years. They pretty good friends until this Daniels got into drugs. Then, they start pull apart. Roger and Daniels had argument day before Roger disappeared. Daniels say, 'You going to pay for this. Bad things happen to people who do bad things.'"

Well, well. Another mark on the "guilty checklist" for Daniels. Get enough of those and the cops would put him away forever. "Do you know what he was referring to?"

She shook her head. "It hard for me to believe he do something to Roger. But he was plenty mad at time."

Alexander said, "You said Daniels did drugs at one time, yah?"

"He got busted for pushing to high school kids. Did time in prison, then got paroled. When he got out, he said he learned lesson. He go straight."

Something wasn't making sense to me. "Why would a guy who'd gone straight threaten your husband. Especially if they were friends for a long time."

"Roger never wanted talk about it. He say Daniels making things up. He kine paranoid since he get out of prison. Always think someone after him."

"Was there? I mean, was someone really after him?"

"He not the one who dead, yah?"

"Maybe Kimu want you talk to Daniels, see if he have something to do with Roger's death?"

Alexander nodded and grabbed Mrs. Lau's hand. He squeezed and said, "If this Daniels killed Roger that would put McKenna in great big danger. He can't do that."

"Not if he don't accuse him. He just talk with him, maybe Daniels not even here when Roger killed."

Alexander nodded eagerly. He was being mighty free with my life. What if something went wrong? What if I accidentally spilled the beans? What if—the story of my life, the past few years.

Alexander glanced at me. "I think maybe that what Great-Grampa Kimu have in mind. You were a big-time skip tracer. You're a good liar. You gotta see this through, brah."

Great, now I had a license to lie. What other credentials could I compile? How about a license to skip town? Philadelphia looked good. Maybe New Jersey. Or Bar Harbor, Maine. That would give me more than 5,000 miles. I could get a place with no phone. No TV. I was wondering how well I'd adjust to freezing my ass off in the winter when Alexander seized my hand. Oh, crap, I saw a group hug lurking on the horizon.

He squeezed, "McKenna? You going see this through? Or you going do what you always do and run?"

"Why aren't we turning this over to the cops?"

Emma said, "I already call them. After you here last time. I report Roger missing. They tell me not much hope for finding him unless he return home on his own."

"Did you tell them to search around Sacred Falls State Park?"

Her blank stare gave me my answer. "Why?"

"Call them back and tell them to start looking for him in those mountains. If they ask why, and they will, tell them a friend saw a body get thrown from a plane. Have them check with CrimeStoppers, there's a report on file already. You just can't tell them about Alexander."

Alexander nodded. "Yah, that would end my business." He turned to me. "So you gonna do it?"

There was the missing body. The surfing, dead grandfather. The Fall Leaf Tour. I cleared my throat. "I, uh, was thinking how pretty the leaves on the East Coast are in the Fall. They have that big Tour thing you can do and—"

"McKenna." He sounded like my fifth-grade teacher again—right before she threatened to send me to the principal's office.

"Roger would be kine grateful if you do this." Emma had teary tracks on both cheeks.

My fifth-grade teacher had let me off the hook after I'd promised Penny Sue Kapinski that I'd never snap her training bra again. I told myself that I wouldn't mind freezing my ass off, but the truth was that I'd settled into island style. I'd adjusted to the weather and the slower pace. And now, I was starting to feel again. I sensed an emotional bond between Alexander and Emma. And one between Meyer, Shapiro and Roger.

The voice that spoke was mine, but the attitude wasn't the old McKenna. To make myself feel better, I told myself it was Kimu making my mouth move, possessing me and forcing out the words. "I think I have this Daniels' phone number in Shapiro's business records."

"You won't need that." She pulled out what she'd been hiding in her pocket.

The expression on her face told me she was handing over her last hope of finding Roger alive. My heart broke for this woman I barely knew as I took the small scrap of paper. It was the key to her loss— and she'd entrusted it to me. Through watery eyes, I read the initials "DD" and a telephone number on the paper.

"That his cell. You can reach him anytime with that number."

Yup, it was official, Kimu had taken over control of my mind and he was determined to get me a Darwin Award. I'd disappear from the human gene pool without ever making a contribution. As depressing as that seemed while I watched the bond between these two, I had to admit one thing. I'd almost forgotten about the hunt. How addictive it was. And that I was a hunt junkie.

24

I admit it, I'd originally agreed to help Harris because I'd found her attractive and the thought of spending time with her perked me up. But despite my concerns, something else was driving me forward. It was the old adrenaline rush—a thrill I'd abandoned when my life imploded. But just like an alcoholic, once I'd gotten a taste of my old addiction, my resistance melted.

I wanted the drive back to Honolulu to be a three-way planning session between Alexander, Meyer, and me. I began with, "It's got to be one of three people using that plane. This Daniels character, he's my first choice. He tried to rent it, got turned down, then killed Bob."

Alexander said, "Sounds weak to me."

"I agree. It's a lousy motive. Makes no sense. Kill a guy for a stupid drug run?" I shrugged. "What about Stone or Willows? Is there anyone else who would have had access or known that it was available?"

Alexander said, "Find out who's using the plane and we've found the killer."

"Because they used it to drop Roger's body."

From the back seat, Meyer said, "How come you two want to go see a movie thriller? I thought you was going to talk to this Daniels? I don't like those ones with lots of blood."

I twisted around to face him. "Don't you have hearing aids?"

"Sure, but they ain't working very good today. Why, did I miss something?" He paused. "It probably would be a waste of money for me to go to a movie today, anyways."

Uh, make that a two-way planning session between me and Alexander, combined with a few detours for Meyer. We finally agreed that I would, oddly enough, tell the truth—sort of. Emma Lau had asked me to contact Daniels to see whether he had seen Roger lately. I'd ask him where he'd been the past few days. I'd work that into asking what the bad thing was that Roger had done. And, the tricky one, why had it made Daniels angry? All that assumed he'd even talk to me.

Alexander's point of view was that I'd just be using my old skills. It would be easy for someone with my talents to manipulate Daniels, he said. It'd be easy to wear a dancing bear costume on Waikiki Beach, too. I wasn't about to do anything that stupid, but I had made a promise to Emma. I also realized that if my circle of friends grew much more, I'd go broke buying Christmas cards. That move to the East Coast was looking better.

Alexander said, "Why don't you try Daniels right now? Maybe you can rule him out? Maybe he was gone and couldn't do nothing."

I pulled out the scrap of paper from Mrs. Lau. "Sure. Let's see where Mr. Daniels is right this minute." I dialed the number and waited. Three rings later, I was listening to his greeting.

"Hey, thanks for calling, but I'm busy right now. Leave a message."

"Uh, Mr. Daniels, my name is McKenna. I'm a, uh, friend of Roger Lau and Bob Shapiro. Can you call me when you get a chance? I'd like to ask you a few questions." I left my number and said thanks.

"I got to drop you off. I have a late tour this afternoon."

"What? You got me involved in this, and now you're bailing out on me?"

"Just for the afternoon. I be back on the job tomorrow, boss." He gave me that infectious gleaming-white smile of his.

I turned towards the rear seat and said, "Looks like we're grounded for the afternoon, unless you drive."

Meyer perked up, "Me? Yeah, I can drive. What's wrong with Alejandro?"

"Alexander. He's got to work and I don't drive."

Meyer's eyes got big and he practically blasted me out of the car. "What kind of manure pile is that? How do you get anywhere?"

"I've got two feet and a monthly bus pass."

Meyer chuckled. "Yeah, and a Hawaiian taxi that looks a lot like this truck. Let's go get my car."

Alexander didn't hesitate for a second. He made the next right and we headed off to Meyer's place. Alexander looked pretty happy that I had a new mode of transportation. Obviously, he wasn't getting an adrenaline rush from the hunt like the one that ran through my veins.

At Meyer's apartment building, Alexander made a hasty exit. That left the two of us to ponder what to do next. Meyer wanted to check his messages; I suggested going to Willows Construction, the company owned by Frank Willows. Because it was almost two and it would probably take us a half-hour to drive there, we agreed to do that first, and then come back to check messages.

As it turns out, Meyer was a surprisingly good driver. Sure, he couldn't hear squat, but he paid attention and drove carefully. He didn't seem to mind the horns blaring around him, probably because he couldn't hear them. And he did motor through a slightly red light—but just once. So, basically, he did okay. We didn't hit anything, we only got two one-finger salutes and a couple of glares from other drivers as they zoomed past us on their way to their next accident.

I nearly jumped out of my seat when my hip began to vibrate. The ring of the phone started low, then got louder. I glanced at the display. Dadrian Daniels. I quickly reiterated the canned reason for calling. He sounded cooperative, almost eager.

"You knew Bob, huh? Who wound up with his stuff?"

Okay, that's not why I said I was calling, but he hadn't told me to take a flying leap off of a tall building, so the game was on. "Me. I've got it secured in a storage unit."

"I'm going to miss him. But, he did have something of mine that I'd like to get back."

I thought about the records at my apartment and couldn't imagine what he'd want. I wasn't interested in giving any of it away, but I did want to know what he was interested in. If he was motivated, this might be his pressure point, the thing that would make him talk. "Why don't you come by tomorrow morning around nine? I can take you to it."

"Tomorrow's not good, how about this afternoon?"

"Oh, that could be a problem. I'm not home and don't know when I'll get back."

"How about five? Will you be home by then?"

I checked the time. That was more than two hours from now. And I could always call and cancel. "That should be okay. If I can't make it, I'll call you."

"You've got all of Shapiro's stuff, right?"

"In storage. The landlord handed off everything that wasn't thrown away or donated." I winked at Meyer, who glanced at me for only a second, then focused back on the road.

Daniels said, "Nothing's left in Shapiro's apartment?"

Ah ha, he didn't know that the apartment was empty. He couldn't have been one of Meyer's visitors. "Right."

"Great, see you at five. What's your address?"

I gave him the information and we disconnected.

Meyer said, "Well?"

"We're going to meet him at my place at five. You know, it's really odd. He didn't know that Bob's apartment was empty. If he'd have been one of the one's who broke in—"

"What if he was lying?"

"Why? What would that accomplish? No, he's not the one who broke in."

"I won't have time to check messages if we have to be at your place by five."

"Do it remotely."

Meyer grumbled, "Can't remember the damned code." Then, added, "What if he ain't as stupid as you think he is and goes to your place ahead of time?"

Uh oh. I hadn't thought about that. I called Harris.

"Hey, McKenna. Howzit?"

I laughed. "Getting the lingo, huh? Look, I've just set up a meeting with a guy who's interested in something of his that he said Shapiro had. Can you be at my place at five?"

"Sure. I'm just hanging out, working on my tan."

Sweet. "And Harris, if you see anyone wandering around or looking suspicious before I get there, call the cops right away. I don't think this guy is dangerous, but be safe. Don't question, just call 9-1-1."

We arrived at the construction company just after 2:30. The first thing I noticed was the size of the business. Willows owned a lot of equipment. There were backhoes and small caterpillars, several trucks with Willows Construction signs on the side and guys carting tools into a large storage area off to one side. I hadn't realized it until now, but I'd seen the willow tree logo on construction jobs while gazing out the bus window waiting to get to my destination. In some perverse way, Willows having an interest in Shapiro's small charter service made sense. He was helping to turn these islands into nothing but condos and hotels, why not get some other sources of revenue going?

The office was a mobile home that had been hauled in and converted for business use. It had a sign over the door that proclaimed it as Willows Construction Office and it had construction-type guys wandering past. They reminded me of a bunch of kids kicking rocks as they waited for the end of their PE class. Meyer parked, then peered straight ahead as a worker crossed in front of the car. He appeared riveted by something, but I had no idea what.

I said, "What's the matter?"

"That guy that just walked by? He's one of the one's who came to my apartment."

"You've got to be mistaken. He works here. Look, if you want to wait here, that's fine. This is no big deal, a couple of questions and we're out of here."

"He's one of them I tell you."

I rolled my eyes. These guys all looked alike. Big. Burly. Did I mention big? I'd imagined this to be a fly-by-night operation, but that was obviously wrong. Anything this size would have to be a legitimate business. The best thing would be to meet Frank Willows, ask how he'd become involved with Bob Shapiro, get Meyer to realize he was wrong about the construction guy, then move our scrawny butts along before someone mistook us for vagrants.

"Look, let's go inside and meet Willows. I've got a couple of questions to ask, then we can take what we know to the cops. I've seen this company doing jobs all around town. He's legit, I tell you."

We shuffled by a couple of workers who stood between us and the door. I smiled at them and said, "Got any openings?"

They both laughed as they made way. We climbed the few stairs and opened the door to the office. To watch us, you might even think we knew what we were doing.

The inside of the office was paneled in a dark wood. The walls were covered with photographs of construction jobs and awards that the company had received. A perky receptionist greeted us. She wore a blue tee shirt emblazoned with a large arrow pointing upward and text that read, "Hey, dummy, my face is up there."

Uh oh, mea culpa. My cheeks felt hot as I glanced up. Her hair was straight and dark with blond streaks that screamed, "Did you notice me?" At least, that's what it said to me. It probably told the boys her age that she was hot and interested.

"Welcome to Willows Construction, may I help you?"

I said, "We'd like to see Frank Willows, if possible."

She nodded and said, "Let me see if he's available."

Okay, so I committed another major faux pas by watching how her skintight jeans wiggled as she crossed the room. Even Meyer poked me in the ribs and cocked his head in her direction. I just nodded and enjoyed the view.

A minute later, she returned, followed by a tall man with a well-tanned face and a subdued Hawaiian shirt. He had dark wavy hair and a neatly trimmed mustache. His tan was the result of either working, or more likely, playing, in the sun much of the day. He said, "I'm Frank Willows. And you are?"

I had the immediate sensation of a spider crawling down my back. He fit the description of the man that Cousin Dijon had described. "McKenna. And this is my friend, Meyer Herschel."

His eyes darted in Meyer's direction for a split second when I introduced him. Did he recognize the name? The sense of confidence I'd felt outside had evaporated. The tightening of his jaw and cheeks also had me worried. We couldn't stop now though; he knew who we were, so I went on. "We're here on behalf of Mr. Robert Shapiro, Jr. I understand you're one of his business partners." Just a question or two, then we could go. That's what I'd said.

He fingered his mustache, then said, "Let's go into my office."

The receptionist parked her well-proportioned self back at her desk. She gave me a little wave as we followed her boss to his office. The phone rang and she greeted the caller in a cheerful receptionist's voice. Inside the office, Frank Willows closed the door.

His desk was large and strewn with plans, papers, and other construction-boss-type detritus. I'm sure he considered his office organized, but to me it seemed like pure chaos. Photographs of projects adorned the darkly paneled walls. Framed documents, which appeared to be proclamations of some sort, were scattered throughout. I focused in on the closest one.

"That's a pretty nice thank you note."

Willows managed a smile. "Thanks, City Hall loves their proclamations." He extended an open hand at a couple of chairs, where we perched while he folded himself into the big one behind his desk.

He eyed me suspiciously. "What's your interest in Bob Shapiro?"

"We're here regarding his estate."

"What estate?"

"I mean, when someone dies, someone else has to take care of their affairs. That's him." I pointed at Meyer.

He leaned forward on the desk. "What do you mean died? I haven't talked to Bob in a couple of weeks, but the last thing I knew, he was alive and well. We had dinner at the Pikake Terrace at the Princess Kaiulani."

Was this an act? I said, "Never been there."

"You can have dinner poolside, listen to some good Hawaiian music. Tourists like it. Bob did, too."

I noticed that he used the past tense. As I reached forward and pulled one of his business cards from the little wooden holder, I said, "That was a couple of weeks ago?"

"Yeah, the—" He grabbed his PDA and tapped the screen. "The eighth. We met for drinks at 6:30, then had dinner. Finished up around nine."

I watched his eyes as I said, "Shapiro was in a hit-and-run about nine."

The crows feet at the corners of his eyes crinkled in recognition. Was it sorrow? Anger? Or self-satisfaction? "Really? Did he die right away?"

It wasn't the words that struck me as odd, but the tone of voice. It was almost as if he'd wanted Shapiro to suffer. We were into dangerous territory. What to do now? Ask a question, then get out. "Were you two close?"

He shrugged. "Just business partners. It was a good arrangement for all of us."

"All of us?"

"Yeah, me, Stone, Shapiro."

"And what about Roger Lau?"

His jaw twitched and his tone became sarcastic. "Him? He was just the maintenance guy. Ornery little shit, if you ask me. Always pushing himself in where he didn't belong. These Hawaiians, they…" When he continued, the sarcastic tone was gone and he was the businessman once again. "Well, enough of that. Can I help you with anything else?"

Arrogance is one of my hot buttons, it just irritates me to no end and makes me crazy. This disdain for the Hawaiians struck me as pure arrogance, the kind of haole attitude that gave all of us a bad name. Maybe because I'd recently been called out on that myself, I was doubly sensitive. Right now, my anger was hot enough to fry an egg. It was people like Willows who had made these islands so expensive that the locals had to work three jobs just to pay the bills. I didn't think he had to work three jobs to survive, and I'd call the locals anything but lazy. In a snotty tone, I said, "You can tell me what you did after dinner with Bob Shapiro."

Willows sat up straight in his chair. His nostrils flared, and I think that if he'd have been holding a pencil, he might have snapped it in half. He barked, "Who the hell did you say you were? Are you a cop? Lawyer?"

I'd one-upped him and it felt good. I calmly replied, "No, Mr. Willows, I'm just an interested party." Meyer and I stood and turned in unison; we left him staring after us. It was a movie-perfect exit. I'd have to congratulate Meyer on his timing. And me on my calm—well, at the end, anyway. We'd been right in sync. I read the receptionist's tee shirt again, then winked at her as we left. She smiled and appeared ready to say something cute when the color in her face drained and the smile disappeared.

"Excuse me," she said as she pushed past us.

She closed the door as Willows started yelling. We hightailed it outside. On the landing at the top of the stairs, I turned to Meyer and we gave each other a high-five. He gave me an appreciative nod as we climbed down the stairs. I stopped and stared straight ahead. "Holy shit," I said.

"What?"

Two cars down from where we'd parked was a black sedan. I walked to the back of the car and read the license plate—HSKYFN. It wasn't High Sky Fan as Dijon had remembered it, but Husky Fan. The car had been hidden from us on the way in by a big pickup truck. We hadn't seen it as we'd entered the office because we'd been facing the other direction. I began to inspect the car as quickly as I could. I pulled out a scrap of paper and wrote down the license plate number. I'd made it all the way around the car and was on the passenger's side, just by the windshield when I spotted a parking permit. It was for the Waikiki Sands Condominiums. It was one of those permits that people hang from the rear view mirror, but had been tossed onto the dashboard and probably forgotten.

I jumped when Frank Willows bellowed behind me. "What do you think you're doing? Get out of here, you son of a bitch. You come onto my property and start prowling around like you own the place. Get out of here before I call the cops!"

Meyer strode over to Willows and stood before him. The top of Meyer's head was about even with Willow's chin, but the little guy stared straight up into his eyes. Slowly, deliberately, he said, "Keep your morons away from my apartment." With that, he turned and motioned for me to get in the car.

I opened the passenger door, but before I ducked in I called out. "Oh, about calling the cops, I'll take care of that for you!"

Willows exploded in our direction, but Meyer locked the doors and started the engine. For a second I thought Willows might hop onto one of the big Caterpillar backhoes and hoe us to death, but he held his position and stood, arms across his chest as we drove away.

Meyer said, "I thought we were just going to ask a few questions, then get out. Now you've got him pissed off."

"Me? You're the one who threatened him with that 'keep your boys away bit.'"

"Morons. I said, morons."

"Whatever you say. I don't think he likes having little guys like you stand up to him."

Meyer chuckled. "I guess not. He didn't much like you either."

I read the name of the condominium complex I'd scribbled down and wondered where this would lead. I thought about the encounter. I really didn't have an excuse for my actions other than testosterone had kicked in. Rather than using that one, I said, "Alexander's kupuna made me do it."

25

I couldn't shake the image of Frank Willows glaring at us. Maybe I'd gotten the wrong impression. His anger could be caused by an attempt to hide his involvement or by the indignation of an innocent man accused. Which was it? One thing was for sure, due to his prominence on the island, I couldn't afford to be wrong.

It was almost 4:30 when we made it to my place. I checked with Harris first—no strangers had been around. I grabbed my mail from the box—just bills. Checked the machine for messages—none. I filled two glasses with water—one for Meyer and one for myself. We went outside to relax on the lanai. He grabbed the chair in the shade and I took the sun, which warmed my face.

A few minutes later, Harris joined us. She, too, took a spot in the sun.

Meyer said, "You two aren't worried about skin cancer?"

Unfortunately, the sun couldn't warm away the cold bigotry of people like Frank Willows. "I'm more afraid of people like that jerk. He could drop you into the foundation at a construction site and you'd never be heard from again."

"He might just be angry about being accused of something he didn't do. You did kind of jump the gun there."

Harris said, "Was this Willows? He was pretty upset, huh?"

"I did hit a nerve. Just wish I knew which one it was."

"You should stay out of the sun," said Meyer.

"Dermys do a helluva business here," I said. "My job's to help them send their kids to college." Harris and I gave each other a high five. We all turned at the sound of a car door slamming in the parking lot. "What time is it?"

Meyer glanced at his watch. "Jesus, you don't wear a watch either. Ten 'til five. For chrissakes, he doesn't drive, doesn't wear a watch. Damn native customs."

I chuckled. I stopped wearing a watch the day I quit skip tracing; it had nothing to do with coming to the islands. A man wearing a tee shirt with the familiar plumeria pattern in a wide white stripe across dark-blue material and jeans faded at the knees rounded the corner. He wasn't one of my tenants, so he must be Daniels. His arms were well-tanned and muscular, portraying a man used to hard outdoor labor. He wore black tennis shoes and a pair of wraparound sunglasses.

To my left, I heard Harris growl. Oh, great, she sees a hunk and there goes our relationship. His phone rang just as he turned the corner. He raised his sunglasses and checked its display, then hit a button on the side of the phone to stop the ringing.

"Women," he said. "Hey, where can I find McKenna's apartment?"

"This is it. Meet you at the front door. Go around there." I pointed to my right as I stood.

Harris and Meyer followed me into the living room and waited off to the side while I went to the door. "You must be Dadrian Daniels."

"You McKenna?"

I nodded. "Guilty. Come in." To my relief, we shook hands the old-fashioned way. His handshake was firm, yet a bit clammy. When he was through the door, I introduced him. "This is a friend of mine, Harris Galvin. And this is Meyer Herschel, the manager over at Bob Shapiro's apartment."

While they pressed the flesh, I dragged a couple of dining room chairs the ten feet to the living room where we all sat. We put Daniels on the couch so he could see the boxes stacked around the dining room table. Harris grabbed the other half of the couch, presumably so she could observe his reactions from the side. The expression on his face said, "I get the point."

I started things off. "So you and Shapiro went back a ways?"

His two-day beard growth and his attitude said, "This ain't no job interview, pal, let's get down to business." But we had something he wanted, so he was polite, even though he kept peering past me at the boxes. "Air Force. We trained together."

"So you were a pilot, too?"

"I got booted out. I ran into—some problems."

Meyer jumped in, "From what I hear that might be drugs. You do drugs, Mr. Daniels?"

Harris flinched. Daniels' attitude wasn't one of anger, but more analytical. "I was young and away from home for the first time. Started running with the wrong crowd. Bob tried to get me to stop, but it was too late. I got busted and that was the end of my flying career."

I said, "For one offense?"

His jaw tightened. "It was a big one. Anyway, Bob had something of mine that I'd like to get back. Can I see his stuff, then I'll get out of your hair."

I said, "Yah, we can do that in a minute. But first, I've heard that Bob was having dinner with one of his partners the night he was run down. Do you know anything about that?" During my years of skip tracing, I'd used my Third Skip Tracing Secret a lot. If I was right, Daniels would be like all the others and quite willing to talk about other people. Once the floodgates had been opened, the hard part was getting them to stop.

"About the partners? Yeah, I know a lot."

"Like what?"

"Like they're bad news, both of them. Willows, he's got a temper. And Stone, he's got an attitude. He's a real big MySpace freak."

Meyer said, "He like science fiction?"

Harris shook her head and hid a smile; she probably thought Meyer was cute. I winced, so did Daniels. I said, "The online service?"

Daniels corrected me, "Social web site. Stone's a braggart and a jackass. Guy's a real moron 'cause he gets off on putting info out there that he shouldn't. It was a bad deal for Bob."

"Why's that?"

"Cause they were taking advantage of him. That plane cost him a bundle. It also cost a lot to run it. Every time they took a flight, he lost the income from a paying customer and he had to pay to run the plane. Plus there was his lost time. Really bad deal."

I said, "Weren't you supposed to go on a flight with him the day before he died?"

"Yeah, it was kind of a reunion present for me and my girlfriend. He canceled me at the last minute."

Meyer leaned forward in his chair and stared at Daniels. "He canceled you because he heard you'd been busted for selling dope and had just gotten out of jail. And you wanted to fly the plane without him."

Daniels fidgeted in his seat, then sighed. "Shit. That was you, huh? He told me someone had run a check and found out about it. Yeah, he dropped me because of that. He was afraid that I'd try to smuggle drugs onto the plane. Said he couldn't trust me anymore. You want to know who he shouldn't have trusted? Look at the partners."

Daniels was growing agitated now, but as long as I could push him for more info, I would. He still hadn't told us what he wanted, and I intended to avoid the subject until I had more answers. "We just had an encounter with Willows. Talk about a temper."

"Same with Stone. Though Willows is worse because he holds a grudge. And he dwells on stuff until he's ready to blow. Guy ought to be on meds."

"It sounds like you had a bad encounter with him also?"

He made a dismissive gesture. "Not me personally. I witnessed a blowup between Bob and those two once. Not that long ago, either."

"When was that?"

"Two days before Bob got run down. They all met at his apartment."

Meyer suddenly perked up. "I remember that! The two of them showed up together. I don't remember seeing you there."

"I was the virtual fly on the wall." He smiled. "Bob used a webcam to record it, and I was watching from my place. It was a slick setup and I downloaded it all to disk. Bob put it on a flash drive. They never even knew they were being recorded. Assholes were so focused on being tough guys, they never had a clue."

Meyer barked, "Why'd he choose you? He didn't trust you!"

I was surprised at Meyer's anger.

Daniels worked his lower lip between his teeth. "Bob and me, we had an understanding. At least, until he heard about my arrest. That's all I'll say."

My instincts told me to move on. "What was the argument about?"

"I told you, Stone was taking advantage of the agreement. Lots of inter-island flights that chewed up tons of Bob's time."

"But he just runs a music store."

"He runs a chain of music stores." He began ticking off locations on his fingers. "Maui, Kauai, two on the Big Island, and one here. He was using Bob as a way to move stock between stores."

Harris, who had remained silent until this point, leaned forward and crossed her legs. The movement was slow and subtle, but it instantly shattered the male domination of the conversation. She said, "What do you mean, stock?" Her tone was slow, sensuous, and made the last word sound almost dirty.

Daniels wet his lips and I noticed perspiration forming on his forehead. Whatever he wanted, he knew he wasn't going to get it until we were done. I said, "What stock?"

"Musical instruments. Mostly violins. He teaches violin also."

Meyer and I exchanged a glance. Harris sat back on the couch and nodded to herself. It seemed so innocent on the surface. But, how many violins did you need on a little island? I said, "Violins? How many of those can you sell here?"

"They're, uh, valuable. Kind of like collector's items. You know how people are these days, anything and everything."

"That's BS and you know it."

He shrugged. "That's what he did. And, uh, actually, that's what I wanted to get from Bob's stuff. There was a violin."

I blinked. "What?" I turned to Meyer. "You know of any violin in his stuff?"

Meyer's brow furrowed, then he asked, "How big is it? Is it in a box?"

Daniels nodded enthusiastically. "Yeah, yeah. The boxes are about this long by this high." He motioned with his hands to indicate size.

I remembered the shipping label from the plane's cargo hold. Now, we knew what Stone had been moving. Or at least, what Daniels was willing to tell us Stone was moving.

Someone's cell phone began to ring. Harris reached for her hip and silenced hers. "Sorry, I have another appointment. I'm going to have to go in a few minutes."

We all nodded our understanding, not that she needed our approval.

Meyer said, "Brown cardboard?"

Daniels nodded again.

Meyer's wrinkled jaw worked back and forth. "Nope. Didn't see nothing like that. And I cleaned out his entire apartment."

The blood rushed to Daniels' face and he glared at us. "What do you mean you haven't seen it. I left it with Bob. It was his insurance. Besides, you just described it."

"No, you did," said Meyer. "I just asked if it was in a cardboard box. Sorry, Mr. Daniels, but I didn't see anything like that. I don't have any use for a violin anymore. I can't hardly hear."

Daniels said, "I don't believe you."

Meyer shrugged. "You can believe what you want, but there wasn't any violin in his stuff, and I cleaned everything out. Gave all his clothes and small appliances away, then threw out the little crap nobody would want. Believe me, if I'd have come across a box like that, I'd have checked it out before chucking it."

I said, "So that's what you wanted—a violin?"

Daniels ground his teeth together. "Damn right." He said to Meyer, "Did anybody else get into Bob's apartment?"

Meyer lied, "Nope. Not to my knowledge."

Daniels said, "Fine. Just fine. What a waste of my frigging time. I've got to go." He stood and started toward the door.

"Thanks for the information, Mr. Daniels," I said.

He turned to face me and said, "We're not done, yet." He spun on his heel and slammed the door behind him. I hadn't seen walls shake like that since my last LA earthquake.

"Wow," said Harris. "You hit another nerve. McKenna, you're on a roll. Hey, I'm late and have to run, see you later?"

I offered to walk her to her car, but she just laughed and told me that she was a big girl and could handle herself. Then, she left and headed for the parking lot.

I convinced Meyer that we should go to Ching's for Chinese. I told him about the Mr. McKay's chicken. He seemed more curious than interested in the food. But, the bottom line was that I needed to get away and the walk to Ching's would probably do us some good. Ching's was only about a fifteen-minute walk and we kept up a lively pace on the way to dinner, but heading back Meyer started to fade.

When we finally reached my apartment, Meyer said he just wanted to watch TV. In my efforts to be a good host, I started flipping through channels. Normally, I'd have grabbed a glass of wine and visited the lanai, but I was the innkeeper, so my preferences came second. When we got to the local news station, I stopped. "Hey, that's the same guy I saw the other day."

Meyer, eyes now only half open, said, "I seen him, too."

The guy on the TV was Jack something-or-other. While he droned on about news that wasn't really news, I zoned out. That is, until he said, "And now, let's go to Ruben Ochoa on the North side, where two hikers reported finding a partially decomposed body in the Kalanui Stream earlier today."

"Thanks, Jack. We're here with Connie and Carl, two visitors from the mainland who had been told by friends back home to take the hike to Sacred Falls. That hike is forbidden, of course, because Sacred Falls Park was closed after a landslide on Mother's Day in 1999 that killed eight people and injured many others. What was it like to find a body, Carl?"

Carl grabbed for the microphone and said, "Wow, it was like— Oh, man, it was gruesome."

Connie chimed in, "All mangled and, like, torn up. Eeoow! That's when we called Five-0."

"Five—" The puzzled look on Ruben's face was priceless and broadcast to the viewers that he was completely lost. He pressed his free hand to his ear, probably to better hear the instructions he'd been given, then wrenched the microphone out of Carl's hand and said, "Thanks folks." He faked a chuckle as he walked away. "Well, obviously, some people think that Five-0 really exists. But, sorry, it doesn't." He chuckled again. There were many adjectives that Ruben probably wanted to apply to his interviewees, few he could use if he wanted to keep his job.

He took up a position a few feet from Carl and Connie, then made a valiant attempt to recover and get some real news out of this. He read from a piece of paper in his hand. "The Office of the Sheriff has issued a statement indicating that they will be working to identify the body; however, the body was, as Connie described it, pretty mangled." Ruben suppressed a smile as he continued. "We do know that this was a male and he was wearing overalls or a jumpsuit. The Sheriff also said that the body has suffered significant levels of decomposition." He squinted at the paper; maybe the ink was starting to run? He stuffed the paper into his pocket and continued. "Due to the advent of natural processes, it may take some time to perform the identification. I think what they're saying is that this body is in bad shape, and it's going to take some luck for them to be able to ID the victim. Jack."

"Thanks, Ruben. Your eyewitnesses seemed a bit overwhelmed by this whole event."

"Yes, Jack. They're just a couple from Northern California, Marin County, and don't find many dead bodies, I'm sure." He smiled.

"Which version of the show do you think they're referring to, Ruben?"

"These guys probably watched a lot of TV in the 60s. I'd say they're thinking of the original."

I chuckled at the thought of what they did in Marin County when they were watching "Hawaii Five-0" in those days. Even today, if that area ever went up in flames, the state would be high for a month.

Jack said, "Ruben, isn't the Sheriff asking for anyone with information about who this might be to come forward?"

"Yes they are, Jack. Viewers with any information about a missing male should call the Office of the Sheriff; we'll follow this story and provide a more detailed description as it becomes available."

The anchor shifted in his seat, a new camera grabbed the frontal view, and that story was toast, its two minutes done.

Meyer's voice was tinged with anger, "That must be Roger's body."

"At least now he can get buried." Before we could carry this any further, the phone rang. I spotted the handset, picked it up, and said, "McKenna."

"You see the news about the body?" It was Alexander.

"Could be Roger. It's about the right place."

"Maybe so, maybe not. I'll have Emma call the Sheriff again."

"Good. So you want to know what happened this afternoon?"

"Tell me, brah."

I gave him the short version, which seemed to impress him. After a moment's silence, he said, "So you shook some coconuts down today. Hope none hit you on the head in the next day or so. How's that Meyer guy? He seems okay, but maybe—"

"We're doing fine."

He paused for a few seconds, then said, "Part of me keeps hoping that Roger will still turn up. Alive."

"Emma needs to follow through on this, no delays." I thought about Daniels' visit. Maybe that had been a stupid move. Now, he knew where I lived. He'd seen Harris. Possibilities, all bad, started running through my thoughts. I continued, "Whoever dumped that body doesn't want Roger identified."

Alexander said, "She might be the only one who can ID that body. And if something happened to her—"

We were both silent, neither wanting to think about another victim.

26

Early the next morning as the sun rose, the ocean did a typical transformation from a dull gray-blue to varying, almost iridescent, colors. Turquoise blended with navy in the deeper areas and melted into sandy beige in the shallows. White trailers of surf peacefully strolled onshore in a relentless, never-ending march. Once Meyer was up, we took turns in the bathroom, had breakfast on the lanai, watched nature's beauty unfold, did a quick check on Harris, then decided to head for Meyer's apartment. We pulled into his parking spot in the carport, where I noticed storage areas along the back wall. "Did Bob have one of these?"

"He didn't have enough stuff. Guy wasn't a saver—not of stuff, anyway. These cost another fifty bucks a month and he didn't want to spend the money for something he didn't need. He was real frugal, just stuck to the basics. Even with cable TV." He chuckled and seemed as though he were lost in fond memories for a moment. "Never seen somebody so disciplined with his money."

As we walked through the nearly empty carport area, I said, "Not many people left around here."

"They all work. Leave early, get home late."

We made our way along the concrete walkway to Meyer's apartment, surrounded by the scent of plumeria and jasmine. Meyer opened the door, we both entered, then stopped dead in our tracks.

Meyer yelled, "What the hell?"

The apartment looked like the wake of a hurricane. Whoever had been here had turned over everything that was movable. Meyer had had a small desk against one wall, which now lay on its side, contents scattered over the floor. I said, "Someone wanted to find something real bad."

"Son-of-a-bitch! Goddamn son-of-a-bitch. I'll bet it was that Daniels. I didn't like his looks, and he didn't like that we didn't have what he wanted."

"Maybe Willows sent over some goons?"

"Daniels is the one said this wasn't over."

We surveyed the apartment's chaos. It could take hours to put this back together, even with the two of us working on it. Fortunately, there wasn't much broken glass, though whoever had done this had pulled glasses and dishes off the kitchen shelves. They'd scattered silverware and cooking utensils across the tile floor. They'd even gone through the refrigerator and freezer and pulled out all the food. Fortunately, the food hadn't yet started to rot and they'd tossed most of that into the sink instead of on the floor.

I felt one of the frozen items. "It's thawed. The refrigerated stuff is room temp. This had to happen sometime last night. They probably put this in the sink to keep from tramping on top of it. No footprints that way."

"Son-of-a-bitch probably didn't want to screw up his shoes." Meyer strode to the phone on the wall and dialed. "Someone broke into my place. It's been trashed." He listened, then gave his address. He hung up, then said, "She said someone will be here in a few minutes."

We stepped outside while we waited for the cops. Sure enough, less than five minutes later, two uniformed officers approached. "Mr. Herschel?"

Meyer glanced at one of the two men. "You again. Sorry to bother you Officer Conners, but someone's trashed my place."

Officer Conners stayed with us to take Meyer's statement while the other surveyed the apartment. Conners asked, "Did you just find this?"

"A few minutes ago. I don't even know if anything is missing. But, I know who did it. It was a guy named Dadrian Daniels. He's trying to get a violin back that he says belonged to one of my tenants. After the break-in the other day, I decided to stay with McKenna. We met this guy and he threatened me, said he wasn't done with us. What are you gonna do about this?"

"We can have a conversation with Mr. Daniels," said Conners. "Are you saying that you don't think this is related to the other night's break-in?"

Meyer groaned. "I suppose it's possible." He added, "But this Daniels is the one that made the threat."

"We'll check it out."

The second officer came out of the apartment. "No footprints, nothing. This wasn't vandalism. Someone did a meticulous search."

Everything was moving along fine until Meyer said the dreaded "M" word. "This is all related to the murder of Bob Shapiro."

The cop's instincts kicked into high gear; you could see it on his face. He was suddenly on the alert for a crime, a scam or a lunatic. "Wasn't he the hit-and-run victim who lived in that apartment upstairs?"

"I'm telling you he was murdered. And I think this Daniels character was involved. Maybe—what was his name, McKenna? Oh yeah, Frank Willows. He was involved, too."

Conners made a quick note in his little pad. "Frank Willows, the contractor? Mr. Herschel, he's a very well-respected businessman. You didn't—accuse him of something, did you?"

Shit, there wasn't much I could do except stand around and mentally practice my Pig Latin, ix-nay on the et-thray, eyer-May. He was about to accuse a guy who probably played golf with the Mayor of murder. Next, he'd be telling them about Alexander and his illegal trip to Sacred Falls.

And he did, almost. "And then there's this body that just turned up. Those two hikers found it. That's the maintenance man for Bob Shapiro. I tell you, there's something big going on here and that Daniels is smack-dab in the middle of it!"

"Okay, okay. Calm down, Mr. Herschel." Conners had apparently settled on the lunatic option and was now trying to placate Meyer.

"Officer Conners," I said, "a friend of mine recently submitted a tip report that might help to connect Bob Shapiro's accident with the apartment break-ins and the dead body found up at Kalanui Stream."

To his credit, Conners did another mental shift. "We'll feed this into the system."

A few minutes later, the cops were gone and we were back in the apartment. I said, "This wasn't someone looking for a violin."

"Why's that?"

"Why would you turn over a kitchen table to find a violin? Why dump the contents of a kitchen drawer? The freezer's way too small. Someone was looking for something smaller, much smaller."

"Or trying to intimidate me."

"Then why not spray paint the walls? Why not destroy things? No, they wanted something small."

"Like what? Some sort of fancy spy microchip?"

Duh, that was it. "Daniels told us that Bob burned the video to a flash drive."

Meyer turned to where the little case with the Medal of Honor had been and began rummaging through the debris.

"Shit! He took it! The son-of-a-bitch took my medal."

Who would take another man's medal? Someone who'd been kicked out of the service?

He collapsed on the floor. "Fourteen men got killed so I could be here."

"Which war?"

"Korea." Tears rolled down his cheeks, the lines on his face deepened, etched with the memories of good souls lost.

A surge of sympathy shot through my veins. I didn't know what to say. So, I changed the subject. "They took your computer."

Meyer stood. "I'm sure it was him. He was a shifty son-of-a-bitch."

"Yah, there were some things he wasn't telling us. Like, what's really in that violin. And he did say that we'd meet again. Did you use an online storage backup?"

"What's that?"

Ouch. I'd take that as a no. For Meyer's sake, I was thankful that they hadn't destroyed things. But, the missing computer would probably nearly cripple his business. And what would the missing medal do to him? I glanced around the room. The couch, though undamaged, lay on its side. The perpetrators probably figured that Meyer wasn't capable of lifting or reupholstering his couch, so there was no point in wasting time ripping it apart.

Meyer handed me his key ring. "Do me a favor, huh? Go out to storage cabinet number three and get me a couple of the big garbage bags. I need a minute here."

"Which key is it?"

"Says Master on the side. There's only one."

I took my time as I strolled to the garage. On the way, I fingered Meyer's jailer's ring, resolving to get one of these for myself. It made it really easy to keep all the keys in one convenient place. I stood in front of storage cabinet three sorting through keys. I inserted the Master padlock key into the lock, but it wouldn't turn. My first thought was that corrosion, a common condition in the islands, had frozen up the lock. I examined it closely. It appeared to have been recently lubricated with no sign of pitting or the powder that gets left behind when the corrosion process begins. I tried it again, nothing happened.

I pulled the key out and checked it. Sure enough, it said Master on the side. And so did the one next to it. I tried the second key, slipped it in and twisted. The lock popped open. Meyer must have been mistaken about there being just one Master lock. I grabbed the bags from the cabinet and headed for the apartment. As I entered, I yelled, "Hey, you old coot, don't you know how many keys you've got on your ring?"

"Of course I do, twenty-two. One for each apartment, one for the pool area gate, one for the main breaker box, which, incidentally ain't a Master lock because the manager went cheap and bought an off-brand, one for the car, and one for the storage cabinet. Twenty-two. Now give me that before you lose it."

I was relieved that Meyer seemed to have composed himself. But before I handed over the ring, I counted the keys.

"McKenna, give me the—"

I ignored Meyer while I counted. "There's twenty-three."

"What? Not possible." He grabbed the ring and checked each key. When he got to the two Master padlock keys, he inspected both. "This ain't never happened before."

He rushed out the front door in the direction of the carports; I followed in hot pursuit. In the carport, Meyer stood before the storage cabinet in carport number four. He stared at the key in his hand, then at me.

I asked, "Problem?"

"That cabinet's supposed to be empty. I never rented it out."

He'd known every key on the ring. How could he not know exactly which storage areas had been rented? "That's another Master lock."

"Goddamn." Meyer worked the key between his fingers as he spoke. "A couple of days before Bob died, I was doing some pruning in the courtyard. He came up and asked me if he could borrow one of my big garbage bags. I said I'd get it for him, but he didn't want to inconvenience me. Said he'd grab one and bring the keys right back. I gave him the ring and he returned a few minutes later with the bag."

"So you think he added a key?"

Meyer stuck the key into the lock. "We're gonna find out." He twisted and, sure enough, the lock popped open.

Inside the cabinet was a box just under three feet long, a couple of feet wide and maybe a foot tall.

"Well, I'll be damned," said Meyer.

I nodded. "I think we've found what got Shapiro killed."

27

Meyer pulled the cardboard container from the storage cabinet and handed it to me. He then closed the door, put the padlock back in place, and secured the lock. Back in his apartment, we righted the kitchen table, set our find on top and opened it. Inside, surrounded by crumpled up white packing paper, lay a violin. The highly polished finish shined like a mirror. On either side of the strings, long narrow slits cut into the wood resembled a lowercase "f." Meyer barely looked at it as he raised it up and positioned the violin under his chin. He said, "I played quite a bit when I was younger." He plunked a string and disappointment painted his face.

I said, "You could have it tuned."

Meyer winced. "I can't hear it hardly at all. It probably needs to be tuned."

I nodded. Why didn't I think of that? He lowered the violin and began a detailed examination. He started at the neck and worked his way down to the body. His eyes suddenly narrowed and he said, "What the—" He handed me the violin and said, "Be right back."

He went into the kitchen and grabbed a refrigerator magnet from the refrigerator door, then began rummaging around on the floor. He returned a few moments later with a knife and the magnet. He pried the magnet off the back of the decorative cover and tossed the cover to one side. "Never liked that one anyway." He set it on the table and began poking at one of the f-like holes while he held the small magnet immediately above the hole.

"What are you doing? Have you gone off the deep end?"

"There's a key here. It's got a little metal tag on it, so I should be able to—"

My jaw dropped as a little tag popped up and stuck itself to the magnet. "That's a pretty good trick."

Meyer winked at me, then grabbed the tag between his left thumb and forefinger. He put a gentle pressure on the key. "I was an engineer for forty years. You learn a few things."

"Now what?"

"This was glued on. I just need a little more pressure and—"

I heard a snapping sound and watched as Meyer held up the key and its dangling tag, a satisfied smile on his face.

"Looks like it's for a safe-deposit box."

"Or a locker. There's a number on it." He squinted at the tag. "One, oh, one, seven."

Why would there be a key without some sort of explanation? I glanced around us. Paper everywhere. There was plenty of opportunity for explanation in this mess. I checked each piece that had come from the box; most was large-sheet packing paper, but one single letter-sized piece had escaped our attention as we'd unpacked. I smoothed it out and read aloud:

> Dear Meyer:
>
> If you're reading this, something terrible has happened to me. Unfortunately, I have unwittingly become involved with people who care about nothing more than making money. I don't want to involve you in anything that will cause you danger, so I'm simply going to appoint you as executor of my estate and instruct you to sell or liquidate all of my possessions in the easiest manner possible. My partners may want to purchase my share of the airplane. Please sell it to them at any fair price.
>
> You may also deduct a fee of 10% of the estate to compensate you for the time and effort involved in dealing with my affairs. Once you have liquidated my estate and deducted your fee,

please donate the proceeds, less any expenses that you may incur, to the family of Roger Lau. The only thing that I ask is that the money be used solely for educational expenses for his two sons. Should there be any remaining balance after the boys have completed college, I request the Lau family donate the balance to the Boys and Girls Club of Honolulu.

It was signed and dated by Robert M. Shapiro, Jr., on May 2, 2011. The letter was witnessed by Gloria Yamato. Meyer seemed to deflate as I placed the letter on the table. His arms fell to his sides. I righted a chair and helped him into it.

At this point, we had two options. Call the cops, again. Or try to sort this out before we made that call. My instincts said to play the cards we'd been dealt and stop bothering the cops until we knew something concrete. Otherwise, we stood a really good chance of being ignored when we'd need them most.

Meyer sniffled and said, "Why? Why'd this happen?"

"I think we're pretty close to finding out." I surveyed the apartment. "Maybe we should leave this for another day? I'd like to look over Bob's records again to see what you're dealing with. I'd also like to see what this key fits. And who's this Gloria Yamato?"

He shrugged. His facial features themselves appeared dulled by the shock of seeing Shapiro's letter.

"Let's get out of here. We'll go back to my place and check things out. Maybe we can figure out what you're supposed to do with that key."

We packed the violin back in its box, put the key onto a spare ring of Meyer's and folded Shapiro's letter neatly so that it would fit in Meyer's wallet. Then, we got in the car and Meyer dutifully drove us back to my apartment.

In the moment before we approached my place, my heart nearly stopped. What if mine had been ransacked too? But, when I looked through the window, I saw that everything was in order. No chaos. No turned over furniture. I'd been spared. Apparently, whoever had trashed Meyer's apartment didn't know or care about me, or simply hadn't found me—yet. That put us back to Willows—maybe.

Where to start? My first order of business was to learn more about the big contractor man and his shiny black car. He'd pissed me off, so I put him at the top of my list. I did an internet search for Oahu vehicle registrations, which the counties handle in Hawaii. Unfortunately, I found out quickly that I'd need both the vehicle identification number and the plate number to get anything. But, what about the Waikiki Sands parking permit on the dashboard? I grabbed the phone book and found the number for the complex.

A friendly female voice answered the phone, "Office."

"Is this the Waikiki Sands?"

"Sorry, I thought it was one of the tenants. Yah, this is the Sands."

"My name is McKenna. A black sedan with a parking sticker from your condo nearly caused an accident yesterday and I'd like to get the owner's name."

"You would have to talk to HPD about that, sir."

It wasn't the answer I'd expected, so I lied. "Ordinarily, I would have called them right away, but I didn't get the license number. It might have been driven by someone other than the owner."

"Some of our owners do make a vehicle available to selected renters."

"This car was recently at Willows Construction."

She sounded perplexed. "Why would it be there?"

"You don't have an owner who works there?" I'd fully expected it to be Willows' car. "Was it stolen?"

The earpiece rumbled as if she were repositioning the phone. "What did you say the car looked like again?"

"Black Chevrolet. Late model. In very good condition."

"Did it have nice wheels?"

"Hmmm. Don't recall. Maybe."

"Can you hold on for a minute?"

"Sure."

I heard music, the sweet sounds of an island rhythm by Braddah Waltah. I hummed along and was feeling pretty relaxed by the time she returned. "Nice music," I said.

"Thanks, we pay enough for it." She clucked like a frustrated mother hen.

Hmmm. Not good. "Is it missing?"

"It belongs to one of our owners who lives in Washington. And you're right, it's not here. I'm going to contact the owner. Maybe he let someone borrow it without letting me know. Thanks for calling me."

So the car didn't belong at Willows Construction. "And that accident? It was a hit-and-run a few weeks ago."

"Omigod! Seriously?"

"I think so," I lied again. I'd probably never see the Pearly Gates unless I could afford a good lobbyist. "Can you call me back when you find out? I'm investigating that accident and some related incidents."

"What's your number?"

And that was that. Now we had a line on the car. Was it really the one used in Shapiro's hit-and-run? Who knew? There had certainly been enough time to have any minor body damage fixed, but why was the car at Willows Construction? Meyer cradled the violin while he stared at me.

He said, "Well?"

"The car belongs to a mainlander. I'll bet he's a Washington Huskies fan. It's missing. She's going to contact the owner and see if he loaned it out."

"Why were you talking about Bob's accident?"

"I concocted that to keep her motivated, but, who knows, maybe it's the car that ran him down. I thought it might lead back to those guys who harassed you. Anyway, it's a long shot. Let's look at his business records, I want to nail down where he banks and see if that's where the key came from."

He held out the violin and said, "That's strange. Look at the top seam."

I looked at it. "So?"

"Where the side and the top meet. Look at the seam."

I examined it and said, "Looks like wood to me."

"Cryin' out loud. You may be able to hear, but you can't see worth a damn."

I rolled my eyes and thought, I can see better than you can hear, buddy.

"It's been taken apart and glued back together again."

"What about it?"

Meyer's face turned a bright red. "What about it! They did a crappy job! Disassembling a violin should be done by someone with some skill. Not just a moron with a tube of glue and a knife."

"Huh?"

He shoved the violin towards my face and pointed. "Can't you see how sloppy a job that is?"

Sure. No. Maybe. I shook my head. "Don't tell me you built violins, too."

"I had an instructor who was an amateur violin maker. He was always talking about craftsmanship. I thought he was nuts because he'd spend months making a single violin. Now it seems kind of interesting. Like we might be able to—you know, leave something behind."

I understood. "Well said. I've been wondering more about that lately."

Meyer sighed, "When you're young, you just want to rush through. As you get older, you appreciate the process more."

"Speaking of processes, I need to start going over these business papers again. Maybe you should pay attention since you're the executor."

"I just wanted something to keep me out of the apartment until this was over. Now . . . " His voice trailed off, he started getting that distant look people get when they remember an old friend.

"Okay! Let me see that letter." He extracted it from his wallet, then passed it to me. I set it to the side for easy reference, then grabbed the box I wanted and began poring over the records. I pulled the checkbook and noted the bank and branch. Bank of Hawaii, the branch just a few blocks from Shapiro's place. We checked the business checkbook; same bank, same branch. There was also a business card for a Gloria Yamato, Branch Manager. Now we knew who had witnessed Bob's letter. And where the safe-deposit box was located—most likely.

Next step, call the bank. I dialed the branch phone number printed on the business checks.

"Bank of Hawaii, how may I direct your call?"

"Gloria Yamato, please."

"I'm sorry, but she's unavailable. Can I take a message?"

"I'm calling for the estate of Mr. Robert M. Shapiro, Jr. I've discovered that he may have had a safe-deposit box at your branch. Can you confirm for me that he did have a box there? The box is number 1017."

The youngish sounding voice on the other end had the familiar island lilt. There was a long pause. "Oh, wait, she's just coming in the door. Hang on, I'll put you through."

A minute or so later, another female voice, this one sounding older, answered. "This is Ms. Yamato."

I repeated my question, then she said, "What was your name?"

"My name is McKenna, but I'm calling for Meyer Herschel, the executor of Mr. Shapiro's estate. I believe you witnessed his letter to Mr. Herschel, yah?"

"Is Mr. Shapiro—did he pass away?" Her voice held an edge of suspicion.

I didn't want her calling the police immediately after she hung up, so, at least for now, honesty was probably the best policy. "Yes. And in going through his effects, we've discovered that he may have had a box there. Number 1017. As you know, Mr. Herschel was appointed executor of the estate." I figured there was no harm in repeating the key info a few times.

"Is Mr. Herschel there?"

"Uh, yah. Hang on." I handed the phone to Meyer, who jammed it to his ear.

He squinted, then finally said, "I can't hear so well, but if you asked if I was Mr. Herschel, that's me. Can you talk to McKenna, he can hear."

He handed the phone back to me. I heard an exasperated sigh. "Mr. McKenna?"

No point in making her day more difficult, I'd go with the Mister. "Yah."

"Yes, Mr. Shapiro does—did have a box here. Mr. Herschel needs to show a power of attorney or a directive from Mr. Shapiro as well as his identification. I'll also need something to show that Mr. Shapiro passed away. If he has that, we can let him have access to the box."

The call ended with the usual blah-de-blah, have-a-nice-day stuff. We went through the bank statements and came to a sudden realization. Bob Shapiro had a payment due on that plane any day now. His checking account registers indicated that he might have enough in the bank to cover it, but we didn't know what other bills might be due soon.

At one point, I said, "We may need to go to the bank, you'd better put that letter in your wallet so we don't get caught flatfooted. You'll also need one of those death certificates."

"I got a better place for them." He left the room and returned moments later with his briefcase. He put both items inside and set it on the floor. "Got a few other gems in there."

Great. Now we had luggage to haul around the island. Anyway, most of Shapiro's bills were on automatic payment, so money was coming out, but none was going in. Bob hadn't been able to make a bank deposit in a couple of weeks, so his income was zero while his expenses were exactly the same. This meant that payments on the plane might bounce higher than it could fly. Worse, if the bank paid the overdrafts, the fees would be brutal. We had no idea what bills had accumulated in the past couple of weeks, what might have been paid since Bob's last register entries, or who might be sending past due notices. The plane was in the partnership's name, did that mean that the remaining partners could take control?

Meyer and I must have had the same thought, because we stared at each other and, almost simultaneously, said, "His mail."

28

We returned to Meyer's apartment to retrieve Shapiro's mailbox key. Inside we noticed an increasing closeness. The air felt heavy as we climbed over the disarray. Meyer vowed to make whoever had taken his Medal of Honor pay. Odor from wasting food in the kitchen overpowered our senses, so we bagged and removed the perishables. We righted furniture, then Meyer went into the bedroom. A few minutes later, I found him kneeling on the floor sorting through keys.

"I thought they were all on that big blue ring of yours?"

"These are for the mailboxes. I keep a spare for when the tenants lose one. Happens maybe once a month or so."

This guy was just way too organized. At my place, if a tenant lost a key, they had to deal with the post office to get a new one. That usually taught them not to make the same mistake again. I noticed that each of the keys in the pile had a tag with an apartment number on it. He put each one back into the special little box on its special little hook and gazed up at me. "Gimme a hand, would you?"

I half-expected us both to end up on the floor, but he popped up like a jack-in-the-box.

"Thanks," he said. "There's a key missing for Bob's mailbox."

"Really?" I stared inside his organizer. There were keys on nearly every hook, including one for Shapiro's apartment. "What's that?" I pointed into the box.

"My copy. His original is gone. I had them both in here after I—I found Bob's copy in his apartment."

I pulled the spare from the box and said, "Let's see what's there."

"You go. I want to pick up a few things. Get rid of this food."

I went to the mailbox area. Much like my building, all the boxes were lined up in two rows at about eye-level. The mailbox doors had dulled with exposure to the elements. Each box had been labeled with a miniature name tag. Some had been typed, some handwritten, on weather-yellowed paper. I searched the names on the boxes until I found "Shapiro, R." I slipped the key into the hole, twisted and pulled. The box opened to reveal a big fat nothing. I stared inside for a minute, then, like a fool, checked the name on the box. When I'd read the name again I said to myself, "Dumb shit, they beat you to it."

I closed up and went back empty-handed. Whoever had ransacked the apartment had probably stolen Bob Shapiro's mail. I just hoped that the security for the safe-deposit box was better than this, otherwise that might be empty too.

We agreed to work on the apartment later and went to Bank of Hawaii, where we were directed to Ms. Yamato by one of the tellers. Ms. Yamato wore a sky-blue flowered skirt with a white, embroidered top and a navy blazer. Her name tag indicated that she was Gloria Yamato - Branch Manager. She was younger than I'd expected, probably somewhere in her early forties. She wore her hair up in that tight bun style professional women seem to like when they want to project an I'm-all-business image.

If someone yanked on my hair that hard, I'd probably cry like a baby, but maybe that was how she kept her facial skin tight. She did have nice skin, too. No wrinkles. And she didn't wear much makeup. She carried herself elegantly, in a manner that said, "I don't need it."

She gestured at two rattan chairs on the opposite side of her desk, then asked Meyer for his identification. "And do you have a POA?"

"No, Bob wasn't DOA, he made it through a couple of days before he died. But he never regained consciousness."

I said, "He's hard-of-hearing, you'll have to speak up."

She nodded. "Do you have a Power of Attorney or a letter of authorization?"

"Oh, sorry. I thought you said—forget it. Here." He put his briefcase on his lap and extracted Shapiro's letter. He set the folded piece of paper on the edge of the desk, then closed the briefcase.

I rolled my eyes as he deliberately unfolded the letter, smoothed it out, then scanned it. I whispered to Ms. Yamato, "Big man on campus."

She pursed her lips and gave me a knowing wink. I was beginning to feel as though Gloria and I could order a pizza and have lunch before Meyer had finished his machinations. Finally, he seemed satisfied and passed the letter to her.

"This looks like it's been around a bit." She smiled, then her face turned serious as she read. "This is the letter—that's my signature. This was an unusual request because Mr. Shapiro asked that we add you as a signer on the box in the event of his untimely death—and he didn't want you to know about it. You have proof of death?" She gazed at us with cool, brown eyes that conveyed her condolences.

I said to Meyer, "She needs the death certificate." Then, to Gloria, "We're trying to figure out who killed him. We think there's something in the box that will tell us why he was run down." I'd tried to sound convincing and confident, but Gloria appeared unconvinced.

She glanced over the death certificate, then said, "I'll be right back." She stood and walked with a smooth, floating grace towards a gate into the teller area.

I hissed at Meyer, "What was that all about?"

He nodded as if I were a beginning student in the college of life. "You can never be too careful."

I glanced at the ceiling and wondered if Kimu had been speaking to some of the Hawaiian gods. Maybe, collectively, they'd decided I'd been a bad boy and needed punishment, lots of it. My thoughts were interrupted by the buzz of the gate as someone let Gloria into the super-secret, bank-teller-only area. A minute later, she came back through the gate, this time holding a small card in her hand. She smoothed her skirt with one hand while she handed the card to

Meyer with the other. She said, "I'll need you to sign this. Here, and here." She pointed and I noticed that her well-manicured fingernail had a diamond in the middle of it.

I felt like I was in love, or at least, lust, and wondered what she'd be like when she let her hair down. Would her skin sag? An old Van Morrison song began playing in my head. "G-L-O-R-I-A." Uh-oh, I was being unfaithful to Harris and we hadn't even gotten started.

She smiled at me and winked as Meyer did his thing. I smiled back. Whew, I was becoming a regular Casanova. "Um, there are a few bills that may be coming in for Mr. Shapiro. We're not sure when they all come in or if there'll be enough of a balance to cover them."

She said, "Unfortunately, there's not much we can do about that. The creditors need to be notified of Mr. Shapiro's death."

"We know what regular bills he has; we just don't know his current balance. Can you give Mr. Herschel that?"

She nodded and turned to her computer. A minute later, she jotted down an account number and a balance, then another.

She handed the paper to Meyer, then picked up the card Meyer had signed and said, "Now, let's get you into that box, Mr. Herschel."

Meyer made another big deal of closing his briefcase. While we waited, I glanced down at her left hand and saw the rock on her fourth finger. The stone was almost the size of a golf ball. Crap. Forget her. There were plenty of other women out there for a smooth, handsome guy like me. I leaned back in my chair and said, "I'll wait here."

Meyer grabbed my shirt sleeve and pulled. "Nope. You're going in with me."

Gloria stood and said, "I'll show you the way."

The three of us formed a line on our way to the gate. She floated, I failed at a macho swagger, and Meyer toddled along behind. A smiling girl behind the counter buzzed us in and Meyer signed a card showing that he'd accessed the box today. Gloria took us into a vault lined with boxes. Big ones, small ones. High ones, low ones. Yeah, all kinds, all sizes.

She ran the diamond-tipped red fingernail along the box numbers until she came across 1017. "Here we go. Would you like to use our privacy room?" Over to the side, I noticed a closet about big enough for one of us and a box. I shook my head. No way I was getting in there with Meyer. No way. Sharing the apartment was bad enough.

Meyer caught my bobble-head doll head movement. "No, thanks," he said.

She inserted his key and hers into the box, twisted both clockwise, then pulled on the box. The sucker just kept getting longer and longer. It was like watching a magician pull a broom out of a top hat. She placed the box on the table and said, "I'll be right outside. Call when you're ready."

Once she'd left us alone, we opened the lid. There were two items in the box; a small, computer flash drive and an envelope about an inch thick with the label, "From Mr. Kanakua." I assumed it would be more instructions or perhaps important records from this Mr. Kanakua. Boy, was I wrong.

Meyer picked up the envelope and slipped his finger under the flap. He ripped it open and small white packets filled with a powdery substance tumbled onto the table.

Time not only stood still, but I think it took a vacation on Maui while we stared at the packets. Under my breath, I muttered, "We are in such deep shit."

Meyer pointed. He said, "Is that what I think it is?"

"Such deep shit. Yeah, that's what you think it is." An image of Meyer rummaging through his briefcase flashed into my mind. Why hadn't he just dumped the contents out onto Gloria's desk? That way, she'd have been able to testify that we didn't bring the drugs into the bank.

I tapped Meyer on the shoulder and put my finger to my lips. He shrugged, made a funny face like "huh," then put the packet back into the envelope. I assembled the rest of the little packets, stuffed them back into the envelope and set the proverbial hot potato back into the oven. We shoved the computer storage device into Meyer's briefcase and replaced Shapiro's safe-deposit box. I called out, "We're finished!" Boy, were we.

29

There's nothing quite like stumbling onto a drug dealer's stash to send your adrenaline level into the stratosphere. My heart jackhammered in my chest loud enough to make me barely notice my shaking knees and dry throat. I could only hope that Ms. Yamato didn't see the fear in my eyes. I'm pretty sure she watched us more closely than she had when she'd let us into the cage. I couldn't rid myself of the anxiety I'd felt as I'd stared out through the bars of the bank vault. It reminded me of a convict waiting for exercise time in the yard. Perhaps prison would be better. You'd get amenities, even conjugal visits—assuming you had someone to conjugate with. Since my prospects in that department appeared to be dimming with every man that even glanced at Harris, it made sense to me that nothing could make up for the bad food and grumpy inmates.

We stood outside the bank and I breathed in the fresh air. The sun beat down, completely unbothered by the few white puffy clouds that painted streamers across the sky. I let the trades caress my face with their gentle touch and closed my eyes as I drank in the moist air.

Once my knees felt like they could do their job of keeping me upright without constant attention, I asked Meyer, "Do you know what that was in the box?"

He leaned forward and half-whispered, "Drugs?"

I nodded. "It looks like Bob's partners were smuggling and he must have figured it out. That's what Daniels wants. The drugs—not some stupid violin." I glanced at Meyer, who looked hot under the collar. "Sorry."

He waved away my apology. "So what now?"

"We need to find out who those belong to. Otherwise, it just looks like they belonged to Shapiro—or worse, to us."

"So now Bob's going to be labeled as a drug dealer?"

"That's what it's looking like."

I could see the anger boiling inside as he stomped away.

"Meyer! Wait. I have an idea."

"What?"

"We think Stone's doing something funny—maybe illegal, right? Why don't we visit a few of his neighbors and see what they can tell us?"

Meyer stared at me. "Are you nuts? We already pissed off Willows, now you want to go after the other partner? You have gone off the—"

"No! He's not going to know we're there. I used to do this for a living. Trust me, it'll work. If Stone's around, we pretend like we're a couple of mixed-up old farts and walk away. After we snoop around a bit, we check that flash drive from the bank. By then, we should have enough information to point the finger at someone other than Bob."

It took a little more persuasion, but Meyer eventually agreed. Logically, there just wasn't enough evidence to force an in-depth police investigation of both Shapiro's and Lau's deaths. To me, they seemed related. But, the who and why still didn't make sense. If Harris was going to get the reward—oh shit, Harris! I needed to call her with an update. That's when my cell phone rang. It was from the Waikiki Sands. Now what? "McKenna."

"This is Zoe over at the Sands. I reached our owner and he tells me that he hasn't let anyone use his car. He's pretty distraught. Do you know where the car is now?"

"Try Willows Construction. I saw it there yesterday. It looked pretty clean." Or freshly painted.

"Thanks Mr. McKenna, I'm going to owe you one for this." We both disconnected.

"Looks like the car was stolen," I said. "I've told her where to find it. Maybe that will stir things up a bit."

"They'll get rid of it," said Meyer.

"Huh?"

"That Willows character saw you and me at the car. Bet you ten bucks it's gone already."

I hate it when other people are right. I called Harris on the way to Stone's business. There was no answer, so I left a message. Stone Music was in an older commercial section on Kalakaua Blvd., which had been named in honor of King Kalakaua, the Merrie Monarch, whose reign began in 1874 after his predecessor died without naming a successor. This particular stretch of the street was old, but clean. There were no vagrants, no drug deals happening, no hookers on the corner. So, while it hadn't been renovated, as many sections had been with new condos, offices or shopping, it reflected an older feel of the islands. Not one of culture and beauty, but cheap, fast growth.

The king had been passionate about art, music, and parties and had brought in a period of economic prosperity to Hawaii by signing the Reciprocity Treaty of 1875, which eliminated the tariff on sugar. Today, there's even a Merrie Monarch Festival dedicated to the king's memory to perpetuate Hawaiian traditions. But over the years, concrete, steel, and glass had replaced that passion for the arts.

The front entrance to the Kalakaua Commercial Offices building was like any other forty-year-old commercial building, double glass doors on aluminum frames, an overhang that protected you from the elements for a few feet, and a tiled entrance that had seen better days. The directory on the wall immediately inside the front doors said that Stone Music was in Suite 104. We decided to take a walk around. Maybe we could find Stone's suite and see whether he was in.

Suite 101 was around the corner from the directory on the right-hand side of the hallway. Wooden-framed doors with frosted-glass insets that had suite numbers etched into the glass marked the entrance to each business. Small nameplates with the names of the businesses hung on the wall to the left of each door. We passed 101 and its opposite, 102, then bingo, 104. I tried the doorknob, but the door was locked. A sign said that they would return at 9:00 AM.

Meyer glanced at his watch. "Damn near noon."

"Maybe they never came in today. That's good." I motioned to the door opposite Stone Music and said, "Let's see if these guys know anything."

According to the sign, Clacket Insurance occupied 103. Inside, I heard the tapping of fingers flying over a keyboard. The door squeaked as I pressed against it, and a young girl's voice greeted me. "C'mon in, we're here!"

Inside, the elegance of the room startled me. I'd expected more of the forty-year-old low-budget atmosphere from outside the office, but inside, it was modern and tasteful. At least one island watercolor hung on each wall, the furniture included a rattan couch with fluffy, dark-patterned cushions, a coffee table and a side chair. The aroma permeated the air and made me feel energized.

The "girl" behind the desk was actually a woman who I guessed to be in her forties. Her high-pitched, youngish sounding voice reminded me of a high-schooler. "May I help you?" She had a smile that brightened the room.

I said, "Um, yes. We were sort of trying to find someone over at Stone Music."

Her smile faded. "Oh. Them. They're out today."

"Doesn't sound like you think very highly of them."

She turned her attention back to her computer and said, "Try again tomorrow."

"I'm not a friend of his or anything. In fact, we're dealing with the estate of one of Stone's business partners and wanted to get some answers about why he was abusing the partnership agreement."

"He abuses everything and everyone. Now, if you'll excuse me."

"Nasty neighbor?"

Her eyes flamed as she shot a glance in my direction. "He's a freak. Whatever. Please leave. Just—go."

"You're very pretty when you're angry. Actually, you're pretty all the time."

The hardness in her face softened. "I'm not twenty, mister."

"You're a lot prettier than a twenty-year-old."

She bit her lip, but it was a feeble attempt to hold back a smile. "You must have been pretty slick—in your day."

Ouch. Talk about hitting below the belt.

She swallowed hard. "Let's just say I made a mistake once."

"So did Bob Shapiro."

"Who's he?"

"The partner we represent. He was killed in a hit-and-run a few weeks ago."

I saw recognition in her face. "I read about that." She glanced down at her fingernails for a few seconds. They were painted a bright red, but one was chipped. She pushed at the flaking nail. "Do you think Stone had something to do with that?"

"Maybe. There seems to be a lot of strange things that have happened during the past couple of weeks. Did you know anything about Stone personally?"

"I have a boyfriend."

That struck me as odd—or maybe not. "That doesn't mean you never, um, saw Stone."

She glanced at the ceiling; her jaw tightened. "Fine. He asked me out a few times. We went to dinner, but there was always this distance. You know, like he was playing you—or had a scheme. He had lots of those."

"Schemes?"

She nodded and started to turn back to her keyboard.

"Does he ever use drugs?"

"Mister, I've already said too much."

"What about MySpace?" I said. "Wasn't he big on that?"

The color drained from her face, she closed her eyes as if she wanted to block out the world, the question, and a memory. When she opened her eyes, they were wet with tears. "Shit. Yeah, he's addicted to that. You'll find everything about him there."

Surely he wasn't that stupid. And what could he have done to this woman to make her so upset? "What's everything?"

Her shoulders slumped. She shook her head and wiped at a dribbling tear. Her words tumbled out between sobs. "Just—because it's there—doesn't make it—true." She waved us out the door while she muttered something about Stone getting what he deserved someday.

Meyer tugged on my shirt-sleeve, so I started to follow him out. I guess I'm developing a bad case of white-knight complex or something because I stopped in the doorway and said, "We could make him pay, you know."

She stared at me for a long moment, then turned back to her computer. Meyer and I left and stood in the hallway. I had an itch to check out another business in the building, to learn more about what Stone had done to the insurance gal.

Meyer said, "What did she say?"

I blinked at him in amazement. He'd missed that entire conversation?

"Batteries died in my hearing aid sometime this morning."

I spoke loudly, probably loud enough for anyone in the building to hear me. "I'll tell you later. I'm going into this office over here, see if I can learn more about Stone. You want to wait here?"

He nodded, then leaned against the wall.

The next office I entered was for a CPA. There were two desks, two people, and about eight million files scattered everywhere. A man with slicked back reddish hair sat behind one of the desks, a woman with a scowl behind the other. As I entered, the man said, "Did you see the Darrell file?"

The woman retorted, "No. And I told you to file it away when—" She stopped and glanced up at me. She pasted a "Welcome Stranger" smile on her face and said, "Can I help you?"

I nodded at both of them. "Yes, I'm representing a deceased partner of Mr. Stone's and wondered if you might be able to answer a few questions."

The woman said, "I'm afraid not, we don't know much about his business."

At the same time, I heard the man mutter, "Son of a bitch."

I said to the man, "So you know Mr. Stone?"

The woman stifled her laugh, but the man just let it out. "He's a blowhard."

"John!"

"Sorry. He's not a very nice person. Doesn't play well with others."

John had a thin, almost invisible mustache that he fingered as he spoke. I wanted to tell him to stop mumbling, but thought better of it. "I'm already aware of that. He likes to brag a lot, doesn't he?"

John glanced at the woman and said, "What about it, Catherine? He's the one that was shooting off his mouth."

Catherine looked flustered. "It's just him spouting off."

I said, "About what? His business? The partnership? His sex life?"

They each stared at the other, then at me. John said, "Molly, across the way? She's a nice lady. We've known her for years. She's always had a level head. Then, she hooked up with Stone one night. He date-raped her. She's never gotten past it."

Whoa! She'd said they'd just had dinner. "Did she report it?"

"Too embarrassed. Felt like it was her fault. She didn't want to destroy her business by making it public. So, no."

I nodded, pieces of the puzzle falling into place at last. Her reaction, and the lie, suddenly made sense. "Did he put information about her on his MySpace account?"

"Her and a whole lot of others. He's a bastard," said John.

Catherine nodded. "I think Molly's hoping that if the right person gets angry enough at Stone, he'll get his due."

I still didn't quite get this whole MySpace thing. "What did he say about her—and the others?"

Catherine sneered. "He posted details about her and his other conquests."

"He admitted to rape on MySpace?"

"Oh, no!" said John. "He paints a different picture. According to him, he's Mr. Macho and the ladies can't resist him. And he says that these women even post comments about how good he is."

"That's bizarre. What's his MySpace address?"

They both shrugged. John said, "No idea."

The rest of the conversation started turning into a rehash, so I politely excused myself. Back in the hallway, Meyer looked bored. I told him I needed to do a little more checking and left to see what some others might say. Unfortunately, I had no luck with 105 or 106.

That wrapped up the first floor, but at least I had something to look for on MySpace, even if I didn't know what it meant or where to look for it—yet.

I returned to find Meyer standing where I'd left him in the hall, this time looking forlorn. "That girl came by."

I opened my hands in the universal what-the-hell-are-you-talking-about gesture.

He said, "From the insurance agency. The one at the computer. She was crying again."

If what I'd just heard was true, I could understand why. "Let's go. I have some computer work to do." Somehow, I had to find Stone's account at MySpace.

30

ABC Stores are a staple in Hawaii. They're a chain of general stores that carry things like sunscreen, flip-flops and cheap mementos. They also have important stuff for locals like batteries and sunscreen and flip-flops—and junk food. Come to think of it, I guess the tourists like junk food, too. In Honolulu, there are more ABC Stores than hookers. At least, that's the way it seems. Maybe I just hang out on the wrong street corners.

After we had a supply of batteries and had outfitted Meyer with the ability to hear again, we went back to my apartment. First thing, I noticed that there was a message. It was short and to the point.

"Mr. McKenna, this is Molly. From Clacket Insurance. You were here—well, you know. I told my boyfriend about your visit. He wanted me to tell you that Stone's user name is Island Giant. As if!" Try as I might, I couldn't recall having given her my phone number. Or my name.

It only took a minute to jot down the user name, fire up the computer, open my browser, and find the MySpace web site. Their home page had a search box at the top, a member-video section in the left-hand column and a sign-in area in the right-hand column. I didn't have a MySpace account, so I took a chance and typed "island giant" in the search field. Instantly, a page labeled "Find a Friend Results for island giant" included just a thumbnail photo of a dark-haired man with sunglasses and a strategically placed guitar. That's it, that's all he wore. One of the information fields was for location and that said this guy was in Honolulu. I clicked on the photo and got the profile page for Island Giant.

Now, I'm not by any means what you'd call a prude, but this was beyond my comprehension. I definitely had the right guy, because there was a biography area in which he said his friends called him Jimmy. He also described his interests as music, women, and flying. The page included details about Stone himself, including a physical description that sounded as if it had been written by a male-enhancement-drug-email writer. There were three major sections, one on Enhancing the Dating Experience, one for Business and one for something called "No Boundaries."

Under the dating experience section, there were photos of women in various stages of undress. The one thing that they all had in common was that their photos were taken in bed and in poor light. Some had sheets pulled over them; others weren't so lucky. The style of the photos, the looks on their faces, and the location had me wondering if the women might have been drugged. If Stone was date-raping his victims as John from the CPA's office had said, I doubted that any of them could have walked, talked, or said no to anything. One of the photos caught my eye—it was Molly at Clacket Insurance. In the office, I'd thought she was quite pretty, and her smile had brightened the room. But, she was barely recognizable in this photo; almost naked, dazed, eyes apparently dulled by drugs.

If I hadn't just met her, or if I ran into her on the street, I'd never recognize her. There wasn't a doubt in my mind that she'd made a mistake that would haunt her for the rest of her life. I clicked on the photo of Molly, and my browser switched to a new profile, this one for her.

After a huge blowout with my boyfrend, I was looking for fun. Island Giant made sure I got it. He had XTC that made my nite awesum. Jimmy is huge and he did me over and over. Anytime he wants it, I'm ready. Screw my asshole boyfriend, he's so gone.

There was more about Molly and her taste in men. There were also about fifty "friends" who said they wanted to meet Molly the next time they were in Honolulu. I went back to Stone's page and began clicking on some of the other women's photos. They all had similar stories. I remembered Molly's plea—just because it was there didn't make it true. I reviewed a few of the other women's stories. Several of them sounded suspiciously alike. They had the same spelling errors. They used the same jargon.

Had Molly really posted her info? Or was Stone offering up testimonials? John had called Stone a braggart. He'd also said that Stone had no fear of retribution over what he was posting, true or not. I called Alexander's cell phone; he answered on the second ring.

I said, "You need to get over here. We've uncovered Stone's MySpace page—you won't believe this."

"What you doing on MySpace, brah?"

"Later. I'll tell you later. Are you coming?"

"I just finished a tour. I still have to tie down the boat. It could take me an hour to get there. You supplying lunch?"

"You know what, I just might."

I checked out the Business link. There weren't any pictures of women in this area, but it had a photo of Shapiro's plane and more bragging about Stone's importance and how he had saved a small, failing business. He didn't name the business, but it sounded suspiciously like Shapiro's. There was another photo of the partners, the one that I'd found in Shapiro's records. Then there was one showing the cargo hold of the plane. The hold was stuffed full of boxes like the one from Shapiro's storage area. Violins. Going where?

The caption read: "My personal aircraft for delivering musical instruments to my stores on each island." Stone's bio had said he liked flying. Was he a pilot also?

The bio moved on to the music business and lessons offered by Stone. There were details about instruments sold by Stone Music and claims that they sold more violins than any other musical instrument store in the islands. In fact, the site said, they sold hundreds of violins each month. Hundreds? Here? Did he sell on the Internet?

There was a discussion about what a wonderful music teacher James Stone was. He'd taught hundreds of children and adults to play. There were photos of a few of his prodigies; a child playing at a concert at the Iolani Palace, another who had gone on to a recording contract with a "major mainland record label" and another who had been accepted at the Juilliard School of Music in New York. The accomplishments continued and the hype sounded good. Too good, in fact. I wondered how much of it was true. After the date-enhancing section, the show-off tone gave away the author in an instant. Molly's words echoed in my head as I realized that this site was all about Stone's ego and had nothing to do with a legitimate business.

I returned to the Island Giant page and clicked the link for "No Boundaries." I fully expected this to be an invitation-only area, and it was.

Meyer tapped my shoulder. "Finding anything important?"

I think I jumped about a foot. Talk about feeling like a teenager caught with his hand in his pants. I cleared my throat, "Stone's a bastard. He uses date-rape drugs on women, then posts his exploits here. It appears that he's creating fake accounts so that some of the women can brag about him. He likes to brag, but he's careful."

"What's that mean?"

"It means certain women would never report that they've been taken advantage of by someone like Stone. It would be too damaging to their careers. Does Molly strike you as the kind who'd put compromising photos on a web site?"

"No way, no how."

"Exactly. So let's see." I dialed the number and Molly answered on the second ring.

"Molly, this is McKenna, thanks for your message. I found the account."

I could sense her stiffening up. "I have nothing more to say, Mr. McKenna."

"I don't mean to bother you, but would you just answer one question? Please?"

"Fine. What is it?"

"Do you have a MySpace account?"

"God no! Are you kidding? There's no way I would—why are you asking me that?"

"I think Stone might have created one in your name."

There was a long pause, then the sobs began. "Omigod. That bastard. That dirty— That's why I've been getting all that—that—awful—e-mail."

"You've been getting e-mail about, um, dates?"

"I always suspected him, but didn't know what to do. I just started deleting them."

If Stone had used Molly's e-mail as a way to harass her, then her real address must be on the account. "Can you hang on one second? I think I can fix this for you."

"I just want this to stop!"

"Hang on then." I put the phone down and took another look at Molly's MySpace home page. Sure enough, there was a Forgot Your Password link. I clicked the link and got a form that requested an e-mail address. I picked up the phone. "What's your e-mail?"

"Why do you need that?"

"In order to close out your account, I need to be able to access it. It looks like all I need is your e-mail to request the password."

She gave me the address, which I entered, and then clicked the button. A polite little message telling me how wonderful it was for them to be serving my needs greeted me. "Check your e-mail."

A sniffle, a pause. "What?"

"I need you to tell me your password."

"I have no idea what it would be. I didn't even know he'd started an account in my name."

There must have been a welcome message sent out by MySpace, which Molly had most likely trashed without reading it. "Check your e-mail, you should have it by now."

A few seconds later, she said, "Oh, Christ. The password, it's CrankyBitch, capital C and capital B."

"You're not one of those."

"Wait'll I tell my boyfriend. He'll kill him."

"We'll get him for killing Bob Shapiro. I'm just sure of it. Don't make your life any worse by dwelling on this."

"That's easy for you to say." She hung up and left me listening to a dial tone.

Meyer lurked over my shoulder again. "Well?"

"I think we're in business." The first step would be to see what was in the No Boundaries blog. I went back to Stone's page. The No Boundaries area was only available to invited friends of James Stone. Since Molly had just suffered with the harassment instead of trying to find the source of the problem, she'd never even known to come here. Never known that she was a "Friend."

I clicked the No Boundaries link.

I entered Molly's e-mail address and her password.

A few seconds later, I was rewarded with access to Stone's innermost secrets.

31

The deafening boom-boom-boom of a rap beat blasted from my speakers. The screen background color turned jet-black and crimson. I listened to the words of the rap song in awe. "Pushin' drugs, pushin' fun, gettin' it all around. Kill the cop, kill the fed who try to bring us down!"

I muted the volume and stared up at Meyer. "Jesus. Talk about vicious."

He stood with his mouth agape. Finally, he nodded. "I call that crap music."

"It's so—angry."

Meyer pointed at my screen. "What's that?"

I'd been so disoriented by the music that I hadn't noticed what he was pointing at. But there, right in the middle, as part of the background, was the chalk outline of a body. The shape reminded me of the popular Hollywood-style body outlines so frequently used on police TV shows—the ones that real cops seldom use.

I started reading the text, which was difficult because it was red text on a black and crimson background. The chalk marks were in red, so it blended in with the words on the page.

> If you've got a yearning to cross the Stoneman, you've got a
> yearning to die. Nobody messes with the Stoneman. You don't
> steal from me. You don't cheat me. You don't mess with me at

all. If you do, you're dead. Just like Shapiro. The stupid son-of-a-bitch thought he could steal my product and learned the hard way. Wound up face down in the street because he got greedy and stupid.

I read it again, just to be sure I wasn't hallucinating. A confession? Online?

"Is this guy insane?" I pointed at the screen. "I've never seen anyone do something so stupid. Read this."

The lines on his face were etched with sadness. "Can't. The writing looks like a big blur to me."

I read it to him.

He sat, his jaw slack. A tear formed in his eye, he wiped it away, then sniffled. "I'd call him a sociopath."

I countered, "I'd call him an asshole."

Meyer chuckled. "Okay, he's a sociopathic asshole."

I said, "This is just the first thing I found. I'm going to document it. Give me some time to get through the rest of his site."

I created a new folder on my computer and named it "Shapiro Case." Then, I started another folder under that one, and titled this one "Stone." I opened Microsoft Word, then went back to Stone's web page. I copied the text and pasted it into Word. I made a note that it had been copied from his site, listed the URL and the date and time.

I went on to the next page. A chill ran down my spine when I saw the photo on the page. It was Roger Lau. Below his photo, there was a caption that read: "Missing Since May 16, 2011." The photo had been put onto a black and crimson background, on which, once again, there was text. As I read the words, Stone's coldness seeped through.

On May 16, 2011, Roger Lau went missing. He had a wife, two kids, a dog, a mortgage, lots of relatives and, who gives a shit. He tried threatening the Stoneman. Was he so stupid as to think he could get away with that? He must have had no brains at all because now he's gone. Vanished. Disappeared from the face of the earth.

Not exactly a confession, but close. I already hated Stone and his total lack of concern for anyone other than himself. But, how could he be stopped? The answer was in McKenna's Sixth Skip Tracing Secret: people are weak, so use their weaknesses against them. Stone was arrogant, just like Johnny Bakerton had been. Johnny had been so arrogant that he'd forgotten to play defense. Stone's weakness was his bragging and his drugs, and that would bring him down. I'd brought down Johnny; why not Stone? I said, "I need Harris. She's got that user name and password from the original tip. I'm going to go get her. We can turn all of this over to the cops. This is way more than enough to get them to investigate."

I extended my fist. Meyer looked at it quizzically, then I saw recognition. He extended his arm gingerly and we tapped knuckles. Man, were we cool? I half-trotted to Harris's apartment. I peeked through the window and spotted her at her computer. I knocked, she glanced up, then came to the door.

"Hey, McKenna, what's up?" She seemed somewhat distant and uninterested. She was also dressed more conservatively than normal. Too bad about that part.

"We've got it. All of it. We know why Roger was killed. Why Shapiro got run down. We've even got the drugs they were smuggling! And this—" I pulled the flash drive from my shirt pocket. "This came from Shapiro's safe-deposit box. I'll bet it has more damaging evidence on it." I dropped the little drive back into my pocket.

A smile spread across Harris's face and she gave me a huge hug. "You are sooo good! Let's see what you've got." She locked up and we went back to my place.

We did a quick replay to catch Harris up on what Meyer and I had found. Then, it was time to continue on into new territory. We found more about Roger. Stone ranted about what a crappy mechanic Roger had been and how much he'd overcharged his best customers. He claimed that it was a waste of air to even let Roger breathe and now that he was gone, that wasted air wasn't wasted anymore.

"He is so going to pay," said Harris.

I copied everything and put it into another Word file. I said, "If the police investigated and found this, it could be damning stuff. But is it even admissible? And what's it going to prove? That he's nothing more than an asshole in the court of life?"

Harris gave me a wink. "Don't worry about that. Cops all over the country are waking up to these social web sites and online evidence. If Stone's got half a brain, this will scare the shit out of him."

"But he's not going to know about it until we go to the cops."

"Exactly my point. Once he's arrested and hears about this, he's going to get plenty worried."

The next link was titled, Mr. Kanakua. I sucked in a breath as I remembered the envelope from the bank. He put information about his drug connection here? I half-expected to see another face or a chalk outline. Instead, it was a photo of a violin. I'm not much of a violin connoisseur, but it sure looked to me like the one Shapiro had had in his storage closet.

The text on this page seemed like it had been written by someone who was, perhaps, human.

Mr. Kanakua was an original violin created by a Japanese Violin Master in 1998. The original violin was sold for over $10,000 to a West Coast dot-com executive whose kid had been accepted at Juilliard School of Music. The kid took lessons from me whenever he was on-island, which was several months each year from 1997-2001.

The original Mr. Kanakua's front face was made from spruce, the neck from ebony, and the back from spruce. It took the creator nearly six months to build Mr. Kanakua, which he named after his maternal grandfather, a master violin maker in his own right.

Harris said, "Looks like he thinks more of his damn violin than he does of people."

Meyer crossed his arms over his chest. His facial expression became stern. "Watch it, violins shouldn't be blamed for people problems."

Harris rolled her eyes, "Whatever."

Harris and I read the next section together. Meyer went off to sulk.

Our copies of Mr. Kanakua are nearly exact replicas. I obtained the specifications for Mr. Kanakua from the creator of the original in exchange for successfully handling an embarrassing situation in which he was caught in a Honolulu brothel by HPD on the eve of his wedding to a wealthy Japanese woman. By intervening with the arresting officers as they were pulling the creator of the original Mr. Kanakua from the bed of his hooker, he and his bride were spared much embarrassment. In fact, had the bride known about the hooker, she would have canceled the wedding. Of course, had the creator of the original Mr. Kanakua known that the arresting officers were really construction workers in rented costume-shop uniforms, he probably wouldn't have been too happy either.

Construction workers? Meyer had said that he recognized one of the workers at Willows Construction. So Stone liked to play games, too.

We have hundreds of Mr. Kanakua replicas in circulation around the islands. Most of the violins have fabulous sound, just like the original. However, there are some that need a slight modification before their sound is at its peak. These, of course, are the expensive violins and you'll know if you've got one. Click here to learn how to make the modifications to Mr. Kanakua.

I copied the text and pasted it into a new document, which I titled, Mr. Kanakua. I was curious as to what modifications would be needed on a violin to improve the sound, so when I was done, I clicked the link.

Modifications to improve the sound of the special Mr. Kanakua violin.

First, using a sharp, thin-bladed knife, slice completely around the violin between the front face and the sidewall.

Second, remove the top of the violin by sliding out the face plate.

Third, remove the plastic baggies that have been taped inside the violin body.

Fourth, using the small tube of glue from one of the plastic baggies, put a bead of glue around the top of the violin sidewall.

Fifth, slide the faceplate back in place and let sit until set.

I stared at my computer screen. Harris kissed me on the cheek and gave me a very close hug. I couldn't believe I was thinking about getting laid at a time like this, but I was.

"You have hit the mother lode, McKenna," she said.

That's not all I was hoping to hit. "You're right, we have more than enough to get the cops to investigate at least Stone and possibly, by association, Frank Willows. So many things are making sense, the safe-deposit box envelope, Shapiro's death. It doesn't say that he did kill him, but he sure implies that if someone stole one of his violins and Stone discovered it, he would."

"Maybe Shapiro tried to sell the drugs?" said Harris.

I shook my head, "They wouldn't be nice and safe in the bank. They'd be out on the streets. Maybe Shapiro tried to blackmail Stone?"

Harris's eyes lit up. "Wait. You actually have the drugs?"

"Not here, no."

She turned away and muttered, "Damn."

I called across the room to Meyer, "You know those drugs in the bank?"

He moved his head back a smidge, and his eyes narrowed. "Yeah?"

"They came from one of Stone's violins."

"Very funny, McKenna. Just because I played as a kid." He moved closer.

"No, it's true. It's right here."

"What would drugs be doing in a violin, for crying out loud?"

"It was Stone's transportation method. Look, here's complete instructions on how to take that violin apart and put it back together." I read the instructions.

As I read, Meyer walked over and picked up the violin. He examined the area around the faceplate carefully. "That'd make sense. Some moron without any training put this back together. That really irks me. That someone would use one of these as a suitcase."

"That's Mr. Kanakua."

"No way, this ain't Mr. Kanakua. That violin was built by a Japanese craftsman. He—"

I interrupted, "You know about Mr. Kanakua?"

"It's a small world. The violin world."

"I'll bet you don't know this. The craftsman got caught with his pants down with a Honolulu hooker by HPD. In order to avoid spending time in the Hawaiian poky, he gave the specs to Stone. The craftsman doesn't know he was set up by Stone. The cops weren't real. The cops were construction workers."

"See, I told you I recognized those morons."

Like I said before, I hate I told you so's, but I had this one coming. "You're right. Stone got the specs for Mr. Kanakua and he's been making knockoffs to use as mules for his drug trafficking. Pretty damn smart, if you ask me."

"Pisses me off."

"Me, too," said Harris. "I think Shapiro got caught trying to blackmail Stone. Why else would the drugs be in that bank?"

Meyer countered, "My money's on the Daniels character."

"But he was Shapiro's friend," I said.

"He's no good, I tell you. No good at all."

"You think he figured out Stone's angle?" I asked.

Meyer nodded. "Bob was too wrapped up in his business. All he wanted to do was fly. He was too trusting and never would've guessed that Stone was smuggling. Never would've believed he could get caught up in something like that."

"That would explain why Daniels wants the violin so bad. He thinks the drugs are still in it. So Shapiro was hedging his bets by storing the drugs in the bank. That way, Daniels couldn't get to them either."

"Everything points to someone blackmailing Stone," said Harris. "Maybe it was Shapiro; maybe Daniels. But, we can't go to the cops yet."

"Why not? We've got everything we need. It's all wrapped up nice and neat, it's time to give the cops a present."

She smiled and held my gaze. What little secret was she keeping this time?

"Come on, Harris, what more could we possibly need?" I said.

She smiled. "A confession."

32

I felt like a feather on a duck in a stiff wind, no longer sure I could hang on. Legs wanted a confession?

Meyer, who had probably missed her last comment, said, "You gonna call the cops, McKenna?"

I ignored him and spoke to Harris. "This was never about getting a confession; it was about compiling information. I'm ready. I want to turn this in. What's that password?"

Harris shook her head. She was steadfast. "I'm not giving it to you. We need more. A lot more. If we can meet with Stone and get him to confess, think of how much that would be worth."

Worth to who?

"McKenna, what are you gonna do about the cops?"

I yelled, "Shut up, Meyer!" I turned to Harris. There was something drastically wrong in this picture. I'd seen the signs that Harris was changing the game, but I'd ignored them. I'd been warned by Alexander and Julia about her and I'd ignored that, too. I turned away and stared out at the ocean. I needed clarity. I faced Harris and said, "Let's go down to the beach for a minute."

She plucked the flash drive from my shirt pocket. "Let's look at this first. You're not going to want to miss what's on here."

Did she already know what was on that drive? It was no more than the size of my finger. On one end was a USB connector, which she inserted into an empty slot on the side of my notebook.

Windows, my operating system, came alive as it sensed a new member of its little computer world. Only one file popped up on my screen; Harris double-clicked the mouse on the name. The media player started up, said it was loading, then the little hourglass turned into an arrow. Well, I'll be damned. I was looking at a view of a man facing a camera.

"This is Robert M. Shapiro, Jr. Today is Saturday, May 7, 2011, and I'm about to have a meeting with James Stone and Frank Willows. As a witness to this meeting, Dadrian Daniels is watching via the internet and is recording this meeting."

We heard a knock on Shapiro's door. He stood, left the picture, then returned, followed by Willows and another man, the one holding the guitar from Stone's MySpace page. They all sat, Shapiro on the couch, Stone and Willows on chairs next to each other.

Willows spoke first. "Well, Bob, you wanted this meeting. What's up?"

"I know what's been going on, why you two wanted the partnership agreement written the way it was. I was so naive before, but now I realize what you're using my plane for. I want out."

Stone said, "What the hell are you talking about? All we're getting is some inter-island transportation. My stores do lots of business and we—"

"That's bullshit! And you know it. I don't want to transport any more of your 'violins.'" Shapiro raised both hands and made quotation marks in the air.

"Come on, Bob," said Willows. "You know perfectly well that's a legal contract. You don't like it, that's too bad." He started to stand and Shapiro held up his hand.

"Maybe you're not aware of this, Frank, but Jim is transporting drugs, not just violins."

Stone leaped to his feet. "Lying son-of-a-bitch. I'll sue you for defamation."

"I don't think it's going to be considered defamation when the cops see what's in your violins," said Shapiro. "I think that's called drug trafficking. Maybe you're both in it."

Willows ground his teeth. "You got any proof of this?"

Shapiro nodded. "All I need."

"You're the one who did that? Why you—"

"Shut up, Jimmy. Bob's got you by the short hairs. But he's missing something. Shapiro, you try going to the cops and you'll be implicated too. They'll never believe you didn't know what cargo you were carrying. Especially after we explain how it was you who approached us for help in the first place. You're screwed too."

Stone added, "You are so goddamned dead."

Willows held out his hand and put it on Stone's shoulder. He turned to Shapiro, "You signed that agreement. You want out, you've got to buy us out. You go to the cops, nobody knows what's going to happen. Nobody wins. You buy us out, everyone wins."

"I don't have that kind of money."

"Call Daniels' bitch and pay up your life insurance."

Willows grabbed Stone's shoulder hard. "Goddammit, Jimmy, no more threats."

Stone nodded. "I want my violin back for starters."

Shapiro shook his head. He moved forward and sat on the edge of the couch. "No way. That's my insurance. Here's the deal. I keep the violin safe. You stop using my plane. When I get enough cash together, I'll buy you out and give your precious violin back. We part company and life goes on."

"How the hell did you figure this out?" said Stone.

"Things didn't add up."

"Bullshit. Someone tipped you off. Was it Daniels?"

Shapiro tried not to say anything, but it was obvious from the way he glanced away that Stone had hit a nerve. Shapiro would have made a lousy poker player.

"That shit!"

"Jimmy. Remember what we talked about?"

Stone smiled and sat back in his chair. "Fine. Do it your way."

Willows turned back to Shapiro and said, "Here's what we're prepared to offer. You've got 24 hours to turn over the violin. I'm a reasonable guy as long as I'm not pissed off. Unfortunately, you're treading very close to ground where you don't want to be." Willows paused for a moment, then his voice grew in intensity with each word. "If you decide to tell the cops, remember that you're going down with us."

Willows moved quickly from his chair and jammed his knee between Shapiro's legs. Shapiro buckled forward, but Willows gripped him by the neck and shoved him against the couch until his back was arched and his head pressed against the wall. Tears flowed from Shapiro's eyes. He launched a feeble swing at Willows, but his body went rigid when Willows jammed his knee into his crotch again. Willows ground out, "Are we clear?"

Shapiro finally nodded. When he did, Willows let go and stood. "Let's go Jimmy. I think Mr. Shapiro has a better understanding of our arrangement now." Shapiro slumped over into the fetal position on the couch.

Stone smiled. "Yeah, I think he's got it." He leaned forward until his face was inches from Shapiro's. "Don't screw this up, Bobby-boy. Otherwise, you could become another page on MySpace." Stone laughed as he stood. He and Willows made their way to the front door. Stone said, "Oh, don't get up, Bobby, we'll show ourselves out."

In the background, we heard the sound of the front door opening, then the voice of Frank Willows. "You and that goddamn MySpace. You're a damned addict. You need help."

As they walked out, Stone said, "No way, man, it's my outlet. You got that—" Their voices faded away as the door closed.

A few minutes later, Shapiro pulled himself up from the couch and approached the webcam. The picture went dead. The following night, Shapiro had met Willows for dinner. He'd probably refused the offer. Then he'd died. At the hands of Stone? Or Willows? Which one had driven the car?

"Time to call the cops," I said. "This is everything they'll need."

Meyer said, "These guys have already been to my place a couple of times. I can't go back until they're locked up. We all know that. This better do the job."

Harris waved her hands. "Hello. This isn't enough. You two aren't getting it. We need a confession. What we saw was only a threat. We've got to get Stone to admit he killed Shapiro. Then we'll be in business."

I told myself that Harris's concussion was causing her to make these weird judgments—that's why she was doing this. Or were my friends right about her? "Let's take that walk on the beach."

She shrugged. "Sure, hon."

We crossed over the short grassy area and onto the beach. We both pulled off our sandals as we neared the water. Here, the waves cooled the sand, making it possible to walk barefoot comfortably.

Harris said, "You don't like my plan?"

I hated it. It scared the hell out of me. I lied, "It's not that. I love it."

"I knew you'd like that recording. So what's wrong?"

What was wrong? How had she known what was on the drive? I remembered her excuse for leaving shortly after Daniels left, how she'd been pulling away in the last day or so. Had she already met with Daniels? I shrugged. "I just needed a few minutes away from Meyer. He's getting on my nerves."

"Kind of annoying, all that can't hear stuff."

"Yeah, very. He's not even a baseball fan."

"You're kidding. That's like, un-American."

"I know. It's America's game. And we Dodgers fans have to stick together, right?"

"I love that team, my dad took me and my sister all the time."

I nodded. "See, we connect. He's just—"

"I know." She stroked my arm.

"You know what I used to hate?" I said.

"What? When they lost? The food?"

I chuckled. "No, the traffic. It's such a bear there. It's bad here, but going to a game, jeez. Thank God they have the Metro Rail system. I always took it to the stadium."

She smiled and nodded. "That was so convenient. A lot better than fighting the traffic from El Monte."

I gave her a hug. "Let me work on Meyer. I'll get him to come around to your idea."

She squeezed me hard. "Thanks, McKenna, you're a doll."

And a liar. There's no Metro Rail station anywhere near Dodger Stadium.

33

When I returned to my apartment, I found Meyer sitting on the couch. He probably thought I'd send him packing after the way I'd yelled at him earlier. He had his hands folded in his lap like a kid waiting for discipline and gave me an expectant look as I approached. He seemed surprised when I said, "Tell me what happened in Korea."

He glanced away. After a short silence, he said, "Not much to tell."

"Try me anyway."

He got a faraway look in his eyes and he started to tear up again. "We were assaulted from all sides. We took heavy fire and men were dropping faster than we could count. The enemy had stationed a few of theirs up on a hill with a machine gun. We were sitting ducks. All I did was crawl to the top of the hill. Government said I killed three Koreans up there and a bunch of others before our guys turned the tide. Me, I don't remember a thing until a week later when I woke up in an army hospital. All's I know is that our guys didn't need to die that day."

I'd begun to suspect that Meyer had a strength of character that Harris, and even I, lacked. "How many did you save?"

"Fourteen good men died that day."

"But how many didn't die because of you?"

"Bob saved some guys in Vietnam. He was like you, kept talking about the ones who lived. He was trying to help me understand before—well, before I check out of this world myself. He was more than a friend; he kept me going."

Meyer slumped forward in his chair. He wiped at his cheek. "I never knew Bob until I became his landlord, but he makes fifteen because he didn't need to die either. Actually, sixteen when you count Roger. He got medals himself in Vietnam."

"How many, Meyer?"

His jaw tightened and he croaked. "Eighteen survived."

I realized now why Meyer felt such a loss—and what I'd never found in Shapiro's boxes. "What happened to Bob's medal? Why wasn't there anything—"

"I buried that and the photos of the presentation with him. So he'd have it forever. Why'd you want to know about Korea?"

"I'm tired of murder, drugs and liars."

Meyer cocked his head to one side. "Who's a liar?"

"Harris. She's a fraud. I don't know who she is, but she's not from LA. And me, I'm a liar, too."

Meyer shook his head. "You lie for a reason, a good one, to get to the truth. I ain't so sure about her."

I pulled her rental application from my files, unsure if I was angrier with Harris or myself for believing in her. I found the letter from The National Geographic Society. It was signed by Elmore G. Pendergast, Editor. There was no specific contact information for Mr. Pendergast, but there was the toll-free number for the National Geographic Society in the masthead. I searched their web site first and found nothing for an editor by that name. I tried the toll-free number. They, too, told me they had never heard the name before. So, there was no assignment. No letter of authorization. Nothing.

Next, I searched Google for Harris Galvin. Another big nothing. I went to AnyWho.com. No records. I tried everything I could think of and kept getting the same result. No Harris Galvin.

Meyer stood behind me. "What in the dickens are you trying to do?"

"Find something, anything, on Harris. She doesn't exist."

"You didn't check her out when she rented from you?"

"That only confirmed that there was nothing negative. There's nothing at all. She's a ghost."

Meyer shrugged. "Well, she hasn't bounced any checks or anything, right?"

"For all I know, she's part of the witness protection program."

"You think so?"

"Noooo. She played me. I don't know how or why—not yet anyway. Hey, what about the flash drive. Where is it?"

"I dunno, I thought you had it."

We spent the next fifteen minutes tearing apart the room. Thank goodness I didn't have a webcam in my apartment, otherwise, it would have looked as if we were practicing for one of those funniest videos they show on TV. I'd search one place, then Meyer would. I'd forget that I'd searched there, so I'd do it again. Then so would he. Finally, after arguing over who'd lost the video for about the third time, we realized that only one person could have it. Harris.

I stormed out the door and to her apartment, determined to confront her and get the drive back. I banged on her door. Through the window, I spotted her finishing up a conversation. Man, this woman could talk. Her voice drifted through the open window. "Be sure he's got it. All of it."

A pause.

"Thanks. Two o'clock. Where we discussed."

The door opened. I said, "Where is it?"

"What?"

"The flash drive. You must have pulled it from my PC. Give it to me. Now."

"Sorry, no can do. My sister needs that."

And that's when I realized what she was doing. The "who" was James Stone or Frank Willows. The "it" was money, probably a bundle. And at two o'clock Harris would sell that flash drive. How blind I'd been. Harris had a partner and it wasn't me. I was just the patsy. "I won't let you do this. I'm calling the cops."

"Wait!"

"It's too late, Harris, or whoever you are—you're not Harris Galvin."

Irritation flashed in her eyes, then disappeared. She raised her hands in front of her, as if in surrender. "Okay. You figured it out. I'll give you the drive." Her shoulders slumped. "Come on in, I'll get it."

Whoa! She'd given that up way too easily. She was the best liar I'd ever seen, what was she up to? I stepped into her apartment. A small camera bag lay on the floor to one side. Next to it was a toothbrush, a small tube of toothpaste, a sweatshirt, a small makeup bag, and the two-thousand-dollar camera. "You were going to leave after you got the money."

She nodded. "You're just too sharp for your own good."

I glanced around the apartment. "You're leaving everything else? What about all your camera gear? Your furniture? Your clothes? I'd have to get rid of all of this."

As she crossed the room to the camera bag, she said, "The furniture's rented. You could give the clothes away. And the camera gear, well, that's from my last job."

"Job?"

"Yeah, my last job."

What kind of job gave you thousands of dollars worth of equipment?

She reached into the bag and began to rummage through it. "I put the drive in here." She turned to face me, her face grim, a small pistol pointed directly at my chest. She shouldered the camera bag. "I'm sorry. I was trying to keep you out of this, now you'll just have to do me one last favor."

Of course, her last job. "You stole it." How dense could I be? Well, I had nothing she could want. "I don't have any money, Harris."

"I don't need your money. You know, you're good. Almost as good as me. You got me with that Dodgers thing."

I cocked an eyebrow in her direction. "How'd you know I was lying?"

"Your body went stiff when I hugged you. That's a first. I knew something was off, so I came back and checked it out. Nice touch, but it did give me an idea. You, Mr. Professional Skip Tracer, are going to meet with James Stone on the corner of Kalakaua and Kapiolani in just a little over an hour. You're going to collect a briefcase full of cash."

"And then what?"

"Why, honey, I disappear."

"What about me? You're going to leave me with Stone?"

She shrugged. "Well, you'll still have the drugs and you can probably use those to negotiate. I'm sorry about that, but how you two resolve your differences is going to have to be between the two of you. I'm sure you'll figure something out."

34

Harris draped a beach towel over the gun and jabbed it into my back. She did the usual one-wrong-move threat and guided me back to my apartment. When we entered, Meyer appeared agitated to see me and Harris together. On the other hand, after she'd closed the blinds and the slider, which would give the impression that I wasn't home, he didn't seem surprised at all when she pulled out the gun.

He said, "Guess this means you two ain't on friendly terms anymore."

Harris pushed me down onto the couch. "No, we're all still friends. For another hour or so."

I said, "Gonna get close in here."

Harris sat, still grim-faced. "We'll survive. In half an hour, we can leave."

I leaned forward, elbows on knees staring into her eyes. "So, how much was true? You said your sister needs this money. Does she really need a transplant?"

"Don't try to scam me, McKenna. I'm a pro."

"I got that—now. I was just curious about why you'd do something like this."

She shrugged. "Whatever. I wasn't planning this, things got out of control back home, so I had to leave for a while."

"San Francisco."

"Don't get too curious."

But I was. "You never had a concussion, did you?"

She smiled. "Nice touch, huh? I had some headaches, but when you guys kept going on about doctors, I just couldn't resist. Besides, it kept you off balance."

"And there's no sister, is there?"

"All you need to know is that I'm Harris Galvin from El Monte and I have a twin sister who needs a kidney transplant. As the old joke goes, if I tell you anything else, I'll have to kill you."

"You need me."

She shook her head. "I've still got him." She pointed the gun at Meyer.

We sat in silence for a few more minutes, the temperature rising in the apartment. We all jumped when there was a sudden knocking on the door. I said, "That's Alexander. I called him and asked him over for lunch."

Alexander called out, "McKenna! I know you in there. How come the place is all shut up?"

She whispered, "Send him away."

"Where? What do want me to tell him?"

"McKenna, come on. Open up. It's me."

"Send him away." She pointed the gun at Meyer's head. "Tell him to go get lunch or something."

Good idea, Legs. I went to the door. "Hey, Alexander, change of plans buddy. Can you go get us some lunch? I'll buy—pay you when you get back. I'm not, uh, dressed right now."

"Fine, you want your usual?"

"Yeah. Get me a Magnum burger and some Volcano fries. Get three, Meyer's here, too. And don't worry about the expense, I'm buying."

"What? You don't eat—"

I interrupted him, "I know they're expensive. But, this is a special occasion. Magnum burger, definitely. Volcano fries, no question. I'll fill you in over lunch."

There was a short pause. "Okay. If you say so. I be back in maybe twenty, thirty minutes. Depends on how busy they are."

"What was that all about?" Harris glared at me, then pointed the gun at my face.

"You—you, told me to have him go—get some lunch."

"Where's he going?"

"There's a restaurant down on Waikiki, he likes it there."

"You'd better not be lying."

I shook my head. "It's one of his favorite places. They've got pretty waitresses in short shorts. He might not be back for an hour or so. If they're busy, he'll have to wait. He may even have a beer while he's there. With the parking and everything, he could be gone a long time."

Harris appeared satisfied. "All right. We'll give him two minutes, then we're going. Give me your cell phone. I don't want you making any calls."

Ugh. So much for Plan B. I could only hope that Alexander had understood my coded message—go to Lulu's Restaurant.

35

Perfect, I thought. Just goddamn perfect. Here I stood on a Waikiki Beach street corner waiting to meet a killer. No cell phone. No way to escape without getting Meyer killed. And wearing a goddamn Giant's hat. I'd feel better standing around in that stupid dancing bear getup I always joked about—at least with that no one would recognize me.

I glanced across the street and up to the second floor. The bitch was in Lulu's Restaurant, smiling at Meyer, sipping a cool drink, enjoying the trades as they drifted through. From her vantage point she could see my every move and keep her gun close enough to quickly kill my friend. If I screwed up, Meyer would die and Harris would disappear.

An ABC Store occupied the first floor of the building with the restaurant. Next to that stood one of Waikiki's many skyscraper hotels, the Park Shore. I suppose Stone could have taken a room and be watching over me. Or maybe he'd hidden behind me at the zoo entrance. Or on one of the other street corners. Would he find my behavior suspicious? Would he recognize the box I carried? And where was Daniels? No matter how hard I tried, I couldn't shake the memory of the conversation with Harris.

"It's simple, McKenna. I'll be sitting in that restaurant at the window. I can see your every move. If you do something to scare off Stone or if you try to tip him off about where I'm at, I'll shoot Meyer and disappear in the confusion. You, on the other hand, will be watched by Mr. Daniels. Because he thinks you lied to him about the violin, he's quite willing to kill you if I tell him to or if you do something that he considers, um, uncooperative. Your only chance to save both of you is to play this exactly the way I told you to. You tell him you're just the drop man, I'll be watching from somewhere and if he pays up, he gets the safe-deposit box key as well as the flash drive."

"But then I won't have the drugs or the evidence. I won't have any leverage!"

"Sorry about that, hon, guess you're out of bargaining chips."

Meyer had remained silent. He and I most likely had the same questions. Are you intending to kill us? How will we stop him from killing us? And the ever popular, what if he double-crosses you? Crap, that put us back to the first question.

"There's a dead-man's switch. If I don't stop it, my e-mail service sends an e-mail to the police with a copy of the flash drive file attached and links to Stone's web pages. And there are images of Stone's web pages, too. So it won't do him any good to delete the pages from MySpace."

She'd even given Meyer her good camera, saying that it would give him something to hang onto. Actually, I think the fancy Nikon with the big lens and flash attachment was meant to serve as a prop. It would divert attention from the real action. He'd be viewed as the tourist sugar daddy, she as arm candy. The men would envy him, the women would despise him, all for flaunting a woman like Harris.

Harris was so thorough and yet, she'd involved me. I'd asked, "Why'd you need me? You could have pulled this off all on your own."

"Actually, you were a good investigator—found the plane, the people, in no time when I wasn't one hundred percent. And you had the connections through Alexander. I don't know if I could have done this without you."

So I was good for something—screwing up my friend's family.

She pointed her gun at Meyer. "You're driving, by the way. I won't be needing a car."

Meyer's jaw dropped. "You don't drive either?"

She said, "It's a little trick I picked up from McKenna. There are plenty of ways out of Waikiki if you don't want to drive. And there are just as many ways off the island. The cops can't watch them all."

Had she thought of everything? How depressing, the woman was a planning genius.

I waited, every now and again stealing a glance at the restaurant across the street. Nothing. Just tourists. Surfers. Couples strolling arm-in-arm. A family with five sunburnt kids that ran in every direction made their pass on their way to the Honolulu Zoo. Dad was oblivious. Mom looked like she was trying to herd cats, her frustration ready to overflow. The main entrance to the zoo was just a few hundred feet behind me. Soon, they'd be having a great time. They'd watch wild animals from around the world. I'd be here, completely panicked. I checked. Two-fifteen. Harris still sat up there with Meyer. But, there was no sign of Alexander. He must have misunderstood. I was so screwed.

Someone planted a vice-like grip on my shoulder, then spun me around. He wore jeans, a tee shirt and a light, nylon jacket. The jacket hung on one side, as though he'd stuffed a gun in the pocket. And, thank goodness, he carried a briefcase in one hand. Had he brought the money?

"That my violin in that box?" His breath smelled of alcohol, lots of it. His dilated pupils and the way he swayed on his feet reinforced the obvious—he'd gotten loaded for the occasion.

"That's it, you have the money?"

"You're not very bright, old man. But I'm feeling benevolent—here in the midst of frigging Waikiki." Stone leaned over and whispered, "Don't worry, I'm not going to kill you right now. Where's Daniels?"

"Daniels?"

"Don't screw with me, I know he set this up."

I shook my head. "I'm just here to deliver and collect."

Stone shrugged. "I know he's doing this for that little bitch, Molly. I'll deal with her after I'm done with you. Hand it over."

Oh, shit, she was Daniels' girlfriend. She'd gotten my number from him. "Not so fast. I need to see the money." Where were the cops when you needed them?

Stone did a half-assed survey of the area. People moved in every direction. Some crossed the street toward the beach. Others strolled back to their hotels or downtown. The same thing with the zoo. Harris had picked her location well. This was a completely open, yet completely private meeting area. No one cared. No one wanted to be bothered by the other people. And she could sit and watch it all from the comfort of a second-floor window seat.

Stone's senses were obviously dulled. He seemed unconcerned with whether we were being watched or not. "How stupid do you think I am, old man? I ain't showing you nothing until I see that violin and its contents. It had better all be there. Understand."

I did, and it wasn't. The drugs were still in the safe-deposit box. Where the hell was Alexander? Where were the cops?

He swayed more than a palm tree in the wind. "Some people don't like my business. You apparently don't mind it, not if you want money. Or maybe you and Daniels think you can replace me. Let me give you a hint, you're too old for that shit. Besides, Daniels will screw you over the first chance he gets. Now give me my goddamn package and we can all go away happy."

I breathed a sigh of relief, he wanted to talk, to intimidate me first. Well that wasn't going to work—I was already intimidated.

Stone leaned into me again, his face now just inches from mine. "It's going to cost you your life if you keep up this shit."

I considered holding my nose, but resisted the temptation. "The money?"

Stone grabbed my shirt. Uh, maybe I could be intimidated more.

"I'll bury you right here if you give me any more lip, asshole. Now, one last time. Are you gonna turn it over or are you gonna die?"

A couple walking by eyed us over their shoulders. The man started to turn in our direction, but the woman grabbed his shirt sleeve and yanked him away. I said, "Like Shapiro? Did you make him the same offer?"

I detected the faintest bit of surprise on his face, his eyes flashed an emotion, probably satisfaction. "Yeah. Like Shapiro. My partner made him a generous offer. He didn't like it. I straightened it out."

"With the hit-and-run."

"What the hell, you're gonna be dead in about fifteen seconds. Screw it. With the hit-and-run."

A drunk in a trench coat and wool cap staggered in our direction. He'd probably get picked up for vagrancy before someone helped me. In his left hand he held a paper bag, which would contain his bottle and sustenance for the night. I muttered, "You have a witness."

I could see the rage build in Stone's face as he glanced sideways. He yelled, "Get the hell out of here, scumbag! You're coming with me, asshole."

He pulled me closer—I felt my feet leaving the ground. I realized how strong Stone was and felt my own weakness in comparison. For what seemed like the hundredth time, my brain screamed, "Where's Alexander?" I also realized how foolish I'd been to think for a moment that I could manipulate this maniac.

"Look, maybe we can work something out."

"Too late. You're gonna be on MySpace real soon. Real soon."

Stone shoved me away and reached into his jacket pocket. The drunk staggered closer. Stone barked at him, "Beat it!" He pulled out the gun and aimed at my head. "Think you're funny, asshole?" He released the safety. "Go to hell!"

The drunk grabbed Stone's arm with one hand and thrust upwards. I damn near peed my pants as a blast from Stone's gun shattered the urban calm. Panic erupted. People screamed. I dropped my box. Everyone else ran for cover. The paper bag in the drunk's other hand ripped as the drunk drove a six-inch blade into Stone's stomach.

Stone gurgled, "What the—"

From behind me, I heard a woman scream, "No! You son-of-a-bitch!" It was Harris. She stood just twenty feet away, Meyer in tow.

Stone's voice died in his throat as the bag reddened with fresh blood.

The drunk said, "That's for Molly."

I grabbed the briefcase as it slowly slipped from Stone's fingers.

The drunk thrust upwards again. He said, "And that's for Bob."

Simultaneously, two cops yelled, "HPD, drop the weapon!"

From what seemed like out of nowhere, police cars and cops emerged. In my panic, I dropped the briefcase. I'd survived Stone and Harris, and now I might get shot for grabbing a leather bag?

Finally, Harris would get what she deserved. I turned to give her a self-satisfied smile, but she was gone. And Meyer's body lay on the ground.

Everywhere, cops had their guns drawn. Stone's weapon was at his feet. The drunk released the lifeless body and let it crumple next to the gun, which he kicked toward the police. He raised both hands, and I clearly saw the face of Stone's killer, Dadrian Daniels.

36

While one of the officers handcuffed Daniels, another checked Stone's body for a pulse. He glanced up, his jaw set. The officer dealing with Daniels was named Cano; the one with Stone was Routman. Cano advised Daniels of his rights as Routman called for an ambulance. Dark blood spread across the sidewalk, a red trickle of death inching toward the gutter. Bile rose in my throat, but somehow I kept myself under control.

Sirens blared in the distance, gradually growing louder. The officer approached me and introduced himself, then said, "Are you okay?"

I nodded in stunned silence, then pointed at Meyer.

The officer helping Meyer to his feet gave us a thumb's up. My guy said, "He should be okay."

"Can I go see him? What happened to Harris?"

"I'm going to need to ask you some questions after we get the scene secured. But you can wait together. Who's Harris?"

"The woman who kidnapped us. She was with him!" I pointed at Meyer again.

"Can you give me a description?"

"Uh, blonde. And great legs." I realized how stupid I sounded the moment the words were out of my mouth.

A few seconds later, the officer raised one eyebrow and held back a smile. He must have seen the stupidity I felt reflected in my eyes. "You want to think about that description for a minute, sir?"

I cocked my head in Meyer's direction. "I'll wait with my friend."

When I got to where Meyer stood, we hugged. A manly hug, of course. No wimpy hugs here. I searched for Alexander. Nowhere in sight. Cano escorted Daniels, hands behind his back to a car. Routman held his position until Cano returned with the traditional crime scene tape.

Suddenly, I spotted Alexander. "What happened to you?"

Alexander hugged me, then spoke rapidly. I'd never seen him this animated and wondered if it was because he realized he'd screwed up. "You? Pay for lunch? Magnum, PI burger? Volcano fries? Talk about sending a signal."

"Hey, I've paid before."

"When the last time you pay for something other than cheap Chinese, yah?"

I grumbled, "It worked." So, he had gotten the message. Guess he didn't screw up.

"Yah, it worked. I went to Lulu's. Harris almost saw me when she walked in with Meyer. You could smell trouble cause they was all stiff and fake-friendly like. The manager's a friend and he knows lots of cops around here. He called in a favor from an off-duty guy."

"So why the hell didn't you do something sooner?"

"Hey, brah, the cops didn't know what you was up to. They didn't want to get you killed, yah?" He chuckled, "With what you told me to do, you almost wound up with three Magnum, P.I. burgers from Lulu's instead of a rescue."

I groaned.

Alexander interrupted, "I knew there was a problem when you said you'd pay."

Terrific, being cheap was a bigger clue than my health. What a legacy.

The street had filled with cops and onlookers. Crime scene tape marked off the spot where Stone had died. Tourists snapped photos by the hundreds. The truly anal videotaped the scene. I wondered if someone would try to pitch this to one of the reality crime shows. Even if that didn't happen, I could just imagine the stories about their vacations.

The onlookers made little pointing gestures and every now and again whispered to each other. The cops all seemed to have an assigned duty and canvassed the crowd for probable witnesses. I recognized a woman's face in the crowd, the mascara-stained tears on her cheeks forming tracks of anguish. As an officer neared her position, she drifted away.

Routman stopped in front of me. "What's your name, sir?"

Molly, Daniels' girlfriend, disappeared into the crowd. At least she'd be safe now.

I said, "Wilson McKenna."

"Mr. McKenna, it appeared as though the victim was threatening you when we showed up. Can you tell me what happened?"

"I'm not sure where to begin, Officer. The bottom line is that Harris, the woman who set this up, was trying to blackmail Mr. Stone about his involvement in drug smuggling. And where the hell is she? You guys didn't catch her?"

The officer shook his head as he made notes. "And what was your involvement?"

I tried to maintain my composure, but inside I knew where this was going. Alexander's trip to take Harris into Sacred Falls Park would come out. It was only a matter of time. There was no way around it. "We—Mr. Herschel over there, and me—we'd been kidnapped by Harris. She held Meyer at gunpoint while Daniels watched me. I guess Daniels had his own ideas. He didn't want the money. I guess he wanted revenge for what Stone had done to his girlfriend—he raped her."

"Please, Mr. McKenna, just tell me what happened, what you witnessed."

So, I stuck to what I'd actually seen. When I was done, I slipped and made a comment about Frank Willows.

Routman said, "Again, we're not looking for conjecture. We're just trying to figure out what happened here."

"Oh, so you don't care if Willows is a crook and involved in a drug smuggling ring."

Routman's eyes narrowed. "So you think that Frank Willows, a respectable businessman, is part of a drug ring? Why wasn't he here?"

"I can't figure that part out. I expected him to be with Stone. Maybe they decided that Stone could handle a couple of old duffers on his own and he took the day off. Damned if I know."

"And maybe he had nothing to do with the whole thing. He runs a very successful business."

Obviously, Routman believed what everyone else did about Willows. "I know, City contacts, huge construction deals, big mucky-muck."

Routman let out an exasperated sigh. "I'm sure one of the detectives will be speaking with Mr. Willows."

"Remember to check Stone's MySpace page, there's a lot there. Some of which will link him to Willows. If you've got a piece of paper, I can jot down the address."

He pulled two business cards from his notepad and handed them to me. "Keep one and put the address on the back of the other."

I jotted down the information. "He basically confesses to everything online. You guys should really check this out."

Routman nodded as he listened. "I doubt that we'll be able to do much with it anyway based on what you described. Besides, Mr. Stone is now dead."

I handed the card with the info back to Routman and he stuffed it into his notepad.

Routman surveyed the crowd, then motioned for a tall man dressed in jeans and an aloha shirt to approach. Routman said, "Detective, this is Mr. McKenna. He's stated that the female suspect kidnapped him. She held the friend hostage while the male suspect, an ex-pusher named Dadrian Daniels, watched him. He was supposed to exchange this box, which has drugs in it—"

I said, "Actually, there aren't any drugs in there. They're in a safe-deposit box."

The detective wiped at his brow with a handkerchief. "You put drugs in a safe-deposit box?"

"Um, no, that would have been Bob Shapiro. It was his box."

Routman had a confused look on his face. "So the drugs that were supposed to be in this box are in a safe-deposit box in a bank?"

"That's where we found the flash drive, too."

The detective said, "In the bank?"

"With the drugs. We think that Bob Shapiro put them there for safekeeping. Stone wanted his drugs back, that's why he was here."

The detective sniffled. "So, you're in possession of drugs that belonged to the victim or his killer and you have a flash drive with a video as proof of the drug connection?"

I nodded.

"And what's on the flash drive?" The detective sniffled again, stifled a sneeze, then began massaging the back of his neck.

"An argument between Bob Shapiro, Stone, and Willows. It shows motive for them wanting to kill Shapiro."

The detective shook his head. "Who's Shapiro?"

"A hit-and-run victim from a couple of weeks ago. Stone confessed to his murder before he died."

Detective Sniffles pulled out his phone and punched a speed dial button. "It's me. I'm gonna be awhile." He disconnected and said, "Mr. McKenna, we're going to need to run through this again. This time, from the top. And, please, don't leave anything out."

37

I admit it, I was on overload. So many things had happened today that establishing the details for the cops became a real chore. They talked to me, to Meyer and, ultimately, to Alexander. The questions went on and on, the sun began to feel unbearably hot, and even the trades and the onlookers began to feel hostile. Finally, another detective, this one married to another of Alexander's cousins—imagine that—showed up and vouched for all of us. After what felt like an eternity, we were free to leave.

Alexander, Meyer, and I decided to return to Lulu's. We grabbed three window seats and listened to the music while they drank beer and I sipped a glass of wine. The breezes drifted through as the sun sank towards the ocean horizon. A live band started playing Hawaiian music and we listened and nursed our second drink until dark.

Under normal circumstances, the waitress would have probably had the manager move us along. But, because Alexander was friends with the manager, they allowed us to take up space. None of us wanted to leave and reenter the real world—where killers and drug dealers proliferated.

At one point, the manager came over and delivered Harris's camera to our table. We all stared at it, wondering where it had come from.

He pointed at Meyer. "The lady he was with? She dropped this off a few minutes ago. She left a note."

Alexander reached out, but the manager pulled his hand back. "Sorry, brah. It's for your friend." He handed me the note and winked. "Good for you, McKenna. That's one hot girlfriend you got there."

I planted my hands on the table and half rose. "Is she still here?"

"No, man, she split soon as she handed that off. Told me to wait maybe ten minutes." He stared at me, then Alexander. "At least she's a good tipper." He held up a twenty, winked, then walked away.

I turned my attention to what he'd handed me. It was a white greeting card envelope with my name printed neatly on the front. The envelope was sealed and on the back, over the flap, there was a hand-drawn heart. I opened the envelope and pulled out the card.

The front of the card was a beautiful sunset with the word "Sorry" embossed in large, flowing letters. The inside had no verse, just a graceful, cursive script that I recognized. I read what Harris had written aloud. "Hi hon, sorry I caused you so much trouble. I took advantage of a wonderful friend. Hugs, Harris. PS Guess I should have stuck to my original plan instead of getting sidetracked by that damn plane." My voice felt tight, so I cleared my throat. "She, uh, drew a little smiley face after the PS."

Alexander pulled the card from my hand and read it. "The cops need this. Maybe they can analyze the writing or find a fingerprint."

I yanked it back. "I'll hold onto it. I can turn it in tomorrow. But, you can keep the camera for me."

Throughout all of this, Meyer simply sat and nodded as he gazed out the window.

Given that the camera signified Harris's power over Meyer and me, I think we were both glad to have Alexander take control. From the safety of our open-air nest, we followed the activities of tourists as they wandered in apparent random patterns. The restaurant had filled now, and people lined up to get in.

The band and the restaurant crowd had nearly reached rock-and-roll-concert level when Alexander said, "We gotta go!"

No sooner had we vacated our table than it was wiped clean and replacement customers seated. The natives were truly restless and wanted food and drink in Waikiki.

Our solemn little procession made its way to Meyer's car in silence. Alexander must have sensed that I, and probably Meyer, wanted the perceived comfort of an additional warm body. Once we were safely in Meyer's car, Alexander began to walk away. "I gonna go get my truck. Meet you at your place in a bit."

"Thanks." He was no more than a few feet away when I jumped out of the car. "Alexander! I'm sorry about having to tell the cops about Sacred Falls."

He waved his hand dismissively. "No problem, brah. That detective that's married to my cousin? That's Jarod. He says he thinks they can overlook my 'mistake' in exchange for my testimony. I would have to do that anyway, so it all work out."

He turned in the direction of his car and walked away. Meyer drove us to my place. As Meyer parked the car, he said, "Guess I should be getting ready to move back to my own place, huh?"

I remembered to speak loudly, "Yah, but not tonight. It's already late and you never did finish cleaning up your place. Tomorrow, I can help you out. Maybe we can get Alexander to come over and lend some muscle."

"Thanks, I'm not ready to go back yet. Tonight was just too familiar."

"From the hilltop in Korea?"

He nodded. "I killed one of those Koreans with my knife. It was the only way."

"Officer Routman said that some woman told you to lay on the ground back there. Is that true?"

"It was your friend, Harris. She was gonna shoot Stone, but that Daniels guy got him first."

"What? Why would she do that?"

"We talked a lot while we were up in that bar. She promised me she was gonna fix this. All I'm gonna say is that Harris Galvin, or whoever she is, realizes she made some bad choices here. She ain't gonna cause you no more problems. Besides, she did what I couldn't."

"I don't understand."

"You remember the sixteen good men I talked about?"

"Yah, the soldiers, Shapiro and Lau. So what?"

"She kept Stone from making it seventeen."

"Sorry, I don't follow."

"You, moron! She kept you from getting yourself killed."

He considered me a good man? I ranked up there with Shapiro and Roger Lau? My throat went tight with emotion as we exited the car and walked to my apartment. I was so tired that I didn't notice the door was unlocked until I'd inserted my key. I had the door opened just a crack when I saw a flashlight beam go out. Faint footsteps approached, then stopped. I threw my weight against the door and shoved with everything I had. I felt a hard connection, maybe with the intruder's head. We heard cursing, then the crash of my TV set as the intruder went down.

"Come with me!" I yanked Meyer's hand and we rushed down the sidewalk as fast as we could. We climbed the stairs to the roof in hopes that the intruder would escape through the parking lot and give us a glimpse of him from the rooftop. At the top of the stairs, Meyer bent over, his hands on his knees. His breaths came in ragged, raspy spurts. He looked as though he was ready to pass out. I leaned him against the wall, then went to the edge of the roof where I could peer down to the parking lot.

There was no movement in the lighted area, nothing at all. I had a sinking feeling that the intruder wanted more than just some of my stuff. That meant it had to be—

"Don't move."

I recognized the voice from the construction office. I whirled to see a shadowy figure pointing a pistol at my chest. I said, "Willows."

He held Meyer up by the collar, then shoved him in my direction.

I grabbed Meyer just before he lost his balance and by some miracle, we avoided crumpling into a lump of old bones. "What do you want?"

"I should thank you, actually. You eliminated that pain in the ass Stone. After Daniels dusted Jimmy, I left there and waited here.

But you never showed up, so I got tired of waiting. Figured maybe I could find it."

"What?"

"Stone's stash. I knew you wouldn't bring it out in public." He smiled. "Stone's been using again—since he killed Shapiro. So you took care of my two biggest problems. But now that puts you two at the top of my list."

I said, "So you were there?"

"I was sitting on a bench in the shade in front of the zoo. I could have taken out Daniels, but I was tired of Stone's egotistical bullshit." He shrugged. "He thought I was gonna back him up, instead, I let nature take its course."

The final break in the partnership. "You shoot us up here and you'll never get away before someone sees you," I said.

"I'm not shooting you here. We're going to take a little ride."

Meyer yelled, "What did he say?"

"Shut up, old fool," said Willows.

"What? I'm hard-of-hearing!"

Willows raised the gun in the air as if to strike Meyer. He spat, "Shut up!"

"Okay, okay. No need to get pissy. I just wanted to know what your intentions were, that's all."

In a loud voice, I said, "He can't hear crap!"

Willows stifled us with a glare and a zipping motion across his lips. Or maybe it was when he pulled the slide on the gun. Anyway, we both raised our hands and nodded. I thought about the security cameras on the roof and hoped that someone would think to check them. Maybe Julia? She'd have film of the whole thing. I wouldn't tell him about the cameras. Or remind him that this would be his second time to be captured on video, but he must have seen me glancing in that direction. Even in the dark light, I could see the rage painted on his face. "Where is it?"

"Where's what?" I tried to sound innocent, but was too tired and scared. Consequently, I did a crappy job.

He pointed the gun at my face and yelled, "Where's the goddamn camera go to?"

Meyer perked up. "Hey, I heard that. You use the same service as me? I use Brinks. You use them, too?"

"Shut up," said Willows. "If you used a service, they'd be here already. Now, where's the computer? In your apartment?"

I wondered if I could still salvage this. "It's a remote storage service."

Willows said, "Bullshit. You ain't that smart."

"I figured out Stone's MySpace account, Shapiro's death. Remote storage isn't that difficult. You just—"

"Shut up. We'll grab your computer on the way out to be safe. Now move." He motioned at the stairs, then pointed the gun at me. "You first. And, if you try anything funny, your friend dies." He pointed the gun at Meyer's head. Not again.

When I got to the top landing, I said, "Why don't you just let us go? We'll give you the drugs. Whatever you want."

"You had that chance with Stone. Now shut up."

I was halfway down the stairwell when I heard Meyer stumble. I glanced over my shoulder and saw that Willows was holding him up by the collar with one hand. He pointed the gun at me. "Move."

I was on the second step from the bottom when Willows commanded, "Stop."

I held my position as he came down two stairs. I was on the second, Meyer on the third, Willows on the fourth. Willows motioned with his head for me to go further.

I started to say something, but he cut me off. "Zip it." He motioned again.

When I reached the landing, I noticed a movement to my right. I saw the reflection of the flash attachment and instinctively moved left. Behind me, a brilliant flash lit up the stairway. Willows' gun went off and Meyer stumbled down the last step. He would have landed face first on the concrete, but an arm reached from the darkness and shoved him in my direction.

Another flash left me half blinded and a second shot also went wild. Willows yelled, "Shit!"

I heard Willows curse again as he lost his footing and fell the remaining two steps. Through the glare that clouded my vision, I saw

Alexander jump from the shadows and slam his fist into the other man's jaw. I thought Willows would go down, but he hit back and landed a punch in Alexander's stomach, then slashed downwards with the barrel of the gun. Alexander raised his arm and blocked the blow. The impact jerked the gun from Willows' hand and sent it into the bushes.

Willows swung wildly. He landed a punch that sent Alexander sprawling to his right. I heard a clatter as he collided with the camera and sent it tumbling across the pavement. Willows stumbled onto Alexander and planted both hands on his throat.

I helped Meyer to the ground and blinked several times to clear my head. A few feet away, Alexander frantically struggled to pry the hands from his throat, but Willows just squeezed harder. Alexander threw a weak punch, but missed, his energy and air almost spent. I searched frantically for the gun, but it was lost in the bushes. There was no time to call for help. Nothing to do but save my friend. The glint of landscape lighting reflected off the lens of Harris's camera.

I found it, grabbed the strap, turned, and swung with all my might. My swing was smooth and fast, just like it had been when I nailed Johnny Bakerton's pitch. Willows looked up just in time to see the camera smash squarely into the side of his head. A loud crack split the night, Willows slumped over, blood bubbling from his temple and Alexander pried himself from under the dead weight.

Several tenants rushed into the area. A few gawked at the scene. Julia burst through the crowd and secured Willows by pulling his hands behind his back. She pinned his wrists and kept him immobile with the practiced ease of someone used to self-defense. She said, "There should be cops here in a couple of minutes; I called when I heard the first shot."

Alexander leaned against the wall, rubbing his arm where he'd been slashed by the gun. He stared at me. Or rather, at my feet. I said, "I'm okay."

His jaw fell open.

"What?"

He pointed at the ground.

I looked down and saw the body of the camera. The back hung open, the flash attachment hung limply from the body and one of the straps had separated completely. Uh-oh.

Alexander mumbled, "Harris's camera."

I cradled the half-opened body in my hands as if it were a baby and passed it to Alexander. "You were in charge of it, not me."

Alexander turned the camera over to look at the back, but it just flopped around. The flash lighted the pavement in a blinding, momentary burst of light. "How am I gonna explain this to the cops?" The flash lit up the courtyard, again. "Oh, man."

"Flash works," I said.

Alexander fumbled with the camera's corpse.

I shrugged, "Look at it this way, that's one helluva photo finish."

Oddly enough, Alexander didn't think that was funny at all.

Maybe my timing was off.

38

It was nearly one in the morning by the time the police let us into my place. Both Meyer and I were exhausted and sacked out right away. I dreamed that night of surfing at dawn. The sun's rise over the horizon was only what you could call majestic. The old man with long hair straddled the surfboard next to mine. He faced the rising sun, soaking up the rays with his face.

Dark clouds on the horizon approached, but he waved them away. "You like my office?"

I said, "Who are you? What am I doing here?"

"Surf flat today. You have good mana. That why you here." A wave approached, so he turned toward shore and began to paddle. As he slid away through the water, he called to me over his shoulder. "Try on your knees; otherwise, you might have to paddle back."

I gripped my board, watching other surfers glide past me. My board was twice the length of theirs, I had no idea why. Finally, I made it to my knees as a small wave approached. I began to paddle and rode my little wave about halfway in before I fell off the board. But, I'd done it—I'd surfed Waikiki!

I sat straight up in bed and glanced at the clock. Four in the morning. The sun wouldn't be up for well over an hour, but I went out to the lanai and watched and listened. The nighttime ocean performed a symphony of sights and sounds, each moment different, each second a magical sequence of events that nature might never repeat.

As the sun rose behind me, foamy wavelets drifted onshore in a steady rhythm. I wondered which beach Kimu Ioneki was surfing at this moment.

Meyer didn't rise until almost nine. He stepped out of his room with a cheery, "Good morning, McKenna!"

I grunted, "Morning." Which, technically, it was, at least until noon. "You must be ready to go home."

"Home? Yeah, I am. I'm ready to leave, skedaddle, hit the road—"

"What did you do, take a happy pill last night?"

"Vamoose, move on out—"

"Meyer!"

"What? You don't want me to leave? Sorry, but I got an apartment of my own to get back to. It's a mess, if you recall. You were going to call that Alejandro fellow and see if he might lend a hand to an old man. You know—"

"It's Alexander. I'll call him." I didn't need any more synonyms for anything, including moving, helping others, even getting a cup of coffee or Joe or anything else. Crap, now I was doing it. I stood and said, "Are you packed?"

"Yes sir! I'm packed and—"

"Let's go." I stood and started for the door. "I'll get a ride back with Alexander."

Alexander did show up to help and, thank goodness, after Meyer saw the mess in his apartment, his desire to regale us with his good humor waned. By the time we had the place back together, he and I were both tired. Alexander seemed more bored than anything, but returned me to my apartment, where he dropped me off so I could take a long afternoon nap.

As we sat in the parking lot, I said, "I've been dreaming of your Great-Grampa Kimu."

He said, "I know. I knew since you denied it. You got all weird on me."

"I dreamed I went surfing last night."

Alexander put his hand on my shoulder. "That why you look so tired. So, you ready to talk about why you came here?"

I caught a glimpse of the ocean beyond the apartment building. Watched a gentle wave roll in. I smiled, free from the weight I'd been carrying. A lone surfer rode a wave nearly to the shore. "Yah, finally." We talked for nearly two hours after that. It was time to share my story with my best friend—my wins, my losses, and my regrets. I could only hope he'd still like me after he knew who I really was.

It took a couple of weeks for everything to get sorted out, but in the end, it looked like Willows would spend a lot of time in prison for conspiracy to murder Bob Shapiro and Roger Lau and, of course, several counts of assault, attempted murder, etc., etc., ad nauseam. And Harris? She'd vanished.

I heard from Meyer that he found a manager for the complex, someone who could help reconstruct his lost records. It would take them some time, but they did have enough documentation to begin rebuilding what had been destroyed. After everything that had happened here, I think he was glad to leave the islands. He said the first thing he would do was pay a long-overdue visit to his brother in Minneapolis. I bit my tongue.

I pitched and got a job to write the entire story for the Advertiser as well as the follow-up stories for the trial. I knew it wasn't going to win a Pulitzer, but I was pretty stoked over it. Do they still say stoked?

We turned the drugs over to the cops and that made them happy. Stone's businesses were raided and the cops busted his drug ring. Stone wouldn't care—he was dead.

When Alexander called to tell me that he'd arranged the boat ride, I tried to back out, but he refused to accept no for an answer. Besides, he told me, Julia would be there along with Kira and the keike. Julia? Bathing suit? Sure, I could do this.

Alexander's boat was a 42-footer. We had a perfect day—86 degrees, a few wispy clouds in the sky, trades at 10-15 mph, and almost flat seas. We all met at the Kewalo Basin, where Alexander moored his boat, Kimu's Dream.

Alexander said he planned on taking us around the island to Kane'ohe Bay where we'd have lunch, do some snorkeling and scuba, then head back. Once we'd anchored in the bay, he readied the boat for the party while Kira, Julia, and I sat around the miniature dining table and gabbed.

Kira had been curious about how we'd figured out who had killed Shapiro, but her next question caught me off guard. "McKenna, you never been one do nice things for other people. You always for McKenna only. Why you get involved?"

"I, um, did it because of Harris's sister."

Julia gave me a playful punch in the arm. "You thought you were gonna get lucky with that blonde wahine."

"Okay, guilty. It started out that way. It was later that I thought I was helping her put together money for her sister's operation."

Kira said, "So why you not back out once you suspect trouble?"

Obviously, Alexander hadn't shared the details with her. "It was too late. By the time I figured it out, she already had her plan in motion. Julia, what's going to happen to Daniels?"

"My boss decided to represent him on the murder charge. He thinks this is gonna be high profile."

I said, "Good. Daniels made some bad choices, but in the end, he was just trying to help Bob. I'm glad he'll get a good attorney."

Julia nodded, "If Stone hadn't raped his girlfriend—"

Silence settled around the table.

I cleared my throat. "You know what really irritates me? I have to rent that damned apartment again."

The boat rocked as a small wake caught us broadside. We all rolled with the wave and Julia's shoulder brushed mine. I'm not sure how it happened, but right after that my hand wound up on her thigh. She gave me an affectionate glance and took my hand in hers.

Holy cow. She wanted me.

To my surprise, she removed my hand and said, "I like you, but do that again and I'll break your arm."

Shit. Busted. "Got it. No funny business." Guess I really was going to miss Legs.

Acknowledgements

The following people have all helped me in the creation of this book in one way or another. I'm sure there have been others that I am missing here. To those I've missed, I apologize sincerely—I should have kept better notes. To those listed here, I give a warm mahalo (thank you) for your kokua (help). First, to Kathy Ambrose, my wife and the person who has put up with countless hours of being ignored while I struggled to create a character and story worthy of the time. She's also read innumerable revisions as I stumbled along the way and always let me pursue my dream.

Thanks also go to Ed Stackler, an excellent fiction editor, for the idea of making Harris a woman and for his guidance on the elements of building a good story. I can only hope that I've hit the mark and not missed it entirely.

This manuscript began years ago and was then put off to one side as I went on to other projects. As a result, I've lost track of the early readers. However, I owe thanks to the members of the St. Phillips Neri Writers Group in Tucson, AZ for their feedback. Those members include Mary Ellen Barnes, Clark Lohr, Molly McKinney, Ellie Nelson, Constance Richardson, Shirley Sikes, Bert Steves, and Jim Turner. Most recently, I want to thank Diana Amsden, Judith Berg, Dee DeTarsio, Brae Wyckoff and Jill Wyckoff for reading the manuscript and for their suggestions. I'd also like to thank Bobby Ramos for the information he provided about Kalaeloa Airport and Dillingham Field. He was extremely helpful and patient in answering questions and discussing the workings of both airports.

About the Author

A painting of three mountains inspired Terry Ambrose to write his first short story when he was a child. The painting was titled "The Three Sisters" and the story, which he called, "The Great Spirit," was about how the sisters angered a powerful god, who then transformed them into mountains.

Terry started his business career skip tracing and collecting money from deadbeats. During his first day on the job, he learned that liars come from all walks of life. He never actually stole a car, but sometimes hired big guys with tow trucks and a penchant for working in the dark to "help" when negotiations failed.

Much like his protagonist in Photo Finish, Terry is a baby boomer, has a quick wit, and likes to follow a hunch. He and his wife live in Southern California where they run their own small business. Terry enjoys walking, swimming, and writing. In addition to working on his next novel, he is reporting on real-life scams and cons. Learn more on his website at TerryAmbrose.com.

Made in the USA
Monee, IL
04 March 2022

92302495R00156